THE MAKING OF GENEVIEVE

JUDY LANNON

Paperback ISBN: 979-8-218-36027-6

Ebook ISBN: 979-8-218-36028-3

Published by Outer Beach Press

Lannon is a genius at understanding human behavior and putting it on the page. I highly recommend *The Making of Genevieve*. There may be a small piece of Genevieve in many of us.

Barbara Conrey
USA Today bestselling author of
Nowhere Near Goodbye and *My Secret to Keep*

ACKNOWLEDGMENTS

I would like to thank my readers. Your continuous support, positive reviews, and words of encouragement instill in me the belief that I can write something that ignites discussions about life with laughter, joy, and maybe a few tears.

I am incredibly grateful to my BETA and ARC readers for their indispensable suggestions, astute observations, and meticulous tweaks. Thank you!

Thanks go to my copy editor and proofreader, Joyce Mochrie, owner of *One Last Look*, for doing what you do so well—catching mistakes, especially keeping those last names straight!

I also want to thank my graphic designer, Brandi Doane, for "getting me."

A large collective thanks to the Women's Fiction Writers Association. You have been a lifeline for me and so many others. This group absolutely ROCKS.

And last, but certainly not least, my family … my husband, my daughter, and my granddaughter. You have each provided me with what I needed when I needed it. Whether you were the sounding board for my thoughts, the expert I relied on for technical help, or the person who brought me a glass of wine, your support was invaluable. Thank you!

GOING HOME

"PEOPLE ARE USUALLY THE HAPPIEST AT HOME." — WILLIAM SHAKESPEARE

"Hello." I hope my voice doesn't quiver, giving away the exhaustion I feel.

"Good morning, Genevieve. It's me, Sara. How are you feeling this morning?"

How the hell do you think I am feeling, Sara? This is what I want to say to my daughter. I received my death sentence yesterday, so I am ready to take off someone's head. That is what I would like to say … and oh, I would like to say so much more. Instead, I struggle to sit up in my hospital bed, fluff my thinning hair, which has gone from a brilliant silver to a dull gray, and steady myself. I remember saying to someone many years ago that I didn't mind getting old, as long as I didn't look old. Even at ninety-four years old, I still feel young at heart, but my body and my looks are starting to betray me.

"Well, dear, considering our news, I would say I am a bit out of sorts, but the thought of going home after thirteen days in this damn hospital is better than all the drugs I'm getting. Will you be meeting me at the house?"

"Yes, I'll see you there later this afternoon. Unless you want me to come and stay with you until you're ready to leave. The front desk said that you should be ready to be discharged around three. I hate they are making you come home in an ambulance. It's not like you can't sit up in a car. Jessica will already be there and have the house perfect for your homecoming."

Sara has been with me for the last nine days, every day, working out of my hospital room since she got back from her company conference. Every day, I wake up, and there she is. She is a blessing and a burden at the same time. I feel like Sara has taken over my life … well, what brief life I have left. But I am not quite sure where I would be if I didn't have her to lean on. Leaning on someone is not a trait that I am comfortable with. But Sara has been a rock, which is a surprise for me. I think she has tried her best to keep a safe emotional distance between us. But that is all water under the bridge or over the dam, or whatever that saying is. All that mother–daughter bullshit.

"I will see you this afternoon, dear. Goodbye." I hang up the phone, lie back down on the bed, and close my eyes. I realize this might be the last time I am alone while I am still alive. And now, I grasp that I just might be afraid to be alone while still alive. When I was young, I never enjoyed being by myself. It was only as I got older that I realized I am my best company. Now I am not so sure.

"Mrs. Austin—Genevieve, I'm sorry to wake you, but I need to check your blood pressure." I hear someone, but I don't recognize the voice. Oh, dammit, I am not on the beach. It is not the summer of 1939. I am in the hospital, and they are ruining a perfectly wonderful memory.

"Yes, of course. When am I getting out of here?"

"Just a few more hours. Your blood pressure is elevated, but that's to be expected with the excitement of going home," the nurse says.

No, it is not the excitement of going home. It is the excitement of remembering that summer—the summer of 1939. That was the summer I met Nicholas Reynolds. That was when I introduced Nicky to my family. He was a new summer kid. Emma, Trey, and I always made friends with the summer kids. We would all go to each other's houses, have sleepovers on the big porches most of our houses had, and explore the beaches that were our backyards.

Well, that was usually the case, except when it came to the extremely wealthy summer kids—the Ollrichs, the Vanderbilts, the Bergwinds, and plenty more. My sister, brother, and I were out of their league. Yes, our home was a beautiful, Newport, Rhode Island, oceanfront home with eight bedrooms, four bathrooms, and an upstairs sleeping porch, my favorite spot in the house. Our formal dining room could easily seat twelve for dinner. There was a game room, an enormous, stone fireplace in the living room, and a state-of-the-art kitchen for that era.

The backyard sloped down to our soft, sandy beach, which stretched for miles along the Atlantic Ocean, bearing the brunt of large waves rolling directly to the shore. This was our year-round home. We didn't vacate on Labor Day, only to return at the end of the following June. We had gardeners to care for the one-acre property, and a woman who cleaned for us twice a week in the summer, less in the winter. But we didn't have a full-time staff, chauffeur, or polo ponies—actually, no ponies at all—despite my constant demand for some.

Most of these summer Newport families were wealthy Irish Catholics, and we were French. I found out at an early age that sometimes the two don't mix, at least back then. I discovered that being called a frog was not a term of endearment, so my sister, brother, and I stayed clear of those kids. I remember when Trey was about six years old, asking my father what it means when someone calls him a frog. Pops had gone through the roof, yelling, "What Irish Mick called you that? I'll shove my fist down his lying, Irish mouth. Remember, never trust anyone Irish."

"Edward, stop that talk this very minute." My mother was always concerned about keeping up appearances. "Someone might hear you. Children, ignore what your father just said."

"For Christ's sake, Margaux, there isn't a house within shouting distance to us," Pops said, heading straight to the liquor cabinet to pour a Scotch. My parents rarely argued or raised their voices to each other. I think it was then that I had decided that no Irish Mick, whatever that meant, was going to be any better than me.

I started reading every *Harper's Bizarre*, *Marie Claire*, and *Ladies Home Journal* issue I could get my hands on. Mom was happy to see me reading, thinking I was interested in fashion advice and how to make a happy home. I was interested in what the rich were eating, drinking, reading, where they vacationed, what music they listened to. Anything that would put me on an even playing field with anyone who thought they were better than me. The articles in those magazines helped me to learn the best wines and spirits to serve at a cocktail party, what records to play, the best appetizers to serve. But I took it a step further ... I mean, why not? I learned what grapes are used to make champagne or chardonnay. What regions those grapes are grown in. Same thing for spirits—best Scotch, gin, and why?

Oh dear, my mind is wandering. I suppose it might be the effects of the morphine they have started to give me. It is quite a delicious feeling.

Nicholas Reynolds. Oh, he was a handsome, young man. He came to Newport in early June that summer, earlier than the other summer families. Nicky was from New Orleans. His parents bought the house just down the shore from us to escape the stifling, Louisiana summer heat. We were ... we are ... the same age. He was, and probably still is, tall, but not taller than me.

When I was much younger, I hated being the tallest kid in my class—not just the tallest girl, but the tallest kid. But by the time Nicky came along, I had accepted my looks, which included my body. The models in my fashion magazines were tall and thin, and they helped me see myself in a different light. Even as a teenager, I was a confident, headstrong person. If only I knew then what I know now and how my life would evolve, I wonder if I would have made different choices. Not better choices, simply different choices.

SUMMER OF 1939

"LIVE IN THE SUNSHINE, SWIM IN THE SEA,
DRINK IN THE WILD AIR."
— RALPH WALDO EMERSON

Margaux Lemaire stood over her gas stove stirring a large pot of fish chowder, wondering why she was making chowder on a hot, June day. Brownies should come out of the oven in a few minutes, adding to the warmth in her big, farmhouse-style kitchen. She gave the chowder one last stir, put the lid back on the pot, and wiped her hands on a blue-and-white-striped dish towel. Glancing at the kitchen clock, she turned to look out her kitchen window. *It's almost five o'clock. Edward should be home for dinner in an hour. Where are the children?*

She stared outside her window, beyond the row of blue hydrangeas and rosebushes with pink blossoms ready to open, past the lawn, and out to their beach, never tiring of the view, which was as fickle as the sea. But today, the white sand glistened, and the waves were gently crashing along the shore.

Margaux noticed two of her three children on the beach. Emma, fourteen years old, was sitting on a blanket, reading her Nancy Drew novel, and twelve-year-old Edward III, Trey, for short, was skipping stones at the edge of the Atlantic Ocean. *I*

6

never have to worry about those two. It's the other one, Genevieve, I worry about.

She scanned the shore and the waves, looking for any sign of her sixteen-year-old daughter, when she saw Genevieve coming out of the ocean a few yards to the left on their beach. Genevieve was laughing, saying something to another person who was getting caught up in the waves. Margaux watched as her tall, tan daughter gracefully maneuvered the waves and came onto shore, wearing her white, one-piece maillot. She thought about the argument she and Genevieve had bathing-suit shopping earlier in the year. Margaux wanted her daughter's suit to be conservative, a style that would show less leg.

"But Mom, those are so out of style. Look at what the French women are wearing, and we are French, *c'est bien ça?*" Margaux had learned a long time ago to choose her battles with her willful daughter. She had to admit that Genevieve looked striking in her new suit with the higher-cut legs.

I wonder if I had a premonition when I named her. Genevieve fits her so well. My mother was furious that I would give a baby a name meaning tribal woman, but I chose it for the old Welsh meaning white wave, Margaux thought as she stepped out to the back porch and rang the bell hanging next to the back door —a signal to come back to the house.

"What's for dinner?" Trey yelled before his bare feet hit the porch steps.

"Fish chowder, corn on the cob, and brownies and ice cream for dessert. Make sure you get all that sand off your feet, and if you have sand in your bathing suit, drop it on the porch and go get cleaned up," Margaux said, giving her son a brief hug.

"Mom, I'm not getting undressed in front of you. Turn around."

"Trey, I have seen you naked."

"Mom, turn around."

Margaux turned around, but not before getting a peek of her son running through the kitchen, up the back stairs, with a hint of the beginning of his summer tan, except for his baby-white butt. She smiled, taking in this special moment.

Emma is just a minute behind her brother, feet already free of sand, and no sand in her suit. She rarely ventured into the ocean.

"Emma, did you tell Genevieve to come up?"

"I did, but she didn't listen, as usual," Emma said with a touch of jealousy in her tone. But just then, in walked Genevieve, wrapped in a beach towel, wet bathing suit in hand, and long, blonde hair dripping down her back.

"Genevieve Lemaire, get your sandy feet and dripping hair out of my kitchen. Why are you carrying your suit? And why won't you wear a bathing cap?"

"Sorry, but you are always telling us to not wear our bathing suits inside if they are full of sand, and mine was full of sand from body surfing. And you know I will never wear a bathing cap," she said, twisting her lengthy, blonde hair over the kitchen sink to wring out the saltwater.

"I invited a new summer kid over after we have dinner, okay?" This was more of a statement than a request as Genevieve dropped her wet suit back out on the deck, tightened her towel, and went up the stairs to her room. But first, she turned, looked Emma dead in the eye, and said, "Oh, by the way, I do listen. I just might not respond like a puppy, like you, Emma."

"Genevieve, who is this boy you want to invite over, a friend of your brother?" Margaux asked as she handed a bowl of chowder to her husband, Edward. He reached across the large, oak dining room table for an ear of corn, listening to his family's dinner conversation.

"Not my friend, but he's a nice guy. I think he likes Genevieve," said Trey, holding a cloth napkin to his mouth to cover up the large mouthful of corn in his mouth.

"Mom, he's a new neighbor, and I am being neighborly, that is all. You are always telling us to be nice to new people."

"What's this fellow's name, and where is he staying?" asked Edward. Edward gives the appearance of not listening, but he always had a pulse on his family. At least for now.

"Nicholas Reynolds, Nicky for short. His parents bought the Bellingham house. They're from New Orleans, Louisiana. Nicky goes to the Isidore Newman School for boys. And he's not Irish, Pops, so you should like him," replied Genevieve, giving her father her sweetest look.

"Children, your father and I don't care what nationality a person is. We look for their character and strengths. Isn't that right, Edward?" Margaux said, giving her husband a not-so-sweet look.

Edward glanced from Genevieve to his wife, took a sip of his wine, and said nothing.

"Genevieve, Nicholas may join us for dessert and gin rummy on the porch."

"Thanks, Mom. I'll run over to his house and let him know." Genevieve pushed back her chair, picked up her plate, silverware, and glass, and placed them in the glistening, white, enamel kitchen sink, letting the screen door slam behind her as she raced off the porch to Nicky Reynolds's house.

The Reynolds home, known as the Bellingham, was a close distance to the Austin home, which didn't have a name, other than the Austin home. For long-legged Genevieve, the run down the beach to Nicky's house barely winded her. She bounded up the steep staircase, counting each of the twenty-two steps out loud, and then sauntered across the meticulously maintained lawn to their back porch. The house was situated to get the best views of the Atlantic Ocean from as many windows as possible. The Bellingham house reeked of wealth, but that thought never entered Genevieve's mind. She was surrounded by wealth.

Nicky answered with her first knock.

"Hi, come on in." He smiled, flashing his perfect, white teeth with an air of complete relaxation. "My parents want to meet you," he said, leading her onto the side porch where his parents were seated, sipping after-dinner cocktails.

"Mama, Daddy, please meet Genevieve Lemaire. Genevieve, please meet my parents." Mr. Reynolds stood up, walked over to Genevieve, and gave her a once-over. "Nice to make your acquaintance, Genevieve. Nick here tells me you live down the beach a bit. So, Genevieve, what type of name is that?"

Before Genevieve could respond, Mrs. Reynolds rose out of her large, white, wicker rocker and stood next to her husband, putting a hand on his arm. "Honestly, Robert, leave this poor girl alone. She's not here for an interview. So nice to meet you, dear. I'm happy that our Nicky has found a friend here in Newport. What are your plans for this evening?"

Genevieve smiled her sweetest smile, giving Nicky's flashy, white smile a run for its money. "Thank you, Mrs. Reynolds. Nicky and I are joining my parents, brother, and sister for dessert and gin rummy on the porch. It's something we enjoy doing together on summer evenings."

"Should Nicky be concerned about getting fleeced at this little, family card game?"

Again, it was Mrs. Reynolds who tried to smooth out what was obvious. Her husband was an arrogant bully, hiding behind a charming smile and a smooth, affective tone. "Never mind that. You two run along, have fun, and Nicky, darling, no nighttime swimming. I expect you home no later than nine o'clock."

Nicky leaned over to kiss his mother's cheek. "Yes, ma'am, I won't be late." He barely glanced at his father as he ushered Genevieve out the door. They walked silently across the lawn, and only after running down those twenty-two stairs did either of them speak.

"I'm sorry about my daddy. He was raised in a different time and tries to hide his Cajun heritage. He's got a chip on his shoulder and feels he needs to be better than anyone else, and they sure as heck should know that."

Genevieve sensed Nick wasn't defending his father, but that he was apologizing for him.

"Ha, who cares? My dad will be thrilled to hear your French."

"French? What do you mean?"

"You said Cajun … isn't that French?"

"Well, I suppose so. We don't give that much thought, but if it makes your father happy, then *c'est une bonne chose*."

Genevieve smiled. *Yes, it is a good thing*, she thought.

THAT SUMMER, Nicky and Genevieve were inseparable. Their days were filled with scheduled activities, but they always found time to swim and body surf if the waves were just right. They strolled along the ocean's edge, searching for beach glass in the soft, white sand that stretched for miles, sharing stories that only best friends could.

Genevieve loved to bring each new edition of her magazines to the beach, where they would lie on a blanket, side by side, critiquing the new styles, arguing what was great and what was hideous. Nicky leaned toward most of them being hideous. Rainy days were spent on either of their family's porches.

Mr. Reynolds was gone all week, which made for a friendlier environment than when he was home. Mrs. Reynolds always had pastries from the bakery, a pitcher of sweet tea, and a stack of books for them to read. Both Genevieve and Nicky loved to read. They formed a book club, just the two of them—Beach Book Readers. Each would take a turn reading a book, while the other read something different, then they would swap. They spent many rainy days, or summer evenings, discussing, bickering, and sharing their opinions on their most recent read.

The Lemaires' porch was much more spirited. Trey always had a few boys his age roughhousing out there, while Emma, if she came down from her room, would curl up in a corner rocking chair with a book, trying to ignore the surrounding mayhem. There were always fresh-baked cookies on hand, lemonade, and board games.

This is where Nicky felt the most comfortable. He loved being with this family. They treated him as one of their own right from that first night of dessert and gin rummy on their porch. As an only child, he was smothered by his mother and had what seemed to be an unreasonable standard to gain any attention from his father. With the Lemaires, he could just be a teenage boy living at the ocean's edge, loving summer and friends.

Genevieve felt at home at Bellingham. She loved to listen to Mrs. Reynolds talk about her Southern culture, their cuisine, and her family's lineage. Helen told Genevieve all about her beautiful childhood home, the Clarkesville Plantation. In her Southern drawl, she described each room in vivid detail—the furniture, the chandeliers, the great fireplaces, and the upgrades to the home, as she could remember. "Mama and Daddy wallpapered the great room, which nobody did in those days. I'm sure it was Mama's influence on Daddy that sealed the deal."

But one thing that she impressed upon Genevieve was that she understood the history of her home, Clarkesville Plantation, and what that represented to her. She talked about the inequality between the races and detested the horrors of the treatment of people of color. "No one is better than anyone else, no matter what color their skin is. If there is one thing for you to carry with you, Genevieve, it is just that. We are all created by the same God."

Every Fourth of July, the Wellington family invited all the neighboring families to their summer home, which was situated on a bluff high above the Atlantic Ocean. Genevieve, Emma, and Trey loved this day. Each family brought a picnic basket loaded with fried chicken, potato salad, coleslaw, and lots of home-baked desserts and gathered on the Wellingtons' lawn, which was speckled with Adirondack chairs and small tables for their guests to relax and enjoy the day. They played croquet, some played tennis, others played badminton, while many of the older men could be found placing bets for the best chip shot on the putting green.

As dusk approached, a huge bonfire was lit on the beach below and then the fireworks! The Wellingtons spared no expense on this yearly display, proudly showing off their love of country and American pride.

There was much to celebrate this year—the Baseball Hall of Fame was dedicated in Cooperstown, New York, American Bobby Riggs won the Men's French Tennis Championship, and the Great Depression was well in the past. However, this summer, the summer of 1939, there was darkness looming. The kids were blissfully unaware, but their parents were mentally preparing for what might be in the future for the men, the sons, the brothers, and fathers.

"Nicky, let's check out the house before the fireworks start," Genevieve said as she grabbed his arm and pulled him toward the house.

"Gen, I don't think we should. The Wellingtons might not like that." This was his first Fourth of July in Newport, and he didn't want to miss anything.

"Come on, do not be a scaredy cat. I do it every year, and each time, it just gets better." They entered through a side door, away from the guests' vision, and stepped into a solarium. Washed-out, gray bricks on the floor felt cool on their sandy feet, and windows that reached from the floor to the ceiling opened wide to let in the ocean breeze.

The room was decorated with potted palm trees in each corner, the lush green contrasting with the chintz, floral sofa and armchairs. The room gave off an air of wealth and privilege. But this wasn't Genevieve's favorite room.

"Follow me," she whispered, forcing Nicky to be a conspirator in her plan. They tiptoed through each room, while Genevieve lovingly touched the fabrics, the marble on the fireplaces. She let her hand rest lightly on teak side tables and sat briefly in one of the twelve carved, mahogany, Chippendale chairs. As they moved from room to room, Genevieve whispered what the style of most of the pieces were, and if she didn't know what they were, she made a mental note to find out.

Suddenly, the sky exploded with fireworks, sending Nicky running out the door they entered with Genevieve reluctantly following.

July turned to August, and August hinted at fall.

Knock, knock. Nicky stood just outside the Lemaires' back screen door, waiting to be invited in. Mrs. Lemaire had told him more than once to just come in. "Family doesn't knock," she said, but he knew what his parents would think if they'd heard this.

Trey came to the door in a pair of navy-blue shorts, a wrinkled T-shirt, and bare feet. He appeared to have grown a foot that summer, now as tall as Emma, but still not up to Genevieve's height, which was his goal.

"Hi," said Trey as he opened the screen door, pushing his shaggy, blond hair out of his eyes. "If you're looking for

Genevieve, she's already swimming. She's crazy, you know. She left early for the beach. Want some breakfast?"

"Thanks, Trey, but I already had mine," said Nicky as he turned to leave. He wasn't looking forward to what he knew he had to do.

Nicky stood on the shore, scanning the water for a glimpse of Genevieve. She was nowhere in the water, at least as far as he could tell. A bit of panic started in the pit of his stomach. Nicky knew Genevieve was a strong swimmer, but she was alone, and the waves were much larger than yesterday. And then he glanced to his right and there she was, walking toward him. He felt such relief to see her as she waved to him.

She casually walked along the shore, stopping every few feet to inspect a shell. Most went back to the sea. Genevieve was particular about which ones would go home with her. Nicky waved back and then just watched her. He took in her tall, somewhat gangly shape, long, tanned legs and arms, her wet, blonde hair dripping down her back. As she approached him, Nicky noticed that her nose, which some would say was too large for her symmetrical-shaped face, had a subtle, pink hue to it. *Too much summer sun*, he thought to himself.

"Hi, you started early today."

"I did. I could not sleep. I feel like … well, I don't know what I feel like, but I feel something," she said, shrugging her shoulders and then showing him the only shell she decided to keep.

"I don't think I've ever seen one like this. Do you know what it's called?"

"It is an Angel Wing shell. I've seen them, but never in perfect condition. Look, not even a chip or a crack." Nicky took the shell from her hand and felt the smoothness on the inside, the texture on the outside.

"Gen, I need to tell you something," he said, rubbing the shell between his thumb and forefinger.

"Oh, okay, what?" Genevieve was bent over, examining more shells. Nicky knew she wasn't listening. He touched her shoulder. She glanced up at him and sensed something was wrong. Was this why she felt off last night and early this morning?

Genevieve stood up and gave Nicky her full attention. They were still the same height, and she could look him right in the eye.

"So last night, Daddy came home. He's never home during the week, and I don't think that Mama even knew that he was coming home. From the moment he walked in the door, he was in a foul mood. He told us we are leaving Bellingham on Friday and won't be back until next year. And then he said maybe not even next year. That maybe he would sell Bellingham."

"That is stupid. Why did he say any of that? School doesn't start for weeks. And even I know how hot it is in New Orleans in August."

"I don't know why he said any of it. I tried to ask, but he told me it wasn't any of my business, and I should go to my room. I told him I was going out, but from the look he gave me, I just went to my room. I tried to listen. I think Mama was crying. Daddy was just yelling something about how we had to leave, and she needed to pull herself together."

Genevieve stood, staring at her best friend, trying to process what he just told her.

Friday, he said Friday. Does he mean next Friday? It cannot be this Friday. That's tomorrow. Genevieve was sure she misunderstood what Nicky had said.

"We leave tomorrow morning. I have to pack today. Daddy has already booked us train tickets. We flew here, so I don't understand why we can't fly home." Nicky was staring out at the ocean when he said this, afraid that he might cry.

"Well, it's not right, not fair. What if I asked my father to talk to him? I know … maybe you could stay with us for the rest of the summer." Genevieve was excited. There was a problem. She solved it. *That's what I do*, she thought. *Make a plan, solve a problem.*

"Gen, Daddy would hate that. He'd probably kill me for even mentioning it. It's done, my summer is over. I need to get home." Resigned to the inevitable, Nicky handed Genevieve's shell back to her and began to walk away.

"Wait, Nicky, wait. I will see you before you leave, right? I can help you pack, and then we can swim and walk together to make plans for next year. You should come for dinner. That is what you should do."

"Thanks, but I have to help out at home. I need to be there for Mama. I don't think that I can come for dinner. It just doesn't seem right to leave her alone on our last night in Bellingham."

"Will you at least meet me tonight, after dinner? Tell your mother you need to go for a walk, and I'll go to bed after dessert and then sneak out at nine. We can meet at the bottom of your stairs. Please, you cannot just leave me like this." Genevieve was beside herself. She wasn't thinking about how hard this must be for Nicky. She was only thinking about herself, how hard it was going to be for her.

Genevieve could barely eat her dinner. Her mother had made baked stuffed cod, salad full of their garden vegetables, and their summer favorite—corn on the cob. She pushed her food around on her plate while Trey retold the story of how he and his buddies spent the day sailing out of Narragansett Bay.

"Pops, do you know why Mr. Reynolds is making Nicky and his mother leave tomorrow and why they aren't coming back?"

Her father glanced at her mother, took a sip of wine, and put more butter on his corn. "I don't know why. Maybe Nicky needs to start school early. He's on the football team, so perhaps early practice." Genevieve knew this wasn't the reason for an early departure, but she also knew when to not push the envelope with her father.

Her mother remained quiet and finally said, "I am sorry to see them leaving. I so enjoy having Nicky around, and Helen Reynolds is a lovely neighbor, even though I've barely seen her this summer. Who's ready for dessert?"

"None for me. May I be excused? I just want to go to my room." Genevieve put on a perfectly dejected face as she cleared her place and left the dining room.

Nicky and Genevieve met at the bottom of his stairs. He told his mother he was going for one last walk, while Genevieve climbed out her window to the front porch roof and then down the pink Clematis vine, her mother's favorite.

"Hi. Did you have any trouble getting out?" Nicky asked as they walked down the beach.

"Only if I ruined my mother's Clematis vine, then I'll be in trouble." Genevieve was conflicted about what she was feeling, and it wasn't concern for the vine. She felt a mix of sadness and anger, and a third emotion that was unfamiliar and confusing. "How about if we become pen pals? We can write to each other as often as we want, and we can keep our Beach Book Club going."

"That sounds like a plan. Leave it to you, Genevieve Lemaire, to always have a plan. I'm going to miss that. I'm going to miss you." They stopped walking and just stood side by side, watching the swell of the ocean that they had swum in together more times than anyone could count.

"Well, looks like you know me pretty well, Nicholas Reynolds. And I will miss you, I will miss us." She reached into her shorts pocket, pulled out the Angel Wing shell, and handed it to Nicky.

"Keep this to remember our summer together. Just rub it

between your fingers, and you will smell the ocean and think of all our fun."

Genevieve handed Nicky the shell, closed his hand with hers, gave him a quick hug, and turned to leave. He watched her walk down the shore in the moonlight. She turned just once, waved, and then continued toward her home.

Newport Hospital

"When all is lost, there is still a memory." — Dejan Stojanovic

Beep, beep, beep. *What the hell is that sound? I can barely open my eyes. What is happening?*

"Genevieve, dear, can you hear me?"

That is Emma, I hear Emma. I am awake.

"Oh Emma, yes, I can hear you. You are loud enough to wake the dead." My sister still annoys me, but we do love each other. As much as a Lemaire is capable of loving anyone.

"Well, Genevieve, from where I'm standing, you are far from dead."

Oh, dear sister, I think, *don't be so sure of that.*

"Emma, anyone our age is quite close to dead. Get me my hairbrush out of the Chanel bag over on the chair. I must look like holy hell." I might feel like hell, but I do not need to look like it.

"Aside from sleeping, what are you doing to pass the time? How many days have you been here?"

"Too many days, possibly ten. I've lost track. It's incomprehensible that with all the tests, poking, and prodding, these idiots cannot come up with a diagnosis. What am I doing to pass the time? I am reminiscing. Things that I haven't thought of in years are coming back to me. It is quite strange and yet reassuring at the same time. Do you remember the summer we met Nicky?"

"Of course I do. Who could ever forget that summer? He was so handsome, with that jet-black hair and those intense, chocolate-brown eyes. Oh, and his nose. I think they call it a Roman nose. My, my, I had such a crush on him, but he barely knew I was alive."

"A crush? I never knew that. I just remember you had your nose stuck in a book all summer."

"I remember when he left," said Emma. "It was like the air was sucked from our house. I felt like we were just going through the motions, with our golf and tennis lessons, the beach, shopping. All the things we did before Nicky just seemed so different after Nicky."

I feel like I am looking at my ninety-two-year-old sister for the first time. I never paid much attention to her when she was younger. Well, I knew her, but only on the surface. But Emma is right. Things changed once Nicky left. I thought I was the only one who felt the void. He was such a large presence in our life that summer.

Mom had kept the three of us busy with our different lessons, which I enjoyed. I knew that my skills in golf and tennis would come in handy, as I aimed to level the playing field with the affluent summer crowd in Newport. I practiced on the tennis court with Newport's high-society teenagers and teed off with them on equal ground at the club. But there was one place that did not matter to me who was watching or who I was competing against, and that was horseback riding. Only a few had a slight advantage over me—the teenagers whose parents had paid to have their thoroughbred shipped to Newport for the summer. They had the luxury of knowing their horse and vice versa. The rest of us were assigned to ride one horse for the season, which I took as a challenge. I loved a good challenge in those days. Actually, I still love a challenge. Just a bit more difficult to rise to it.

"I remember how you would run to the mailbox every day after Nicky left. If there wasn't a letter from him, you would mope around."

"I did not run to the mailbox, and I certainly did not mope. But there was a time when his letters meant so much to me. As we got older, they became a lifeline when times were so tough."

"Nicky is a good friend, Genevieve. Have you two spoken recently? Does he know you're in the hospital?"

"Emma, you sound like my kids. I will tell Nicky when I feel the time is right."

"Oh dear, speaking of time, I am going to be late for mass. I will check in tomorrow to see how you are doing. Oh, and I will pray for you."

"Emma, it is not too late for you to join the convent," I said, as my sister, now taller than me, smiled and walked out of my hospital room. I hate that I have shrunk a bit, and she hasn't. Life is not fair.

I straighten my blankets, trying to not get caught up in all the wires hooked up to me. My hands are black and blue, and my arms are bruised from all the different tests done on me. I brush my hair, without a mirror, and hope for the best. Emma's brief visit, and the attempt to brush my hair, have wiped me out.

I lean back into my down pillows that Sara brought from home and think about my life and where I am now. I know what's wrong with me. I don't need a doctor's diagnosis to confirm it, but I am paying enough for all these tests and treatments. I want to get my money's worth and make them figure it out.

As I start to doze, I think about what Emma said about Nicky. How old was she that first summer, thirteen, maybe fourteen? Emma, who grew up wanting to be a nun. Saint Emma had a crush on Nicky Reynolds. I chuckle. Sleep comes to me quickly, or is it all the meds I am getting? With sleep comes memories.

Nicky and I wrote faithfully, as we had promised each other on that moonlit night in August 1939. Once we both started school, our letters were full of what our days were like. Nicky's schedule was jam-packed more than mine. We talked about books—some that had been assigned to us by our teachers, and others we had chosen for ourselves. That winter, we individually saw *Gone with the Wind*, swore not to talk about it until we both saw it, and then our letters were full of how much we loved the movie. I identified more with Rhett Butler than I think Nicky did. Oh, sure, Scarlett O'Hara was a schemer, but Rhett … well, he just thought about what he wanted and did it. I am drifting. It is lovely. Who is singing?

1940

"THE MOST IMPORTANT THING IN LIFE IS
LEARNING HOW TO FALL."
— JEANNETTE WALLS

"Happy birthday to you, happy birthday, dear Genevieve, happy birthday to you." Genevieve pulled back her long, blonde hair, made a silent wish, and blew out all seventeen candles on her birthday cake. All chocolate, just the way she liked.

From behind her group of girlfriends came a loud and clear, "You look like a monkey, and you smell like one too."

"Mom, get him out of here."

"Trey Lemaire, stop that right now, or no cake for you." Margaux was trying to act shocked by her son's behavior, but secretly, she loved that her only boy was a mischief maker. She watched Genevieve open her presents, laughing, thanking each person, even if she didn't like that gift. *Where does she get this confidence? I certainly wasn't like that at her age. I don't think I'm even like that at this age.* Genevieve was maturing, growing out of her gangly arms and legs. A year of braces was all she needed to get her smile perfected. She was so full of life, so full of energy. *I hope she can harness that before she gets herself into trouble*, Margaux thought as she cleared away the dirty cake dishes.

Genevieve's party came to an end. Emma helped clean up, while her sister relished the attention she had received all day. Genevieve loved having the focus on her. Trey was trying to sneak another piece of cake to his room.

"Genevieve, there's a phone call for you, dear." Genevieve looked up at her mother. Who would call? Her friends had just left.

"I think you are getting your birthday wish. Now go find out who it is."

Genevieve raced down the hall to where the phone sat on a small desk, which offered little privacy.

She picked up the receiver. "Hello."

"Happy birthday, Gen." It was Nicky on the other line. Neither had spoken since he left last August. Long-distance phone calls were expensive, and both of their fathers considered it frivolous, a waste of hard-earned money.

"Nicky," she said with complete joy, a big smile on her face. "You remembered!"

"How could I not remember? You had a countdown in every letter since the start of the year."

NEWPORT WAS a hive of activity on a sunny Friday, with people preparing for the Memorial Day weekend. Margaux took advantage of the quiet house. Kids were in school, and Edward was at work. She took a cup of tea and a warm, cashmere wrap out to the porch, catching the late-morning sun, rocking silently in the big, wicker chair that had come out of winter storage for this "official" kickoff-for-summer weekend.

Margaux looked out over her sprawling lawn to the ocean below and thought about the world she was raising her children in. Europe, which seemed so far away, was marching farther and farther into war. Britain had begun food rationing,

Germany had invaded Denmark, and Norway and the Netherlands surrendered to Germany soon after. Earlier this month, the Summer Olympics were canceled because of the war.

Yet here in the United States, life seemed to move along, as if oblivious to the terrifying events happening on the other side of the ocean. As a surprise, she and Edward had splurged a bit, taking the kids to see the Walt Disney movie *Pinocchio* at the Colonial Theater, and then to dinner at the White Horse Tavern.

The family had celebrated Genevieve's seventeenth birthday the same as they had every year—chocolate cake, lots of friends, presents, and a call from Nicky. Margaux smiled, thinking how much easier it was to plan Emma and Trey's birthdays than it was to appease Genevieve. Emma loved a family dinner at home, hoping to get a wonderful selection of books. Trey, true to his personality, started handing out his list of wants weeks before his birthday.

Margaux felt a chill, pulled her cashmere wrap tighter against her small shoulders, finished her tea, and sat for just another moment. She felt unsettled, worried. The world was changing, and she was concerned for her children. Margaux sent a silent prayer out to the ocean as she stood up and walked back into the kitchen.

She had no sooner washed her teacup and saucer when there was a knock on the back door. Margaux dried her hands on her floral-print apron and opened the door to Nicky Reynolds.

"My goodness, Nicky. Oh my, what are you doing here? Come in, come in. Let me get a good look at you." Margaux was beaming. She had such a warm spot for Nicky.

"Hi, Mrs. Lemaire. Sorry to just drop by, but I couldn't wait to see everyone." His smile was still intoxicating. His striking, brown eyes scanned the kitchen for just a minute.

"Oh, Nicky, well look at you. My goodness, how many

inches have you grown? The children aren't back from school, but sit down, dear, and tell me what you have been up to and why you are here preseason. I saw some activity at your house last week. How are you?" Margaux realized she was rattling on and sensed that Nicky seemed nervous. "Can I get you something to eat? A piece of apple pie?"

"I would love a piece of your pie, please. That will help me know that I'm really here." Nicky ate the pie slowly, washing it down with a glass of milk she had given him.

"How are your parents? Are you all here for the long weekend? It seems like quite a lengthy trip to come from New Orleans to Newport for three days."

"My mother is here with me. She's doing better now that our New Orleans house has been sold."

Margaux sat across from him at the large, farmhouse kitchen table. Something was off here. "Oh, well, that is big news. Are your parents in the market for another home down south?"

"No, ma'am. Newport is our home now. My mother and I will be here year-round." Nicky knew Mrs. Lemaire needed the complete story, but this would be the first time that he would actually say it out loud to someone who had no idea what the past few months had been like for him. Not even his best friend, Genevieve. "You see, my father died earlier this year," he said as Margaux's hand flew to cover her mouth. "He was killed in a car accident. His car got stuck on railroad tracks, and there was a train, just bearing down on him. The train couldn't stop, and he couldn't get out of the way."

Nicky pushed the fork around on his plate, moving the last bits of pie crumbs. The silence in the kitchen was thick, as if a heavy fog had just rolled in. Margaux said nothing. She reached her hand across the table and took hold of Nicky's free hand. He put down the fork, let her hold both of his hands, as he sat at the Lemaires' kitchen table and started sobbing.

This is the first time he had let go, let his words and the reality of his father's death sink in and come out of him at the same time. His cries were guttural, like a wounded animal. He held on to her hands, sobbed, and rocked back and forth in the sturdy kitchen chair. Neither of them knew how long they had sat like that, but eventually, Nicky stopped rocking, stopped sobbing, and let go of Margaux's hands.

She got up to get him some tissues and a glass of cold water. Neither had spoken yet. Margaux was not sure how to comfort this boy, and Nicky was not sure what to say after his breakdown. But at that moment, Margaux heard Trey yelling to his friends. The children would come through the back door any minute.

"Nicky, why don't you go into the bathroom and splash cold water on your face? I'll tell the children to go upstairs to clean up before their after-school snack. That will give you some time to … well, to try to pull yourself together." He went into the bathroom, and Margaux thought, *Why couldn't I have said something more comforting to this boy, this child who just lost his father?* She picked up his plate and glass, shaking her head, as she put them in the sink. Her three children came into the kitchen the same way they'd done year in and year out—loud, disruptive, and wonderful.

The surprise of Nicky walking into their kitchen was almost more than Emma, Trey, and especially Genevieve could believe. They all talked at once, hugging and laughing. Margaux watched for any remnants of what had taken place just a few minutes before, but Nicky showed no signs of pain or tears.

After they all ate apple pie, Genevieve stood up, grabbed everyone's plates, placed them in the kitchen sink, and said to no one in particular, "Nicky and I are going for a walk, alone." She emphasized the word alone with a look at both Trey and Emma. Off they went, out the back door and down to the beach.

This was when Nicky disclosed his story for the second time, but it was easier since it was to Genevieve. He also revealed the complete story, swearing her to secrecy. As Nicky began, he pulled out the Angel Wing shell Genevieve had given him and rubbed it between his fingers. The part that he hadn't told Margaux Lemaire is that the reason his father got the car stuck on the railroad tracks is because he was drunk. He probably would have lived if he hadn't been too sloshed to get out of the car to avoid the collision.

"The conductor said Daddy just stared at him as the train came bearing down on him. He said the train was going too fast to stop. I think he could have gotten out. I don't think he wanted to."

The two friends walked side by side, taking turns talking, Genevieve asking questions and Nicky doing his best to answer. Mr. Reynolds had been drinking more and more, most likely because of problems with his business. Nicky wondered if his father had done this on purpose. Suicide wasn't something people discussed openly.

Nicky talked about moving here, how his life had changed forever, and wondered what he was supposed to do for his mother. "I'm all she has left. It's just the two of us now. I know Mama is worried about money. That's why we are here, and that's why I had to leave school."

Genevieve stopped walking, turned to face Nicky, and said, "That is silly. You might think that all you have is your mother, but Nicky Reynolds, you have me. You will always have me."

"Gen, I don't think you understand. You have your parents, Emma, Trey, and lots of friends from school. It really is just Mama and me, and she is going to need me to be the man of the house."

Genevieve tried to feel what her friend was going through, but it seemed so foreign to her, this pain that Nicky was feeling. She had experienced nothing like that, and she seemed almost incapable of allowing herself to console Nicky. Instead, Genevieve took his hand in hers and smiled up at him. "We will make this summer the best ever." And with that, Genevieve dropped his hand and started running down the beach. "Race you to the next jetty," she yelled.

Nicky watched for just a second and then started running after her. As she raced down the beach barefoot, still wearing her plaid skirt and white blouse from school, blonde hair flying behind her, Genevieve smiled, thinking how happy she was to have her friend close by, and now he would never leave her.

However, the summer of 1940 was not what Genevieve had hoped for. To begin with, Nicky seemed to be with his mother all the time. She was fit to be tied when he didn't go to the Memorial Day parade with her.

"Gen, Mama isn't up for parades or big crowds, so we are staying home tomorrow," is what he'd said when she told him what time to be ready to go. They were sitting on the Reynolds' porch swing, their feet dangling side by side as they slowly rocked forward and back. At that moment, the only sound was the squeaking of the swing and the seagulls squawking overhead as they flew toward the ocean.

Genevieve put her foot down to slow the rocking and turned to look at Nicky. "Well, that is stupid. The parade is fun. Who doesn't want to have fun?"

Nicky set both of his feet on the porch floor. The squeaking stopped abruptly. "It's not stupid, it's what she's feeling. He has been dead for only five months. This is hard, Gen, really hard, for her and for me."

Nicky stood up as if to go into the house, but Genevieve patted the cushion on the swing. "Sit back down, please. I didn't mean to make you mad. I just don't understand why. It's been five months. Surely that is enough time to get back to normal, isn't it?"

TIME MARCHES ON

"YOU ARE THE DANCING QUEEN, YOUNG AND SWEET, ONLY SEVENTEEN." — ABBA

"Dear, I am sorry, but I forgot your name. I would like to get out of this bed for a while. I am so sick and tired of just lying here. My robe is in the closet. Please help me put it on and get me to the chair by the window." *Sick and tired*, I think. That is usually just an expression, but I am sick, and I am tired.

Today is Sunday. I told Sara to stay home today and spend some quality time with her husband. She has been coming here every day, and I am concerned about her marriage. Emma will be at church, so it looks like I might be on my own today. There was a time in my life when I didn't want to be alone. I loved being the life of the party. One would think that after all these years of being on my own, I would not mind being by myself. But being on my own and being alone are two different things.

A nurse, whatever she said her name is, helps me with my robe and gets me and the damn IV over to the window, which overlooks the harbor. The sun is shining, reflecting off the water, and the bright-blue sky gives the illusion of a warm, spring day, but the icy wind blowing in off the ocean tells me it is still February in Newport. I watch the boats moored in the harbor sway from side to side, buffeted by the strong gusts of wind.

It is strange to not have been outside in days. How many days have I been here? At least ten, maybe longer. My mind begins to wander. I try to stay in the present, but it's easier to let go, at least for the time being. Not let go completely. I am not ready to let go completely.

My seventeenth birthday comes to mind. I remember everything. I wore a red-and-white, polka dot, shirtwaist dress with red, leather, swing-dance shoes. God, I loved those shoes. Having a size nine shoe at seventeen was quite a challenge to find anything other than those damn saddle shoes to put on my feet.

Most of the girls from my class came over after school. We danced to Frank Sinatra and Bing Crosby, had cake, and I opened all my presents. It was wonderful being the center of attention, and still is. The best gift was the surprise call from Nicky. Oh, Nicky. Oh, dear Nicky.

I remember how I was so looking forward to him coming back to Newport that summer. I had already started in on Pops about getting my driver's license and had big plans of driving around Newport and maybe to Providence, exploring with Nicky. But then, his damn father had to go and kill himself. He absolutely ruined that summer for me. I could not, for the life of me, understand why Nicky and his mother moped around that entire summer. Mr. Reynolds was the one who chose to drink himself into a stupor, park on the train tracks, and wait until a train came along to end his life. Nicky had told me that, not the story that everyone else believed … that his car got stuck on the tracks and he was tragically hit by a train.

I tried to tell Mom the truth, and she got absolutely furious with me. Told me to never speak of that again. I didn't always listen to her advice, but her anger about this was something I was not going to push. I went along with the lie and Nicky, and I never talked about the truth. But this truth or lie seemed to put a wedge between us. That and the fact that he was always doing something for his mother that summer. He missed so much fun, and so did I. It wasn't fun without him.

Our parents made sure that Emma, Trey, and I were kept busy that summer. We had tennis, golf, and sailing lessons. Funny, I would tell my kids that they overbooked their kids with soccer, baseball, lacrosse, whatever, yet when I look back, my parents seemed to overbook us each summer. I still took riding lessons. My favorite, and Pops', was patiently trying to teach me how to drive. Neither of us had much tolerance for that.

When Nicky could tear himself away from his mother and spend time with me, I always acted like I didn't care whether or not I saw him. But I think I did care. It was an odd feeling because looking back, I didn't care much about anyone but myself. Thinking about the feelings of others was not—or probably still is not—in my wheelhouse.

One major highlight that stands out for me that summer was that Mom finally gave in and bought me a pair of real nylons. They had come out in May, and after much pestering from me, she broke down in July and got them for me. But it was summer. I was not going to wear them then, which I told her. She said I was ungrateful. Maybe, but who would wear nylons in the summer?

Once school began, Nicky and I had more time together. Now that he was here year-round, we sat together on the bus and had some of the same classes. He made the football team, of course, and I had worked two days a week, after school, at the stables to barter for lessons. Pops had said that it was time to "tighten the purse strings," and he was looking at ways to cut back on expenses. I didn't mind helping out since I was where I loved to be—around horses. Even with these distractions, Nicky and I did our homework together whenever possible. It was usually at his house, so Mrs. Reynolds wouldn't be lonely. Honestly, there were days I wanted to wring that woman's neck. She had such a hold over Nicky.

1941

"THE WORLD'S MINE OYSTER."
— WILLIAM SHAKESPEARE

Genevieve turned eighteen in February. Her birthday party was no different this year than it had been in the past, other than Nicky was there, as well as some of the other boys in her class. They danced in the living room to Duke Ellington and Tommy Dorsey, sang happy birthday, and ate chocolate cake. Genevieve noticed the gifts were less extravagant than in previous years. She knew that her family had made some adjustments, but Genevieve didn't seem to understand that others were doing the same thing. Instead of getting a new pair of leather gloves, she got a pair of white, cotton gloves. Hitler was waging war across Europe, she understood that, but what could that possibly have to do with her and her friends?

Genevieve's lack of enthusiasm for her gifts did not go unnoticed by her mother. Margaux bit her tongue. She knew what battles to pick with her oldest daughter, and this was not one of them.

Nicky turned eighteen in March with very little fanfare. He invited Genevieve to dinner at his house; it was just Mrs. Reynolds, Nicky, and Genevieve. Mrs. Reynolds enjoyed

Genevieve's company. She brought an air of optimism to her otherwise quiet life and appreciated the friendship between her son and Genevieve.

Despite the tension in the world, life seemed to move along in Newport. Nicky and Genevieve graduated from high school. Her father finally gave in and allowed Genevieve to get her driver's license. Nicky already had his. They both took turns driving around, relishing the freedom of being adults, as they referred to themselves. But they both knew that their lives were going to change, and they needed to make this their best summer ever.

Genevieve would leave for Connecticut College in August. Her parents had chosen this school for a few reasons. Connecticut was just far enough away to give Genevieve a sense of independence, not that she really needed that. This school offered a secretarial degree, which was affordable for the Lemaires. The escalation of the war was affecting most Americans' bottom line. They looked forward to Genevieve getting a degree in an area that she could branch out in and begin a career with, before she settled down, got married, and had children.

Genevieve, however, looked forward to joining the equestrian team. Nicky held off on college "just for a year," he'd told Genevieve. Through connections from his father's cronies, he had been offered an entry-level job at the First National Bank of Newport. They had discussed— fought about—this decision for most of the spring.

"A bank … a bank? Nicky, you were offered football scholarships at some of the top schools in the country. You could have a full ride at Wesleyan, and we would be near each other. Why would you throw this opportunity away?"

It was a warm, spring Saturday, and her dad had given her the car for the afternoon. She and Nicky drove down the shore road and stopped for ice cream. What should have been a fun outing was turning into an uncomfortable time for Nicky. *Genevieve just doesn't give up*, he thought before replying.

"Gen, this is what I have to do. I don't have a choice." Before he let her interrupt, he said, "My mother needs me, and we need an income right now. The bank will give us both that. Can you accept that, please, and finish your ice cream? It's dripping down the front of your shirt."

Genevieve glanced down at her chocolate ice cream trickling onto her white, linen shirt. She rolled down the driver's side window, tossed out the ice cream, gave her sticky arm a lick, turned on the ignition, and pulled out of the parking lot, hoping that if she went fast enough, Nicky's ice cream would land on his lap.

But these spats never lasted. Nicky and Genevieve were too close to let life get in their way. Nicky started working at the bank a week after graduation. It was hard for him, working inside all day in the summer. He felt like his life was slipping away from him. He secretly would have loved to accept one of those football scholarships, attend college, and join a fraternity … all the things his father had done. But Nicky Reynolds knew that this wouldn't happen. His mother had plans for him, and he also knew that he did not want to become his father. He envied Genevieve, who seemed to have her whole life opening up for her, and he knew she would take whatever was offered to her and fly with it.

In early June, the whole Lemaire family packed up the Buick and drove to Connecticut College for Freshman Family Day. As an incoming freshman, Genevieve would stay in a dorm room while the rest of the family stayed in a local hotel. Genevieve was bursting at the seams to get there. "Pops, can you drive any faster? Let me drive. I want to get there before we miss everything."

"SHALL we get you back to your bed, Genevieve?"

"Oh, who are you?" There are so many damn different people coming in and out of here. It is like a revolving door, and they just expect me to smile and do what they say. Well, I am not dead yet, so I am not about to change.

"No, not just yet, but you can get me a blanket and a bit of juice, preferably with vodka and ice. Thank you." Before the poor, stuttering fool can form a sentence, I wave her away. "Fine, just the blanket then." The blanket is comforting. I feel like I am in a cocoon, all tucked in. It is so refreshing to be out of that damn bed. What I would give to just get away. I need an adventure, not beeping machines and hovering nurses.

I still remember how excited I was to get away from Newport for my first overnight at Connecticut College. It was Family Day, but I was more excited that there was a dance that night, and my overly protective parents and pain-in-the-neck sister and brother would not be going. Freedom, at last!

Pops drove so slowly, I thought I would die, but I didn't. However, I will die soon, but enough of that.

Mom helped me get settled into my overnight dorm room. There were three other girls already there with their mothers, so it was crowded and hectic. But once the mothers left, we all looked at each other and started laughing and jumping up and down. Betty, Jane, and Sally—we became immediate friends, not knowing that day would lead us to become lifelong friends, but we did. Sadly, I am the last one left.

After the obligatory family picnic, tour of the campus, and speeches, we could finally go back to our room to get ready for the dance. Before I could get away, Mom stopped me, put her hands on my shoulders, and looked me straight in the eye. She could do that. Mom was as tall as me. "Genevieve, remember who you are and how we raised you. Hold your head high and act like a Lemaire." I remember thinking, *Just let me go*, but in hindsight, I should have listened to my mother.

The four of us were buzzing with energy as we tried to get ready in that small room, the sound of our laughter echoing through the shared bathroom of the dorm floor. It was hectic. Betty, Jane, and Sally each wore a dress that was appropriate for what part of the country they were from and, of course, their age. So, nothing too daring. Actually, there was nothing daring between any of their dress choices, or shoes, for that matter.

I had packed the dress that Mom and I decided on—a simple, light-blue, gingham party dress with puff sleeves and navy-blue, kitten heels. But when I showed Nicky what I was wearing, he told me to leave room in my suitcase for something else. God, that man had good taste even back then.

The girls gasped when I came out of the bathroom stall, ensemble complete. I was wearing a strapless, pink, chiffon tea dress cinched at the waist with bright-red high heels. My hair was swept to the side with a red rose, and my lipstick matched both the shoes and the rose. Nicky had found the perfect dress and shoes for me in his mother's closet. The rose was my idea. "She won't realize it's gone, and you'll look stunning in it. Those college boys won't know what to say. I bet they won't even be able to speak," he said, folding the dress into the bottom of my suitcase and hiding the shoes under my other clothes.

I felt incredible. These days, they say something about how I felt my power. Well, let me tell you, I not only felt my power, I embraced my power and walked into that dance with my head held high, accompanied by my three new but frumpy friends. Nicky was right, maybe too right. I think I scared those wannabe frat boys away. Nobody came over to talk to me; they talked to the other girls. I didn't care. I was better than all of them. I knew it. They knew it. All except one—just one—and that one would be my undoing.

"Hi there. Are you alone?" He was just about my height. I was five foot ten without my heels, but the extra couple of inches they added made me almost as tall as he was. Tall and handsome. The most intoxicating blue eyes I had ever seen and a smile that gave mine a run for its money. At that very moment, I thought about how our children would be blessed with our smiles, completely forgetting how much Pops had paid for my braces.

"I wouldn't say that I am alone, but at the moment, it appears that way." I extended my hand. "Hi, I am Genevieve Lemaire."

"Michael Austin. Nice to meet you, Genevieve," he said, shaking my hand gently. I think he actually gave it a little squeeze. "Do you want some punch, or would you like something a bit stronger?" he asked with a wink.

"Nice to meet you, Michael Austin, and a glass of punch would be lovely." As we walked over to the punch table together, Michael put his hand on the small of my back. I felt such a tingle up my spine. Nobody had ever done that to me. He casually guided me to the table and handed me a glass of punch. We moved to the side of the table and talked about who we were, where we came from, and where we were going. Every so often, one of his buddies would walk by and slap him on the back or the shoulder, grinning. I was so naive then, thinking that they were just being nice, not realizing that they were probably thinking Michael Austin was about to get lucky that night.

I was completely smitten with him, but I also knew that it was important that I hold my own with this man. This might have been the forties, but I was not about to ruin my life for a little fun with a handsome stranger. Michael was from New York. He told me he had been invited here by a friend who was attending Yale that fall. I was impressed. Getting into Yale was no easy feat. I smiled my most charming smile and asked him if he was also going to Yale. I am sure if I could have, I would have crossed my fingers and toes. What a prize ... a Yale college man! And that is when this incredibly handsome man told me he would be going to Harvard. *Even better*, I thought.

But he kept talking and said he was going to be a senior in high school that fall. He had early acceptance to Harvard, but the terms were that he could take two preliminary classes while attending high school, and he must graduate with his class, meaning, he had another year. I was confused by this. This is the first boy I met away from home, and I felt like he was a fake. Was he just putting on a show? He took my hand, smiled, and said, "I hope you aren't disappointed."

I was disappointed; he was younger than me. Why would I be interested in someone younger than me, although the Harvard angle was interesting. *What the hell*, I thought, *this is just a dance.* We danced a lot that night. We talked a lot that night, and I felt something I had never felt before. I felt Michael was listening to me. Nobody did that, except for Nicky. Oh, I could not wait to tell Nicky all about this night.

The dance was ending. Michael and I exchanged phone numbers, but the chance of us seeing each other again seemed slim. He would be in New York City for the summer, working, and then back to high school for another year. I would be in college in Connecticut, which was almost a three-hour train ride from the city. He said good night and gave me a kiss on my cheek. I remember thinking, *Why in the hell do you have to be younger than me?*

SUMMER 1941

"IF THERE EVER COMES A DAY WHEN WE
CAN'T BE TOGETHER, KEEP ME IN YOUR
HEART, I'LL STAY THERE FOREVER."
— WINNIE-THE-POOH

"Pops, let me drive. We will never get home at this rate." Genevieve couldn't get home fast enough to tell Nicky all about her night.

"For Christ's sake, Genevieve. First, you couldn't get to Connecticut fast enough, and now you can't get home fast enough. What is it with you?" He glanced over at his wife in the passenger seat, completely exasperated. Genevieve did that to him. Margaux looked at her husband, gently smiled, and shook her head no. In other words, walk away from this battle.

Genevieve sulked in the back seat, tapping her finger against the window, Emma read, and Trey slept. They arrived home early Sunday afternoon. The kids jumped out of the back seat, and Genevieve started to head straight to Nicky's house.

"Genevieve, who do you expect to take your suitcase up to your room?" her mother asked. Genevieve was about to ask her mother to do it for her and then remembered the red heels and the pink party dress. She reached into the trunk, picked up her suitcase, and ran up the stairs with it. Genevieve took the heels and dress out, folded the dress gently, and hid both in an old chest tucked in the back of her closet. She stuck the red rose, now dried out, in the frame of her mirror. This would be a reminder of her night … meeting Michael Austin.

Nicky was sitting on the beach in front of his house, staring out at the ocean. The sun was shining brightly, the breeze off the ocean was gentle, and there wasn't a cloud in sight. It was a beautiful day. The beach was peaceful and uncrowded, a welcome change from the usual high-season crowds in Newport.

Genevieve ran up to him, slamming her body into him, knocking Nicky out of his trance. "Jesus, Gen, you scared me, and you could have hurt me," he said, brushing sand off his T-shirt and arms.

"Oh, Nicky, aren't you happy to see me? I have so much to tell you," Genevieve said, not waiting to hear if he was actually happy to see her. She thought, *Of course he is. Why wouldn't he be?*

"How was the dance, Gen? How were the dress and shoes? Did you get caught?"

"I did not get caught, thank goodness, and the clothes … Oh, Nicky, you were so right. Nobody could stop looking at me. The stupid boys were afraid to even talk to me. They are mere boys. I am a woman," she said, lying down on her back in the sand, laughing.

"Then you had a good time. I'm happy for you, Gen. And I am sure you looked like a movie star." Nicky seemed a bit off, but Genevieve didn't want to take away from her moment, so she ignored it. She was completely fixated on telling him every single detail, which she did, from her new friends, to the rose in her hair, to how fabulous she looked.

"Did I tell you I looked fabulous?"

"Only fourteen times," he said, pushing her playfully.

Genevieve sat up and glanced at Nicky. "I met someone."

"You told me. Sally, somebody, and somebody."

"Sally, Betty, and Jane, but not them. Someone else. Someone I think I might like."

Nicky stared out at the ocean, waiting for her to continue because he knew she would, whether or not he wanted her to.

"His name is Michael Austin. He is very, very handsome and charming, and he is the only one who had the guts to come over and introduce himself to me."

Silence from Nicky.

"He's from New York and headed to Harvard. Quite impressive, right? We look amazing together. Nicky, are you listening to me?"

"Of course I'm listening. I'm sitting right next to you. So, when do I get to meet Mr. Harvard?"

"Well, that I don't know. I mean, he's in New York, and I'm here for now. Then I am leaving at the end of summer, so there is no telling when you will meet him. But it is exciting, Nicky. I have never felt this way. It is so exciting, but also confusing. There is a lot to be sorted out. But I loved how he listened to me … really listened to me. Like you do, Nicky. You are my best friend, and now I think that I have met someone who could be a best friend, possibly more. Do you know what I mean?"

"I know what you mean. Mr. Harvard might be your first love. I'm happy for you, Gen, I really am, but I feel like there's more to this story than you're telling me."

"Okay, there might be just one little thing, but I don't think it's really very important, and who cares what people think?" Genevieve sat up, wiping sand off her legs. Nicky stared at her. He wasn't going to beg her to spill it.

Genevieve knew this look from Nicky, one she knew all too well. She sat up straighter, peered out at the water, and said, "He is younger than me, not a big deal."

"How much younger? He starts Harvard in the fall, so what, a couple of months younger? You're right, that's not a big deal. Look at us. I'm a month younger than you, but I'm so much more mature than you are," Nicky said, joking.

"He starts Harvard a year from September. He needs to finish high school." Her tone made him cringe just a bit, but he had to ask. Nicky knew this tone from her. She would get defensive, put on an air for show … Genevieve the warrior; do not mess with me.

"He is a senior in high school? Did he get kept back or something? I'm confused. How could he know about Harvard already?"

"Early admittance, with the stipulation that he graduates from high school. Michael is so smart, he is taking two preliminary classes with Harvard while still in high school. He turns eighteen in September. Seriously, age is just a number. It is how a person acts, how they present themselves, what they want to make out of their life. That is what counts. Michael wants to be someone, and I believe he will do something wonderful. Maybe I can do something wonderful with him. I said we look great together. I think we could be a power couple. But enough about me. It is time to focus on you. I am going to make it my mission to find your someone who makes you feel as special as Michael makes me feel."

"Really? And how are you going to do that?" Nicky asked as he gestured to the empty beach.

"Rich summer girls will be our focus. Stick with me, Nicholas Reynolds. You are in for a wild summer."

He leaned over and gave her a kiss on her forehead. "I gotta get home. Please don't do anything crazy … please, Gen."

True to her word, Genevieve did her best to find a "Michael Austin" for Nicky. The work started at the Fourth of July picnic, which was held every year at the Wellingtons' home. The party was full of wealthy summer families, along with the local families. Genevieve walked around the perimeter of the lawn, scoping out who was there and who had matured over the winter. She was looking for someone worthy of her darling Nicky. She did find him some dates that summer, but none of them seemed to work out. Nicky would take a girl out for ice cream or to the movies, but after each date, he told Genevieve nobody could compare to her. Genevieve understood. After all, there *was* no one on this earth who could compare to her.

"Nicky, maybe you are being too particular. Start slow, get to know someone. Don't try to find what Michael and I have. You need to look for someone who can make you happy. Stop comparing." Genevieve and Michael had been writing to each other daily, which intensified this budding, long-distance relationship.

Nicky was confused, not sure of what he wanted, but he knew he hated the awkwardness of these lame first dates. Rarely was there a second date with any of these girls. Genevieve was his best friend. He didn't think he was looking to compare or replace her with anyone, but this confused him even more. He was happy that she had found someone to share her thoughts with, but it must be exhausting sharing your thoughts with two people—himself and Michael Austin. *Oh wait,* he thought. *This is Genevieve. Genevieve loves talking about herself to whoever will listen.*

July became August, which meant summer would start to wind down in Newport. Many families with kids starting college would leave before Labor Day. Nicky was feeling especially melancholy, knowing Genevieve was one of those who would soon leave.

Nicky was adjusting to the bank, taking on more responsibilities and saving his money. His dream was that one year from now, he, too, would leave Newport before Labor Day to start his new life, in a new place, in a new school. Football was no longer an option, but he knew he would find something to give meaning to his life.

This was something that he didn't talk about with Genevieve. He talked to his mother about his future. Helen Reynolds, a staunch Catholic, reminded him of what she wanted for him, but she suggested he talk to their parish priest for advice and that he should pray for guidance. Nicky did pray, every night and every Sunday at church, sitting next to his mother. So far, he hadn't heard a word from God.

"Nicky, where are you?" Genevieve was standing on the Reynolds' porch, yelling for him to hurry up. "You are missing all the fun at the beach party. Hurry up." No answer. She peeked into the kitchen; neither Mrs. Reynolds nor Nicky were there. Genevieve had been in this house so many times, she felt completely comfortable going from room to room, looking for him.

She went up the stairs to his bedroom. The door was closed. "Nicky." Genevieve knocked softly on his door and then opened it. Nicky was lying on his bed with a book open on his stomach. He was shirtless, tan, and muscular. For one split second, Genevieve felt a rush of heat in her cheeks, but when he sat up in surprise, she pulled herself together.

"Gen, what are you doing up here?" He looked surprised, but not the least bit uncomfortable with her being in his room.

"Why aren't you down at the beach? The Kennedys have outdone themselves. Everyone is there. Come on ... get up, get dressed. I will meet you downstairs." Genevieve turned to go.

"I'm not coming, Gen, and not everyone is there." He sounded annoyed with her.

Genevieve turned to look at him. She was wearing a white bathing suit top, white shorts, and her signature ponytail. He noticed how tan she was, how flat her stomach was, and the slight muscles in her thighs. *God, she's beautiful,* he thought. That thought surprised Nicky. He knew Genevieve was a natural beauty, but seeing her today, in his room, looking the way she did made him uncomfortable. He didn't know what this feeling was, good or bad, but he felt something.

Nicky stood up but didn't approach Genevieve. Instead, he closed the book and put on a crumpled, white T-shirt from the end of his twin bed. "This beach party is for people who are starting college this fall. I am not starting college this fall, in case you forgot." He didn't mean to sound as harsh as he did, but Genevieve didn't seem to notice.

She stayed for another minute, gazing at him, and pivoted to leave the room. Before walking out the door, she turned to him and said, "I am sorry that you are not coming. It won't be the same without you. Promise me you will come for dinner tomorrow night. It is the last time we will see each other for a while."

"Of course I'll be there. Have fun today." Nicky peered out his second-story bedroom window and watched Genevieve walk down to the beach to the party. He took note as she went from person to person, laughing, talking, smiling. *Man, can that girl work a crowd*, he thought, smiling.

COLLEGE BOUND

"LIFE ISN'T ABOUT FINDING YOURSELF. LIFE
IS ABOUT CREATING YOURSELF."
— GEORGE BERNARD SHAW

Margaux Lemaire knew Genevieve had been corresponding with a young man she had met at the college dance, but she knew very little else. Genevieve was coy about her relationship with him. She had told her mother that his name was Michael Austin, he was going to Harvard, and that he was from New York City.

After she and Edward got Genevieve moved into her dorm room, Margaux took her daughter aside. "Genevieve, your father and I have raised you to act responsibly in all situations. Just because you are away from home doesn't mean you should forget that. Make us proud, dear." She wasn't overly concerned about this Mr. Michael Austin. He was miles away, studying at Harvard, and she was sure he would have very little time to court her daughter. She hadn't shared any of this with Edward. *Some things are better left unsaid*, she thought as she got in the car and waved goodbye to her daughter as they drove away.

Michael came to see Genevieve in Connecticut for the long holiday weekend in October. They had been talking on the phone much more, now that she was away from her family. He was excited at the thought of seeing her again. Was she as beautiful as he'd remembered?

Genevieve was equally excited to see Michael again. She knew he would be as handsome as he was at the dance; she had no doubt. Genevieve had quite a weekend in store for him, which was to show Michael who she was ... someone he would never want to leave.

Michael had arrived by train late Friday night and stayed with his friend at Yale. Genevieve had told him they were going horseback riding Saturday morning, so dress accordingly. He had no idea what that meant. After talking to his friend about his fashion dilemma, he packed his pleated khakis, a blue-and-white-pinstriped, button-down shirt, and a navy-blue, V-neck sweater.

He was a city kid. Michael didn't come from money, and he knew literally nothing about horses, but none of this would deter him from impressing Genevieve. Michael seemed to have an innate ability to acclimate quickly to any situation that he was put in. Surely, he could handle a girl and a couple of horses.

They met at 11 a.m. at the barn. Genevieve looked stunning in skintight, white jodhpurs, black, knee-high boots, and a white blouse tucked into her pants. He didn't know how she got that blouse tucked in, but he knew he would like to find out.

Things were awkward, but only for a minute. After a brief hug, they both started talking and fell into an easy, playful, flirty conversation. Genevieve saddled up both horses, knowing that Michael was watching her. How could he not? She smiled and thought to herself, *I am in my element.*

As Genevieve helped Michael up into the saddle, she showed him the basics of riding a horse, emphasizing the importance of being gentle on the bit. They slowly rode away from the barn, Genevieve in the lead. She turned occasionally to see how Michael was doing. In her mind, he looked relaxed, comfortable, yet confident. They trotted along for a while at a slow pace.

Michael was enjoying the fall colors of Connecticut, so different from the city, but he was also deriving pleasure watching Genevieve from behind, straddling a thousand-pound animal, controlling him with only her knees. He had read about this, the bond between women and horses. He was grinning, thanking the Lord for letting him witness this firsthand.

But that's when Genevieve yelled, "Let's go." She gave her horse a kick, and off they went, galloping down a trail into the woods. Michael's horse took off, following close behind Genevieve. He had no power in his knees or legs. He just tried to wrap his legs around the sides of his horse and hang on to its mane.

Genevieve and her horse took a sharp turn to the left. Michael's did the same, but Michael didn't. He lost control on the turn and flew off, hitting a tree at the bend. He jumped up, hoping Genevieve didn't see what had just happened. Michael was humiliated, furious with himself, as he dusted the dirt off his pants and sweater. He looked up to see Genevieve riding toward him, leading his horse.

"Are you okay?" she asked as she jumped down and came over to him with what seemed to be genuine concern. "What happened? One minute you were right behind me, and then the next, you were gone."

"I guess I was just feeling a little too comfortable with old Ace here," he said, taking the reins from her. Michael was skilled at covering up anything that might be considered a flaw, at least to him.

"Her name is Grace, not Ace, and I am glad you are okay. Let me help get you back in the saddle, and we can ride slowly back to the barn."

"Genevieve, it's so nice to see you up and out of that hospital bed. How do you feel, dear?"

"Oh, Emma, is that you? It feels good to be out of that damn bed. I thought you might be Sara. I think she is on her way. Emma, she really needs to stay home and focus on her marriage. The last thing this family needs is another divorce."

"Dear, I'm sure your daughter's marriage can survive your hospital stay. By the way, the divorces in this family are all on your side, not mine. And yours, dear sister, was a doozy of a divorce. It's funny that you bring this up. I was thinking about you and Michael last night after dinner."

I glare at my sister. "What on earth would make you think of that?"

"I was sorting through old photos. I'm trying to get them all organized, with names and dates on the back, and put them into albums for my kids. There was a black and white of you and Michael that you had sent to me ages ago. It's from the day you took that poor man on the horseback ride from hell. I wrote on the back: *Genevieve, age 19, the day Michael Austin should have run for the hills.* I'm sure everyone will get a kick out of that."

"Emma, I do not appreciate that. Nobody is going to get a kick out of it because they won't know what the hell you mean by that. Head for the hills? And for your information, I was eighteen that year, not nineteen. I was born on January 5, 1923. I started at Connecticut in September 1941, which is around when that picture was taken. You do the math. You have been terrible with numbers and dates your entire life."

I was not going to let Emma off the hook, but I didn't blame her for getting my age wrong. Yes, it was a long time ago, but I remember Michael had lied to his parents about when we met and how old I was, which seemed to have set us on a trajectory of fudging dates for years to come. At one point, his poor mother, Rose, thought I was almost two years older than Michael. He should never have lied to his parents. There was so little I knew about him then.

The first time that Michael had come to visit me at Connecticut College was magical. It was the first time I was alone with a boy my age, other than Nicky. I found out then that Michael's parents had held him back a year from starting elementary school. His birthday, in September, made him younger than the other children starting first grade. They had felt it was in his best interest to spend another year at home before "feeding him to the wolves," as he put it.

This delay now put him as one of the oldest kids in his senior class, which is what helped him earn the early decision to Harvard—that and his excellent grades. I felt somewhat better knowing that he was now closer to my age, even if he was months younger than me. Even though I had told Nicky that age did not matter, it actually did matter to me. I could not imagine explaining to family and friends that I was dating a younger man. That just was not done in those days.

Once we had figured out the age difference and laughed about the horse incident, we seemed to fall into place with each other. Michael was so easy to talk to. He loved to read and hinted that he liked to write poetry. I found that charming but would have preferred that he had a love for athletics. He played tennis and played well, which I discovered that weekend.

We talked about our families. Michael's oldest brother had died in a car accident last Christmas, which left him at home alone with his parents. His other brother was at Annapolis and only came home during the holidays. He talked about how different things were for him now at home. His parents were very distant. He felt like he was on his own. We were so different, but I didn't see that then. Once, Mom had said that people were meant to stay in their own lanes.

SECRETS

"WHEN THINGS GO WRONG, DON'T GO WITH THEM." — ELVIS PRESLEY

I know I am leaving this damn hospital soon, maybe today, but I am confused, and that is not like me. I am, however, quite aware that I am moving in and out of my past and my current life. The facts are, I am in the hospital. I have cancer. Despite no history of cancer in my family, I am the first one to be diagnosed with it, a situation that seems almost ironic. Leave it to me to take the lead in disrupting our family's long-standing streak of avoiding cancer. I have caused a lot of disruptions throughout my life. The biggest one is a secret shared by just two of us.

I remember the night like it was yesterday. One evening, in late March, a few of us "locals" were home for what was known as Interim Week, which is now called Spring Break. We were supposed to stay on campus for that week, but so many of us were looking for a reason to blow off some steam—away from school, away from the war, away from life. I can remember sneaking rum out of my father's liquor cabinet, tiptoeing out the back door, and racing down the shoreline to what was called Townie Beach. A small bonfire was lit, and I was surprised at how many of us had shown up. I went straight to Nicky.

"Please tell me you haven't seen Emma here. I will hate it if she's here," I said, sitting down next to him, opening the bottle of rum and taking a swig. God, it was awful.

"Haven't seen her. Give me some of that," Nicky said, also taking a swig and grimacing. "You're right, that's awful," he said, laughing.

We spread out towels and blankets, sharing our stolen booze and gradually working ourselves into a pleasant buzz. We sat around the bonfire, drinking, laughing, forgetting the world. Nicky and I were sitting close to each other, sharing the rum, and one thing led to another. We held hands, leaned in close, and shared our first kiss. I was not sure if it was the rum, but my whole body seemed to tingle. We kissed again, this time more passionately.

Without saying a word to each other, we got up and walked hand in hand down the beach, away from our friends, until we came to the Hamilton boathouse. It was a gray-shingled, weather-beaten structure sitting on low pillars directly on the beach. The front door was painted bluish teal, now faded by the sun. The inside was lined with wooden shelves for all the beach needs for any age—pails and shovels, flippers, fishing poles, and bait buckets. If you needed it for the beach, the Hamilton boathouse had it. During the off season, they stored small anchors, oars, beach chairs, umbrellas, and cushions. The rafters were lined with canoes, resting for the winter, until they were needed again.

It was unlocked. We stumbled in, laughing and bumping into each other. We kissed again, and this time, it was much more passionate, almost desperate, as if we knew there was no turning back. Nicky pulled slightly away from me. "Gen, are you sure we should do this?"

"Yes," was all I said as I took off my sweatshirt and watched him do the same. He piled up some of the chaise lounge cushions, gathered beach blankets, and we fell onto them together.

Again, I remember hearing him say, "Gen?" and again, I said yes. I would not be the one to back down. We fumbled with zippers, buttons, hooks, pants, and shirts, then pulled the beach blankets over us and clumsily and innocently lost our virginity to each other. After we lay in each other's arms, Nicky was stroking my hair, and I wanted to stay like that forever.

"Are you okay?" He finally spoke, sat up, and looked at me.

"Of course I am, you?" The spell was over. The reality set in that I had just had sex with my best friend in a neighbor's boathouse. I didn't feel the least bit guilty or slutty. I don't know what I felt. Was I in love with Nicky? At that time, I felt something for him I thought could be love, but I had no idea what it was like to be in love, and it confused me. Love still confuses me.

"We should get back to the others," I said, trying to figure out how to get dressed without him seeing me naked. How ironic. I just had sex, naked sex, and now I don't want him to see me naked.

We slipped back to the party without being missed. Neither of us drank any more rum, and after a few minutes, Nicky said that he should probably get home. His mother would be worried if she found out he wasn't home. He gave me a quick kiss on the cheek and said, "See you soon, Gen." That was it. I was thinking, *Shouldn't he be fawning all over me after what we just did?* Instead, he is going home because of his mother. *Give me a break*, I thought as I gathered my beach blanket, empty bottle of rum, and walked alone down the moonlit shore to home.

The next afternoon, Pops drove me back to school. Once I was back in my dorm room with my friends, I almost forgot about the night with Nicky in the boathouse. We were completely occupied with year-end exams, preparing for graduation, and spending our free time debating what we would do after we graduated. I planned on spending the summer in Newport, as always, and would figure out my life in September. What do they say … something about best laid plans?

THE DORMS at Connecticut College were abuzz with year-end school activities, despite the fact that the United States was fighting a war overseas. Americans were learning how to cope with the changes they were facing in their day-to-day lives. This included labor shortages at colleges, resulting in the students volunteering to help fill in the gaps.

Genevieve was more than happy to assist at the stables. She got up earlier than most to get the horses' stalls cleaned out and feed them breakfast. Many days after her classes, Genevieve was back at the barn to help wherever she could. There was no communication between her and Nicky, but she and Michael talked a few nights a week when possible. Michael was busy himself with school and work.

She didn't give much thought to either Michael or Nicky. Genevieve was excited about her future … excited about making her mark on the world. She wanted to be remembered for her remarkable achievements. She knew she was headed for a life that didn't begin with being a housewife and a mother— she wanted a career in interior design. Genevieve didn't know where to start, but she did know that it didn't start with telling her parents. She figured they would go through the roof.

Genevieve was mucking out a stall after her last class for the day when she got a nagging feeling. She felt that something wasn't right and tried to shake it off. Showered and back in her dorm room, she was looking at her calendar showing all of the upcoming events, and that's when she realized there was one very important event she had missed—her period. She put the calendar down and sat on the edge of her twin bed. At first, there was no emotion, no fear, no panic. But that lasted only a few minutes.

What the hell, she thought. *There must be a mistake. This cannot be for real.* She rechecked the calendar, counted days on her fingers, and rechecked again. That's when fear and panic set in. She paced around the small dorm room, thinking, *What do I do? What on earth do I do?* Genevieve knew the social stigma around unwed pregnancies. Never mind that having a baby was not in her life plan. She did not want to be a mother.

Her fear and panic were rising, and the room was closing in on her. Genevieve needed air. She left her room, walked down the hall, ran down two flights of stairs, and raced across the common room and through the front door until she got to the green directly in front of the school. Genevieve felt like she was in a dream, watching people walk around campus, some in groups, laughing, not a care in the world.

Genevieve was perspiring. A bead of sweat had begun to drip down her spine, despite the cool, Connecticut breeze. She started walking, not thinking about where she was headed. She just walked, losing track of time, until she found herself at the Thames River, on the edge of the New London Seaport. Genevieve sat on a bench, staring out at the water. The sound of gulls overhead and the muffled conversations between fishermen with their lines in the water brought her some clarity. Her panic was subsiding.

Okay, Gen, get a hold of yourself and think. Do not let this get the better of you. Think, she yelled inside her head, while tapping her right temple with her finger. She knew that the first order of business was to figure out if she actually was pregnant. *This could just be a fluke*, she thought, until the night with Nicky flashed before her eyes. *Dammit, that was so stupid of us. What were we thinking?* You weren't thinking, Genevieve, you never do. You just jump right in, consequences be dammed.

Oh, how she hated that little voice in her head, which, in this case, was spot-on.

Genevieve was off the bench, pacing in front of it, trying to come up with a solution to her situation. She couldn't go to her family doctor or the college doctor for a pregnancy test as they would tell her parents. And then Genevieve remembered a pamphlet she saw being handed out on campus for Planned Parenthood. She had just glanced at it before tossing it into the trash. But she remembered the words "confidential consultations." *That's it*, she thought. *I am going to them.* The next day, she was on a greyhound bus to Hartford, on her way to a pregnancy test—alone.

A week later, Genevieve and her dormmates, Betty, Jane, and Sally, were sitting together on the big, leather couch in the common room, working on a plan for the four of them for the weekend. Graduation was approaching, and they wanted to spend as much free time together as possible.

"What about taking a bus to New York City for an overnight? I think I have enough money saved for this splurge," said Sally.

"Too expensive for me," Betty said.

"Same here. What about you, Genevieve?" asked Jane. "Genevieve, are you even listening to us? You have been so mopey lately."

Genevieve looked up. "I am not mopey. I have never been mopey a day in my life. New York sounds fine to me."

"Of course it does," said Sally. "Then you can see Michael," she teased.

"Phone call for Genevieve Lemaire." It was the dorm mother. "Oh, there you are, Genevieve. There's a call for you, dear." As Genevieve got up, her footsteps echoed across the highly polished, marble floor as she followed the dorm mother to the community phone.

"Hello."

"Hello, is this Genevieve Lemaire?"

"Yes," was her shaky reply. Genevieve had a sick feeling. She knew who was on the other end of the line.

"I'm calling from Planned Parenthood and wanted to give you the results of your recent blood test. Is this a good time to talk?"

"Yes." The panic was returning. She turned and glanced at her friends, who were looking back at her, wondering who she was talking to.

"Miss Lemaire, your test is positive. Planned Parenthood's policy is to always conduct three tests from your blood sample before final determination. This assures us of 99 percent accuracy."

Genevieve just held the phone to her ear, not responding. *Positive. This must be a good thing*, she thought. *I am positive that I do not want to be pregnant, so yes, this is good.*

"Oh, thank you so much. This is a relief."

"Miss Lemaire, you do know what a positive pregnancy result means, don't you?"

"Yes, I think so." Genevieve was hoping her friends couldn't hear her. "But if you could just confirm that, I would appreciate it."

"A positive test means that you are pregnant."

Silence. Genevieve couldn't move. She couldn't speak. The phone fell out of her hands, the receiver dangling from the cord, swinging in the air.

"Genevieve, are you okay?" Sally started toward her.

"Oh, yes, of course. Silly me," she said, reaching for the swinging phone. "Hello, are you still there? I am sorry. I dropped the phone." Genevieve wasn't sure how she had found the strength to speak as she waved Sally off.

"Miss Lemaire, I understand your circumstances. Would you like to make an appointment to come in and speak with one of our counselors?"

"Oh, thank you, but that won't be necessary. If I change my mind, I will let you know. Thank you again. Goodbye." Genevieve hung up the phone and stood for just a minute with her back to her friends. She took a large, deep breath and turned around, smiling.

"Looks like New York is out for me this weekend. I need to go home tomorrow."

The girls all started talking at once. "What happened? Why do you need to go home? Is something wrong? Who was that on the phone?"

Genevieve did her best to smile. "Nothing is wrong, you sillies. A friend from home had not been feeling well, and she just called to let me know she was doing so much better. She asked if I could come visit her, and I said, of course. Well, I am going upstairs to pack and take a bus back to Newport. Looks like New York is going to have to survive without me." She practically ran up the stairs to her room, afraid of tears giving her away.

Genevieve pulled out her suitcase and realized she needed to call home before she put her plan into action … a plan that had been brewing "just in case." She dreaded what was ahead. The first order of business was to call her parents to tell them she was coming home. Then Nicky.

BEACH TALK

"DON'T FEEL SORRY FOR YOURSELF IF YOU
HAVE CHOSEN THE WRONG ROAD. TURN
AROUND." — EDWARD CAYCE

Genevieve woke to the sound of the surf, its rhythm pounding against the shoreline. The salty air carried in on the breeze through her slightly cracked bedroom window, filling the room with its refreshing scent. The weather had changed overnight to a gray, overcast sky with a strong, offshore wind.

She pulled her pink, floral quilt up under her chin, planning her day. The weather had thrown a kink in her plans. Genevieve was not to be deterred. *I do not care if there is a fucking hurricane today. Nothing is going to stop me.*

It's Saturday, and the entire Lemaire family was home. They were just sitting down for breakfast when Genevieve came downstairs in her bare feet and fluffy robe.

"Good morning, sleepyhead," said her dad as he buttered his toast. "What's on the agenda today, since it was so important that you needed to come home?"

Genevieve gave him a kiss on the head and said, "Pops, is it a crime if a person wants to come home instead of heading to New York City with a bunch of girls for the weekend?" She knew he would flip if he found out she went to the city, unchaperoned. This was an excellent decoy for why she was home.

"Well, good for you, dear," said Margaux. "Would you like to help me with some baking? I got roped in to baking pies for the church fair this afternoon."

I think I would rather tell you I was pregnant than spend the morning baking, Genevieve thought. "Sorry, Mom. You know how I am in the kitchen. I would just be in the way. Anyway, I have plans to meet Nicky today." She poured herself a cup of coffee and sat down at the table, as if she didn't have a care in the world.

Trey was chatting up a storm about something, and Margaux was asking Emma to put her book down while at the table. Her parents talked about so and so who'd just enlisted, when they would have to start gas rationing, and how unfortunate the weather was for the church fair. This all simply floated in and out of Genevieve's thoughts. She had a lot more on her mind than the stupid fair. She was meeting Nicky at 10 a.m. and was still rehearsing in her head what she would say.

At 9 a.m., the weather cleared. The sun replaced the gray clouds, and the wind calmed down. Genevieve showered and put on a pair of loose jeans rolled at the cuff, with a long-sleeved, white turtleneck. She pulled her lengthy, blonde hair, still wet, into a ponytail and rummaged around in her closet for her summer sneakers. The sneakers were nowhere to be found, so she left the house barefoot, with a large beach blanket in her oversize straw bag, grabbing a gray, hooded sweatshirt on her way out.

She could see that Nicky was waiting for her, standing with his bare feet at the edge of the water. Genevieve adjusted the straw bag on her shoulder and walked toward him, still not exactly sure how to break the news to her best friend. He turned, waved, and walked toward her.

"Hi. Here, give me that bag," Nicky said, taking it from her shoulder. They walked side by side in silence, which seemed awkward to Genevieve. They always had something to say to each other, especially if they had been apart for a while.

"This looks good. How about stopping here?" she asked, taking the bag from him. She spread the blanket out on the sand, which was still damp from the morning mist. They both sat down and faced the ocean. Genevieve's mouth was dry and her hands damp, despite being cold. She felt nauseous but pulled herself together. What were her options? None. With every bit of strength she could muster, Genevieve stood up and said, "Nicky, there is something that I need to tell you."

"I have to tell you something too. You go first." He was staring out at the ocean, dreading what he knew would send Genevieve into a tailspin.

"I am pregnant."

Nicky snapped his head so quickly, he felt his neck crack.

"What did you say?" He knew what she said. He just didn't believe it.

"I said, I am pregnant." Genevieve glared at him. The accusation in her voice and the look in her eyes made it clear—Genevieve was pregnant.

"Are you sure? How do you know? What happened?" Nicky was getting a pain in his chest. *This can't be happening*, he thought.

"What happened? What do you think happened, Nicky? Remember the night of the party? Do you remember how we drank rum and laughed about life? Do you remember kissing me? Do you remember sneaking off to the boathouse? Do you remember taking off my clothes?"

Genevieve spoke these words in anger and pain. She didn't want to sound so angry, but it was just pouring out of her. She thought, *Why is he not dropping to one knee, declaring his love for me? Why is Nicky not holding me, telling me he will take care of me? Why the hell am I in this mess?*

"Gen, this can't be happening. Are you sure? Are you sure it's mine?" Nicky regretted those words as soon as he spoke them, wishing he could reach out, grab them, and bury them in the sand. He watched her slowly sit down, tears streaming down her face. Genevieve was quiet. *Genevieve is never quiet,* he thought, the pain worsening in his chest. He sat down next to her and reached out to take her hand.

"I'm sorry. I didn't mean to say that. I am so sorry, Gen, for everything. What are you going to do?"

"What am *I* going to do? Did you really just ask me what *I* am going to do?" Genevieve wiped away her tears and turned to face Nicky. "We are in this together, whether you like it or not. I am pregnant, which means we are going to have a baby, just in case you do not understand what pregnant means. And if you want me to spell out in detail how this happened, I would be more than happy to do that for you."

The two friends sat side by side, Nicky stunned, Genevieve crying. He finally spoke. "How far along are you?"

"Do the math, Nicky. You were there, remember?" Genevieve wiped her nose with the sleeve of her sweatshirt. She turned to look at Nicky and said, "We need to get married, and we need to do it soon. That is what we need to do."

Nicky said nothing. He continued to sit quietly, peering out at the ocean. Finally, he said, "Get married? Get married?" he said again, as if not believing the words the first time they came out of his mouth. "People get married when they're in love. I love you, Genevieve, but I'm not *in* love with you. We can't get married."

"Well, people are supposed to only have sex when they are in love, not just because they love each other," she spat back at him. "Listen to me. I have a plan. We will elope. You can come to Connecticut next weekend, and we can take a train to New York City to a Justice of the Peace. It will kill my parents, but we will tell them we couldn't wait until after the war. We will let them know you are signing up soon, and … well, war makes people do impulsive things.

"Nicky, we can make this work. I know we can. We love each other, for whatever that's worth. I don't need to be *in* love with you. I don't think I even know what that means. Sometimes I think I might be in love with Michael, but I don't know if that is true. Oh God, Michael."

Genevieve stopped talking. Michael … what would she tell him? Well, that doesn't matter right now. What matters is that they make this mess right.

Nicky turned to look at Genevieve, his chocolate-brown eyes filled with tears. He took her hands in his, sighed, and said, "Gen, I need to tell you something, and I need you to not interrupt. Can you promise me that, please?" She nodded her head and listened to her friend, now the father of her baby, talk.

"I will stand by you, but I can't marry you." She started to interrupt, but he squeezed her hands. "Let me finish. Gen, I'm not signing up, at least not for the army or any of the armed services." Nicky looked into her eyes, tears now streaming down his face. He said, "I'm joining the clergy. Nope, you promised not to interrupt. My mother needs me close by, and I can't be overseas fighting some enemy. She can't lose me like she did my father. This way, my mother will always have me. She won't be alone."

Genevieve pulled her hands out of his and screamed, "Your mother? Your mother? It is always your damn mother. You cannot leave her alone, but you can leave me and your child alone?" She stood up, straightened her clothes, and said, "Go to hell, Nicky Reynolds. I never want to see you again," then stormed toward home.

She could hear him calling to her, "Don't walk away, Gen, please. I can't do this without you."

DECEPTION

"CHANGE YOUR LIFE TODAY. DON'T GAMBLE
ON THE FUTURE, ACT NOW, WITHOUT
DELAY." — SIMONE DE BEAUVOIR

"The hospital is never quiet, no matter what time of day or night. All this commotion is keeping me up, and my mind will not let me rest. Damn these memories," Genevieve said to her empty hospital room.

It was late spring of 1942, and it seemed the entire world was upside down. Unfortunately, my world had just joined in. I remember my anger at Nicky. I thought we would be in this together, get married, have the baby. He would come back from war and become a successful banker, and we would live out the life that I expected. I would have a handsome, accomplished husband and a beautiful home that I decorated with a limitless budget, no thought of cost. I might join a committee or two to stay active. We would belong to my parents' club. But that was not what was going to happen. Did he actually say he was becoming a priest to keep his mother happy? Damn that woman … damn her then, damn her now.

I had stormed away from Nicky, toward home, but when I got in front of it, I just kept walking. I remember what an effort it was for me to walk. All I wanted to do was lay down in

"

the sun. I remember thinking that I should just walk into the ocean and just keep walking until I couldn't go any farther, leaving only one option, which was to sink. I was terrified, but not enough to drown myself.

There I was, nineteen years old, pregnant and alone. Nicky's words were all jumbled in my brain. I felt like I was the protagonist in my personal Greek tragedy. The thought of what had happened to my tidy life was overwhelming. My heart hurt, sweat had formed on my spine, and my breathing had become labored. I gave in and collapsed on the sand. I didn't know it then, but I know now that I was having a panic attack. Such a simple explanation to sum up the first worst day of my life. There would be others.

I lost track of time, laying in the soothing sun, listening to the seagulls flying over, lulled by the sound of the small waves rolling in. When my cheeks began to feel hot and tight, and the rising tide was creeping to my feet, I knew I needed to go home. I picked up my beach bag and slowly walked home.

The kitchen screen door slammed behind me as I dropped the bag on the floor. My mother looked up from her baking, asking me if everything was all right. "Of course, everything is fine," I replied. I swear that sometimes she could see right through me. It was as if she could read my mind.

I went to my room and shut the door. The fear and sinking feelings I felt on the beach were slowly subsiding. I paced around my bedroom, tapping my right temple with my finger, saying, "Think, Genevieve, think." Anger began to replace fear. I did not know what was stronger—my anger at Nicky for not telling me he would make everything all right, or my anger at myself for letting this happen. He should have known better than to have sex with me. Why am I alone in this unbelievable situation?

I crawled into my bed, and for the first time in my nineteen years, I prayed like my life depended on it. I prayed to God, begged and bartered for Him to make this all go away, until I fell asleep. My dreams were so vivid. I still remember them. Nicky and I were dancing. I was in a beautiful wedding gown; he was dressed as a priest. Michael was there, dressed as a soldier, and he was holding a beautiful baby boy. The dream woke me from my nap, but by then, I knew what I needed to do. My heart was colder. Anger fueled my determination.

I packed my bag and demanded that my father bring me back to school. Surprisingly, he didn't ask questions. I think both my parents were relieved to see me go. As usual, he drove too slowly, but I didn't berate him. I was not looking forward to what I knew I needed to do. Michael had graduated the week before, and we had already planned for him to come visit me at school before he started working full-time.

I pulled out all the stops, dressing the part of a woman who was on a mission. My pale-blue, shirtwaist dress accentuated my tiny waist—at least tiny for the time being. I unbuttoned the top two buttons of the dress and slipped on my favorite red heels. My long hair hung loosely on my shoulders. That and a light shade of rouge, along with my ruby-red lipstick, surprised even me when I looked in the mirror. This outfit was in sharp contrast to the current fashion style, which was a more masculine, military style, not the least bit feminine, and I needed to use that to my advantage.

My roommates were away for the weekend, leaving our dorm room for Michael and me. That was against school policy, having a male in the dorms, but since when did I follow the rules? I needed to convince a man I did not love to marry me because the man I did love would not.

Everything went according to plan that fateful Saturday in May. It didn't take much to charm the pants off Michael Austin, and I mean that literally. Michael seemed more, how shall I say this, skilled at lovemaking than Nicky, which made me wonder if I was not his first. That thought nagged at me. I completely ignored the fact that he was not my first, Nicky was.

Afterward, I felt melancholy, and once again, I realized this is not how my life was supposed to play out. But I played my part, pretending this was such a magical moment between us. We spent the night together, and I saw him off at the bus the next morning. I let Michael think he had won me over.

Life went on. I graduated from Connecticut and went home to Newport to, as my parents said, decide what I would do with my business degree. Instead, I told Michael I was pregnant, and we needed to get married immediately.

"Pregnant? Genevieve, how did this happen? Holy shit, what are you going to do?" Michael was in shock when I gave him the news. He had come to Newport for the weekend, I am sure hoping that we could include sex on all our dates.

I listened to him, watched him take a sip out of his ever-present flask, and thought, *My God, you sound just like Nicky.* I was disgusted with him, with Nicky, with this entire situation.

"We only have one choice. We need to get married soon. Before you interrupt, we will tell our parents that we don't want to be apart anymore. I will come to Boston and get a job there. We can rent an apartment near Harvard, and maybe you can get a part-time job on weekends or evenings."

"My parents are going to kill me," he said, taking another sip from the flask. He looked like he was going to vomit.

"They will not kill you because we are not telling anyone that I am pregnant. They might be surprised, try to talk us out of it, but we are in love, and this is what we want. Michael, we need to get our story straight. We need to be a team. Trust me … my parents are not going to be thrilled."

"But the timing is off. When are you due? Oh my God, how could this happen?"

I watched him slide into his pity party while I remained strong. I was running on suppressed anger, propelling toward a future of uncertainty, but I made a plan that was going to work. Nobody was going to get in my way. We would get married. Michael would start Harvard in the fall. The baby would come early, and the three of us would start our lives in Boston. End of story. Or so I thought.

"Genevieve," he said, taking both of my hands. "I'm sorry this happened, and you're right, we need to be a team, but I have to tell you something." Michael squeezed my hands so hard that it hurt. "I've put Harvard on hold. Yesterday, I signed up for the air force. I came here to tell you that. This news is so unexpected, but I will do the right thing. We need to get married as soon as possible."

Even though this conversation took place over seventy years ago, I can still remember the words, but more so, I remember the feeling that went through every cell of my body. My insides turned to ice, yet I could feel a trickle of sweat down my back. The top of my head felt like it would explode at any moment. My chest became tight, my breath was raspy, and my knees were ready to buckle. I tried to pull away from Michael, but he wouldn't let go of my hands.

"You did what? You don't mean this, Michael. You would not give up Harvard to go fight some stupid war in another part of the world. Please tell me this is not true. Please tell me." I was gasping for air and felt like I was begging for my life. I think I was begging. Maybe not for my life, but for something. The man I loved was leaving me for the priesthood. I was pregnant with his baby, and the poor fool whom I had tricked into this mess was now leaving me as well.

At that moment, I felt like I was going down, and I might not have the strength to get back up.

But I did get back up and forced Michael to join me in my deceit. Michael and I told my parents our plans, or should I say, my new plan. He would leave for basic training in two weeks, and we wanted to get married as soon as possible. My poor father looked as though he had a thousand things to ask. Instead, he left the room. My mother teared up but remained stoic. She asked the questions, "Genevieve, you just graduated from college. Why don't you wait? Marriage isn't something that you rush into. What's the hurry?" She seemed to direct each of these questions at me, as if she was accusing me of something.

Michael and I became a team that afternoon, lying to my parents and then spreading the same lie to his parents the next day. Michael's mother was inconsolable. She had already lost one son to a horrific car accident. Her second son would leave for Europe in a matter of weeks, and now, her youngest had scrapped his plan for Harvard to fight in this dreadful war. On the other hand, his father gave me a big bear hug and shook Michael's hand. "I'm proud of you, son. I wish I was young enough to go fight for our country."

I returned home to Newport, and my fiancé left for training in Fort Jackson, South Carolina. Things were strained at home between my parents and me. Emma was thrilled that she was going to be my maid of honor, and Trey didn't have much to say.

Before Michael left, we had decided to get married by a Justice of the Peace. The Austins and Michael's brother would come to Newport for the weekend for the small ceremony. My three friends from school would be the only guests. It shocked my mother that Nicky wasn't invited. I had not seen or spoken to him since the night on the beach when I told him I was pregnant. My mother did not press the Nicky issue, and to this day, I wonder if she knew. Did she see me on a path of destruction, hell-bent on doing what I needed to do to save my dignity, my reputation, and my family's good name?

I can still picture the day my mother, Emma, and I went

shopping for our wedding outfits. I had made it clear that I wanted to keep it all simple, including my dress. My mother was on edge the entire day, picking out dresses that were white, real wedding gowns, and I continued to shake my head no. Emma was taking cues from me, leaning toward the plainer, less-embellished dresses.

Once again, this was not what I had imagined for my wedding. But I held it together, going through rack after rack of beautiful dresses, and then I found it. A lovely, champagne-colored, satin dress, no veil, no train, but perfect for the occasion. I tried it on and felt wonderful in it. The neckline showed off my defined clavicle, the cinched waist would reveal to the world this was not a shotgun wedding, and the three-quarter-length skirt exposed my shapely calves. I added matching gloves and ordered my pumps to be dyed to match the dress.

We found a sweet, tea-length dress for Emma in a soft blue, which complemented her eyes, and my mother selected a midnight-blue sheath with long sleeves and matching heels. I was pleased with the shopping trip outcome … well, as pleased as someone who was hiding a pregnancy could be.

My family hosted the Austins for a pre-celebration dinner the night before the wedding. Mrs. Austin gave me a beautiful pair of small, pearl earrings. Emma gifted me a lovely, blue, lace handkerchief, and the morning of the wedding, my mother placed her gold bracelet in my left hand—the one she wore when she had married my father.

"There you go, Genevieve. You have something old, something new, and something blue. Oh dear, you don't have anything borrowed," Emma said with a hint of panic in her voice.

And with that, my father came to me, placed a key in my hand, and whispered in my ear, "Now you have something borrowed … the key to the car for as long as you need."

Oh how I struggled to not run into his arms, to never leave

the safety and love of my family. But instead, I stood up straight, pulled my shoulders back, and said to them, "This is the happiest day of my life." I should have been an actress.

EARLY SUMMER 1942

"SHE STEPPED OFF THE CLIFF TO SAVE HER
LIFE. SHE CHOKED ON THE WORDS, 'I WILL BE
YOUR WIFE.'" — J.L.

Michael and Genevieve spent their two-day honeymoon on Martha's Vineyard. They left after their wedding luncheon, saying goodbye to family and Genevieve's three college friends. It was a cool, late-spring day. The sun was shining brightly, and the winds were calm.

They stood silently at the bow of the ferry, arm in arm. To the other passengers, Genevieve and Michael looked the part of newlyweds. Together, they were a stunning couple, the envy of those who watched them—the old remembering what young love felt like, and the young hoping to find that kind of love. But for Michael and Genevieve, the love between them was overshadowed by what they were facing. Michael was leaving for basic training, and then on to war. Genevieve was expected to carry on as a new bride and somehow mask her pregnancy until the time was right to announce to the world they were expecting. Michael discreetly took a sip from his flask. Genevieve considered jumping overboard.

They checked into the Vineyard Harbor Hotel as Mr. and Mrs. Michael Austin and spent the next two days exploring the island and each other. Genevieve had opted out of jumping overboard. Instead, she chose to embrace her new life. After all, Michael was handsome, funny, smart, and still had a brilliant future ahead of him. He would rise in the air force ranks and come home as a captain. From then on, the world would be their oyster.

Michael was still very conflicted about marrying Genevieve, but he also accepted the reality of the hand he had been dealt. At the end of the day, he was married to a beautiful woman who was full of surprises, and he loved the feeling of being challenged. He put the thought of fatherhood and war out of his mind.

The time passed quickly on the Vineyard for the newlyweds. Two days just didn't seem to be enough time to establish a sound foundation for their marriage. Edward met them at the ferry in Providence, shook his son-in-law's hand goodbye, and then took his daughter back to Newport. Michael went home to say goodbye to his parents before leaving for basic training.

Emma came running into the kitchen. "Genevieve, tell me everything. How terribly romantic was the Vineyard and your husband?"

"Emma, leave your sister alone. She just walked through the door. Good Lord, give her a chance to breathe." Margaux gave her daughter a warm hug and whispered, "I'm glad you're home. Is everything okay?" Not waiting for an answer, most likely because she didn't need to hear about her daughter's love life, she pulled away and said, "You have quite a bit of mail, and most of it is addressed to Mr. and Mrs. Austin. Don't worry, darling, you will always be a Lemaire. Now go upstairs and freshen up before dinner."

It is nice to be home, Genevieve thought as she put her suitcase on her bed. She was exhausted. The thought of a family dinner was almost too much for her to handle. Genevieve took a long, hot shower and went into the kitchen, wet hair tied up in a knot, wearing a pair of old pajamas. She put her arms around her mother, who was at the kitchen sink. *This feels so familiar and odd at the same time*, she thought.

"Mom, do you mind if I just bring a cup of tea and some crackers to my room instead of joining you for dinner?"

She felt her mother's body stiffen as she turned around to look her daughter straight in the eye. "Are you sure everything is okay, dear?"

"Yes, of course. I am just tired. It has been such a whirlwind these last few weeks, but of course, a wonderful, exciting whirlwind," was Genevieve's response as she put the kettle on for tea and went into the pantry to retrieve some saltines.

"You do look a bit pale. Take your tea and go upstairs. I'll check in on you after dinner. Genevieve, is there something you would like to tell me?"

"Not really, other than I have never been happier."

Genevieve curled up in the overstuffed chair in her childhood bedroom, sipping her tea and munching on a saltine, sorting through her mail. It was so odd to her to see envelopes addressed to Mr. and Mrs. Michael Austin. Most of these were cards congratulating the couple on their marriage. She barely looked at them. *Best wishes on your marriage; Congratulations; Weddings are made in heaven.*

Genevieve was getting agitated. *This is not who I am*, she thought. *Have I lost myself, and now and forever I will be known as Mrs. Michael Austin?* Just as she was considering throwing the whole lot into the trash, she had one more envelope to open, addressed to Genevieve Lemaire. She didn't recognize the return address, but she knew instantly who it was from.

Dear Gen,

I hope this finds you well. I heard about your marriage to Michael, and I am so happy for you both. Congratulations. Even though you are now married, I wanted to write only to you. I suppose that's wrong, but I figure I can do a few more wrong things in my life before I am officially ordained. I have four years to do that while I work on my studies, which are focused on philosophy and theology.

Gen, I never meant to hurt you. I never meant for things to turn out how they have. I meant none of this. I only meant to love you. I love you, Gen. I think I fell in love with you the first time I met you. I was just too stupid to realize it. By God … oh, probably not supposed to say His name in vain. But you were, and you are, a force to be reckoned with. You stand up to everything and everyone with such an amazing source of power. I've watched you take on waves like nobody else. Your joy for the sea inspired me to see the beauty of Newport and beyond. Your energy gave me strength when my father died. I'm fairly sure you don't know that, but you did. I realized that even though you have lost someone, you can keep them close. As you know, I was far from close to my father, but the loss was, and still is, hard. Your energy showed me I needed to get through my pain, not wallow in it.

You are my first real friend, my first love. When I think of you, I think of home. When I am with you, I am home. We never had a first dance, never had a special song, but we share so much more than most can even hope for. Please keep what is us in your heart. I know that I will. I wish you joy, good health, and happiness. I wish you love.

Faithfully yours,

Nicky

Genevieve noticed she wasn't breathing as she stared down at the letter from Nicky. She took a deep breath and reread it. She read between the lines, realizing he was saying what he couldn't put on paper. He loved her, loved their child, and would live a life of regret.

I will also live a life of regret, she thought as she slowly folded up the paper. She sat quietly, the folded note in her lap, and placed her hand on her belly, which was still flat. *Oh dear,* she thought, *we have made such a mess of things. But this baby is what will keep me tied to Nicky always, no matter what. This baby is our love letter to each other, our secret to keep.*

Genevieve stood up, walked to her bureau, and opened her large, rosewood jewelry box. She carefully lifted the bottom of the box to reveal the hidden compartment where she placed Nicky's letter. Shutting the box, she walked to her bedroom window and looked out at the sea. The moon cast a dim light over the waves, giving them a dreamlike glow. It was then that she decided to name the baby Nicholas, if a boy, or Nicole, if a girl. *I don't give a damn what Michael, or my parents, will say,* she thought. She finished her tea, now cold, as she plotted the next chapter of her life.

THE FOURTH of July in Newport came and went with little celebration that year. It seemed the entire world was fighting with someone, and the United States was deep into war at this point. Michael came home in August for two weeks before being shipped out to somewhere in Europe.

"What do you mean they won't tell you where you are going? That is insane. Actually, it is cruel and unusual treatment, torture," Genevieve said to Michael as they sat on the beach in front of her parents' house.

"It's what the air force does. I think it's the same for the army and navy. They own us. It's awful and, I agree, torture. But unless you want to run away with me to, oh, I don't know, the swamps of Louisiana, or somewhere, I don't have a choice. I have to do what they say."

Michael took a sip from his ever-present flask, feeling the burn of the alcohol on his tongue, and put his arm around Genevieve's shoulder. "When are we going to tell our parents about your pregnancy? Nobody could even guess you're pregnant, but it's not all that far along, is it?"

Genevieve stiffened, hoping he didn't sense the shift in her body. "No, not that far along. I think we should wait until they settle you, wherever that will be, and then I'll tell them—both sets of parents. I think I will get less pushback if I look somewhat like the poor, young bride, husband overseas fighting for our country, and now expecting their first grandchild. Well, at least something like that. Why not focus on something else, Michael. How long do you think it will take you to move up the ranks?"

"Well, seeing that right now I'm a basic airman, I think it's going to take a long time. Genevieve, I don't know how any of this works. I'm not second-guessing my decision to fight for our country, but I don't feel that the air force is my future. I just want to do what I need to do, come home to my wife and baby, and move on with my life." Another sip from his flask.

"I have no doubt that you will make captain in no time. Now give me a bit of whatever you have been trying to hide from me," she said playfully.

Genevieve had made a prenatal appointment with a doctor in Providence rather than Newport. The last thing she wanted was her family's doctor to find out she was pregnant, even if she was married. She borrowed her father's car and forced Michael to go with her. He did his best to get out of it, but when Genevieve's mind was made up, there was no dissuading her.

After her examination, the doctor told her to get dressed, and he would meet her and Michael in his office. Genevieve knew he was questioning the timing of her pregnancy and felt that she was farther along than she was saying. Despite his doubts, he had to take Genevieve's word for it, since she was his patient.

"Mr. Austin, nice to meet you. I'm Dr. Micah. I believe congratulations are in order." Dr. Micah shook Michael's hand

and motioned for him to have a seat next to Genevieve in front of his desk. "As I said, congratulations. Everything looks to be progressing just as it should be. However, at this point, the exact due date is a bit hard to pinpoint. Firstborn babies decide when they're ready to meet their parents. Some are in a rush, while others like to take their time," he said, glancing toward Genevieve. "But either way, it is my opinion that the health of the family can be guarded and promoted if each child is consciously planned, rather than just born. Keep that in mind for the next one, heh."

As he rose and extended his hand to Michael, Dr. Micah said, "Godspeed, young man. We will take care of your lovely wife in your absence." Michael and Genevieve walked out of the office, loaded with prenatal brochures and a nagging, unspoken guilt between them.

ALONE AGAIN

"I'M GOING UP AND UP AND UP, AND
NOBODY'S GOING TO PULL ME DOWN!"
— LANA TURNER

The summer of 1942 wasn't very different from previous summers for Genevieve and her siblings. While their skin turned darker and their hair became lighter, they filled their days with sailing, horseback riding, tennis, and golf lessons. They swam in the ocean and collected seashells along the shore. Trey spent his free time with friends, Emma read, and Genevieve focused on the next steps in her pregnancy plans, never letting on to anyone about what she was going through.

She wrote to Michael regularly and reread Nicky's note often. She had held off writing to him. It hurt so much, doing this alone, which is how she felt. Genevieve felt all alone. The only solace she had was the overwhelming affection she felt for the tiny, little being growing inside her. She didn't know that she could feel so deeply about anything. Her whole life had been what to wear, what exciting thing to do next, who was doing what. She realized just how shallow she and most of her friends were. But not anymore. Genevieve had changed. She had become protective of the little secret, baby Nicholas.

"Emma, Trey, I want to leave in ten minutes, so be ready. I

don't have all day to spend on your back-to-school shopping." Margaux looked up the stairs to be sure that she was heard. Trey was the first one to come down the stairs, messy hair, rumpled clothes. Emma was right behind him, dressed like any other girl her age, eager to go shopping. Genevieve appeared at the top of the stairs, looking more like Trey than her sister.

"Trey, go back upstairs, brush your hair and your teeth, if you haven't already, and for goodness' sake, put on something that doesn't look like you spent the night in it. Might I suggest the same to you, Genevieve?"

"Mother, I am not going shopping with you."

"I am well aware of that, but it's 10 a.m., and you look like you've been out all night. Is there anything you want to tell me?"

"Oh Genevieve, guess who I saw coming off his early morning swim," Emma said with a bit of wickedness in her voice.

"I don't know, Emma. Who?" Genevieve wished she had just stayed in bed.

"Nicky Reynolds, that's who." Emma was quite pleased to drop this bombshell on her sister.

Genevieve was completely taken by surprise. *What the hell is he doing here, and why didn't he call me? How long has he been here?*

As if reading her sister's mind, Emma said, "He was just finishing up what he called his last swim of the season. He's here for the Labor Day weekend to visit with his mother. Oh, and boy oh boy, does he look good."

"Come on, you two, hurry up. Let's go." Margaux walked out the door toward the car, feeling unsettled. She didn't know what happened between Genevieve and Nicky, but she could tell that Emma's news struck a nerve with her oldest daughter. It was a warm, early September morning, but Margaux felt a chill. *Something just isn't right*, she thought as she stood by the car, waiting for Emma and Trey.

Genevieve went back to her room and sat in the chair, gazing into her vanity mirror. She saw the dark circles under her eyes and was surprised to see a slight, pink hue to her skin, even with her tan. She felt like vomiting. Was it butterflies or morning sickness? *Screw this*, she thought, as she brushed her hair, put it up in her usual ponytail, and searched for something to wear. *What does one wear to confront the secret father of her child*, she thought. She kept it simple—a navy-and-white-striped T-shirt with navy shorts.

To most, Genevieve looked like a beautiful, healthy, young woman, with no hint of pregnancy, and that was the look she was going for. She walked slowly on the beach toward the Reynolds house, remembering how she used to run toward that house. *What am I going to say to him? Why wouldn't I wait for him to come to me? What if he does not want to see me?* These thoughts ran around in her head, but then she remembered his note. Genevieve knew she needed to see Nicky.

Mrs. Reynolds opened the kitchen door on the second knock. "Oh, my goodness, Genevieve, dear. It's so nice to see you. Come in, please come in. How are you, dear? It has been so long since we have seen you. I heard you're married. That's so exciting, and congratulations to both of you."

Mrs. Reynolds kept jabbering on, and it took all of Genevieve's self-control to not scream, "Nicky Reynolds, where are you?" But she didn't need to because, at that moment, he walked into the kitchen wearing nothing but a pair of khaki shorts and a towel around his shoulders, still damp from his shower. He looked older to Genevieve, even though it had only been a few months since she had seen him. His wavy, black hair was cropped closer to his head, accentuating his chiseled features. He was thinner than she'd remembered, yet much more muscular. If Genevieve was looking for a flaw in

Nicky, all she could come up with was he didn't have much of a tan.

Neither spoke, they just stared at each other. "Look at you two. Nothing to say after all this time? My goodness, I can remember when I couldn't get a word in edge wise when you were together." Mrs. Reynolds removed her apron and said, "I'll leave you to get reacquainted." She walked out of the kitchen, gently patting her son on the shoulder.

Nicky went first. "Gen, it's wonderful to see you. I'm so glad you're here. I was going to call, but I just got here yesterday, and there's so much going on," he said weakly as he gestured around the empty kitchen.

"Yeah, looks like there sure is a lot going on, Nicky. I can see why you couldn't pick up the phone." She hated how bitter she sounded.

"Can we take a walk, please?" He sounded like he was pleading.

"You better put a shirt on. You do not want to burn your lily-white skin." She turned and walked out the door.

Genevieve stood at the water's edge, letting the small waves spill onto her feet. It seemed like an eternity until she felt Nicky approach. He stood next to her and gazed out at the ocean. He longed to reach out and touch her, but knew that was wrong. Wrong on so many levels. Nicky turned to look at the woman he loved—the woman he could never have and the life that wasn't meant for him.

"I'm sorry. I am so sorry." He waited for her to respond, not expecting silence. He was prepared for her rage, tears, and punishing words but heard nothing except the sound of gulls and the waves.

"Gen, can we talk, please? Or can I talk and try to explain to you what happened? Please?"

Genevieve wanted to rage, cry, punish him, but she had already done that, on her own, in her room, on the beach or in the car. She had done all of that, but she had done it alone, always alone. Now that she was standing next to Nicky, she felt weak, numb, exhausted. Genevieve felt old.

"No one is at my house. Pops is at work, and the others are out shopping. We can talk there." Genevieve started to walk toward home. Nicky followed.

They sat on the porch, sipping lemonade. Genevieve went first.

"Nicky, we don't have all day to work this out. My family will be back at some point. The fact of the matter is that yes, I am still pregnant, and yes, it is still your child." She took a breath, holding back tears, trying to keep this conversation emotionless. "After you told me your plans for YOUR future, I needed to figure out my future—my future and our baby's future." She hurled these words at him, hating herself for losing control. Genevieve paused to pull herself together, took a sip of lemonade, sat up straighter, and continued.

"I made a plan, and that was to make Michael believe this is his baby. And how did I do that, you might wonder? I seduced Michael. Poor, innocent Michael. He was quite surprised to find out I was pregnant so soon after our first time together." She paused and looked at Nicky. He was sitting across from her, not saying a word, waiting for the rest of the story.

"He agreed we needed to get married quickly. I had it all worked out. We would move to Boston. He would start Harvard in the fall, and I would raise our child. I would have it all—a stunning home, successful husband, and a beautiful, little boy. I do think that it is a boy, you know." Nicky watched as her hand instinctively went to her stomach.

Genevieve stood up and walked to the porch railing. "But you see, that is when my plan fell apart." He heard the catch in her voice. "That is when Michael told me he had turned Harvard down and enlisted in the air force." Genevieve started sobbing, and Nicky went up to her. He gently turned her around to face him and pulled her into his chest. He hugged her and let her cry. They stayed like that for just a few minutes until Genevieve pulled away, wiped her nose on his shirt, and said, "Your turn."

It took every ounce of strength for Nicky to not pull Genevieve into his arms and hold her. Instead, he took a step back from her, and Genevieve sat down.

"I'm not sure where to start, so please just hear me out." He took a deep breath and began.

"That night that we were together in the boathouse … Genevieve, that was magical, but even then, I knew it was a mistake. Not that I didn't love you, not that I don't love you. I do love you, Gen. I love you more than you can imagine, but the wheels of my future were already in motion." Genevieve started to speak, but Nicky held up his hand and kept talking.

"As long as I can remember, I knew that my mother had a plan for me. She had told me since I was a little kid that I was special, and that God wanted me on this earth for a reason. She said that He had a plan, and that she needed to make sure God's plan was fulfilled. I could never tell my father any of this. She said he would kill us both. My father wanted me to go to college, play football, and follow in his footsteps to banking. However, it seems that my mother and God had other ideas. As you know, God and my mother won."

Genevieve listened quietly, thinking that he sounded so sad, but bitter and sarcastic all at the same time. *Maybe it is his Louisiana twang that is emphasizing all his emotions*, she thought.

"I just went along with my mother. She is eccentric, maybe bordering on dotty." He saw the look on Genevieve's face. "Off kilter, unstable." He looked pained saying those words. "I knew my father would win out, no matter what my mother wanted, no matter what I wanted. So, I grew up very conflicted, as if I were in two worlds, trying to please everyone in both of those worlds. I went to mass every Sunday. I was an altar boy. I went to catechism and did all the religious things for my mother. And then I played football and lacrosse, pretending to be a jock, all for my father. That was the only life I knew until we came to Newport and I met you."

He sighed and turned to look out at the sea. "That's when I added another world to my orbit—your world. Your world is the world I thought I wanted to be in. Oh, you made me feel things I never knew existed. How to laugh, really laugh. How to actually have fun, not worry about anything. Things at home weren't good. They seemed to go from bad to worse when we moved here. My father was always angry, and my mother withdrew and stayed in her room when he was here. I didn't care. I had you."

Nicky stopped talking, struggling to hold back his tears. He turned and looked at her, not caring that she saw the tears. "The worst day of my life is the day you told me you were pregnant." She started to speak, but Nicky continued. "I knew then I was leaving to join the seminary, but I was terrified to tell you. I should have told you from the beginning, but … well, I was afraid I would lose you. They put arrangements into motion right after my father died. Our parish priest, Father Nunes, had been helping my mother with the paperwork to get me accepted to St. Mary's Seminary in Baltimore.

"When I told you I had to put college off for a year, I lied to you. I knew what they had planned for me. I knew what I was going to do. I hated lying. But Gen, I don't hate this path that I'm on. My mother had drilled it into me when I was young. And then I went along because my mother needs me, and she has done nothing to hurt me or to steer me wrong.

"But now, after just a few months, I feel like I am doing what I am meant to do. I'm not meant to fight in a war. I'm not meant to go to college to play football or work in a bank.

I'm not meant to be a husband or a father. The hard part for me—the part that I really struggle with—is that I'm not meant to be with you. I know I said I wasn't in love with you, only that I loved you, but I think that was just another lie on my part." Nicky stopped to take a breath. "I love God, that I know for sure. Now I just need to learn how to not be in love with you."

"And what about this baby, Nicky? Where does he fit in God's plan for you? Or better yet, where does he fit in for your mother's plan for you? Do not answer that, I already know. We do not fit in anywhere in your world." Genevieve pushed the wicker rocking chair with her feet, both hands on her belly, gathering what would come out of her mouth next. She rose and went over to Nicky, her heart racing as they stood inches apart, inhaling each other's essence.

"What is done is done. Michael thinks this child is his, and he will raise him as his own. You will not be a part of his life as anything more than his uncle Nicky. I do not care what God's or your mother's plan is. I need you in my life. I have missed you so much these last few months. I cannot imagine a life without you. I do not understand your decisions, but they are your decisions, not mine. You will baptize our child and stay in our lives as my dearest friend." She took a step back, inhaled a deep breath, and said, "Who knows. Maybe God's plan is not about you. Maybe it is about me. Maybe He knows that I am going to need all the help I can get to keep me on the right path, and you are just the man to do it."

SLIPPING AWAY

"TO HIDE FEELINGS WHEN YOU ARE NEAR CRYING IS THE SECRET OF DIGNITY."
— DEJAN STOJANOVIC

"Genevieve, oh, it's so good to see you. Welcome home." Jessica came through the front door, rushing to her mother.

My girls are here. Sara … well, of course she always seems to be underfoot lately. But Jessica, what a wonderful thing to have her here. All the way from Scottsdale. I wish the boys were here, but at this point, I will take what I can get.

It is lovely being back in my home, in my bed, although it is a damn hospital bed. But Jessica has done her best to make it look like my bed, with all my wonderful linens, and, of course, my cashmere throw. I am tired, but Jessica had put out a lovely tray of cheese and crackers and is opening a bottle of Veuve Clicquot. How could I resist? Just one glass of champagne, and I am wiped out.

"Girls, I need to sleep. I am exhausted," I told them.

"Genevieve, you need to have a bit of morphine to help you get a good night's sleep. Hospice showed us how to give it to you."

Jessica's voice cracked, but it was Sara who stood up, got the morphine, and said, "Open wide."

My children have always called me by my first name. I am not sure if it is something that I encouraged when they were young. Rarely am I called Mom. Sometimes Mother, if someone is annoyed with me, but definitely never Mommy. I do love slipping into this delicious state of morphine. One could easily get used to this.

I can hear Jessica and Sara talking in the other room, but my mind is drifting back to the fall of 1942.

Nicky went back to St. Mary's right after our Labor Day "come to Jesus talk." I felt so melancholy, alone, and bored. Nothing was interesting to me—not the idea of riding, tennis, golf, shopping, or getting in a few last swims before the ocean got too cold. Michael's letters were few and far between, each containing only a few sparse words about what was going on in his life. I knew it wasn't his fault, but I could not shake this deep sadness that weighed upon my heart.

I remember one day in September, wandering down the beach, which was deserted except for the seagulls that stayed on the shore year-round, when I found myself standing in front of the Hamiltons' boathouse. My God, how my life had changed since that night in May. I had graduated from college, got married, and was pregnant. Unfortunately, those events did not happen in that order. I was about four months pregnant and knew I would start to show soon. Bathing suit season was almost over, so for now, hiding this pregnancy would be easier.

I stood there staring at the boathouse with my hand on my belly. This baby was conceived by two young friends who got drunk and had sex. Those are the facts. But there are other dynamics that contributed to those facts. I loved Nicky, Nicky loved me. I loved the child we created. I was in a mess, but I felt certain of my feelings for this child. He would be loved, and he would know how much I love him. I was committed to keeping my secret safe. I had no doubt that I would succeed.

TIME TO TELL

Genevieve had decided that the time to tell the parents about the pregnancy was now. She wrote to Michael to tell him she was about to kick off the operation and tell the parents, which was step two of their plan. Step one, get married. Done. Step two, announce the pregnancy. Step three, move to Boston. Step four, have the baby. Step five, live happily ever after.

"Pops, did you check the mail today?" Genevieve asked, hoping there would be a letter from Michael. She needed him to be onboard with what she had to do. But at the same time, she was pregnant and knew she couldn't hide her pregnancy much longer.

"I did. Nothing for you, unless you want to pay the electric bill," her father said as he put his empty coffee cup in the sink. Genevieve knew this wasn't directed at her to contribute financially, but for some reason, her father's remark stung.

"Pops, the reason I cannot help to pay the electric bill is because I am pregnant." This was not how she had planned to share the good news with her parents, blurting it out like that.

Her mother stopped wiping down the counter. Her father

looked at her mother. Neither knew what to say for just a second. And then Margaux put down the sponge, walked over to her daughter, and took her in her arms. It was a good hug. It was a strong *I am here* hug.

"Well, well, well, Genevieve. You are going to make a grandfather out of me," said Edward when he saw his wife's reaction. That's when he knew it was okay to be happy. "I thought you were looking a bit heavier lately." He chuckled. Edward immediately knew he had overstepped when he saw the looks he was getting from his wife and daughter.

"My goodness, dear, this is such a surprise. Michael must be thrilled. Do you know when you are due? Oh, this is exciting. What wonderful news, especially during these times."

Genevieve wasn't surprised by her father's reaction. For the most part, he followed his wife's lead. But she was taken aback by her mother's response. In fact, Genevieve wasn't convinced that her mother was actually happy for her.

"It was a surprise for Michael and me. This was not planned, but we are both thrilled." She could barely choke those words out, trying to give nothing away.

"Of course we are all thrilled. Have you told the Austins yet? Mrs. Austin will be so excited. Have seen Dr. Matthews yet? Of course not. Maria would have told all of Newport by now." Margaux knew what a gossip the family's receptionist was.

"No, I went to someone else." Genevieve glanced at her father, clearly showing that she was uncomfortable with the turn of the conversation in front of her father. "I'm going for a walk, and then I will call Michael's parents."

Once Genevieve was out of the house, Edward went across the kitchen and put his arms around his wife. "Everything will be okay, *mon chéri*. What's done is done. You must remember how young love is—passionate, impulsive, exciting. They will work this out. And my darling, you and I will be there for them."

Margaux melted in her husband's embrace, and for a split second, she wished she could stay there forever. But the sound of Trey yelling "Mom" before he even hit the porch broke the spell.

As expected, the Austins were beside themselves with excitement. There were no questions like the ones her mother had. They were only concerned about how Genevieve was feeling and what they could do to help her. Genevieve was relieved they didn't ask about the due date and doctors. Mrs. Austin joked she was going to learn to knit.

"I told Michael's parents, and they are excited about a new, little Austin," Genevieve said to her parents before dinner. "For now, I would like to keep this news between us. We can tell Emma and Trey when the time is right. Dad, can I use the car tomorrow? I have an appointment in Providence in the afternoon."

After dinner and the dishes were done, Genevieve went to her room. She was emotionally exhausted. She thought she would feel an enormous weight off her shoulders now that the cat was out of the bag, but that was not the case. Genevieve felt sad, and again, she felt alone. She desperately wanted to run down the beach to Nicky's house. She desperately wanted to talk to him. She desperately wanted him. Instead, Genevieve got into bed, still dressed, and placed her hands on her belly. *Don't worry, baby Nicholas. We are one step closer to getting almost everything we want.*

"MRS. AUSTIN, your pregnancy is advancing nicely. I am writing a prescription for an iron supplement that I want you to start on. The baby is going to be on the big side, considering your estimated due date in early March. I know you are young and healthy, but you need to take some precautions. Lots of rest, fresh fruits and vegetables when possible. I realize that might be difficult with rationing, but do your best."

Genevieve left the doctor's office, her mind whirling. *Dr. Matthews thinks my due date is early March, but I know it's more like early February. This is perfect. I will just pretend that the baby comes early. Nobody will ever know differently, except for Nicky, Michael, and me*, she thought.

Genevieve didn't give much thought to Michael. Out of sight, out of mind. She was feeling more and more like it was just her and her baby, Nicholas, and she was getting used to that.

DARK DAYS

"SOMETIMES THE HEALING HURTS MORE THAN THE WOUND." — UNKNOWN

"Genevieve, Mom, you need to wake up for just a minute. We need to give you some more morphine to help you sleep."

Oh, dear, I am back to reality. At this point, I am not sure where I would prefer to be, lying here dying of cancer or reliving the pain of the fall of 1942.

"Why in God's name are you waking me up to give me something to make me sleep?" I am irritated with these daughters of mine, even though I'm the one who signed off on getting the morphine. And where are my sons?

It was Jessica who gave me the liquid that I guess was supposed to help with a peaceful death. Her hand was shaking, and she was holding back tears. I try to tell her I do love her, but my words sound off, my tongue feels thick.

I hear my mother calling me, "Genevieve, are you coming down for breakfast?" It is early December. The weather had taken on a new appearance, and so had my body. There is no mistaking me for looking heavier, as Pops had said. There is no mistaking that I am pregnant.

"I will be right there." I remember wanting to say, "Don't

let Trey eat all the muffins," but as I pulled off the covers, I noticed a large stain of blood on my sheets. I stood up and watched blood trickle down my legs, splattering the floor. My nightgown was stained with dark blood. I felt faint. Immediately, my stomach was seized by a vise. I yelled for my mother, and that was all I remembered.

I woke up in the Newport Hospital. Funny, that is the same one I had just left.

My mother was there when I woke up. My hand went right to my stomach. It was hollow. The doctor came in to confirm I had lost the baby. I could not stop the tears. That is a terrible thing to say to a woman. Like I misplaced the baby. A person loses gloves, they do not lose babies. He told me it was a boy. He told me that even though he was well developed, he wasn't breathing when he was born. I did not have my baby, my child. I did not have Nicholas.

Even now, in my morphine haze, I feel that pain. Oh, not the physical pain that I had felt then, and not the emotional pain that stayed with me for years. But I still feel it. In my heart. I feel it in a little place reserved for Nicholas. No one has ever come close to how that baby made me feel. He is the only person who has ever taught me to put someone else's needs before my own.

I was in and out of consciousness. I am sure they were keeping me sedated. That is what they did to women then. Keep them drugged up, keep them quiet. Actually, they are still trying to do that to women.

Nicky came. I found out later that my mother had called him. He was looking out the window when I woke up. I watched him for a minute and, as if he sensed it, he turned and looked at me. He had been crying. I raised my hand to him, and he came over, took my hand in his. He kissed it. He kissed my forehead and sat down, still holding my hand, fighting the tears that had returned. Neither of us spoke. No words were necessary to express what we were both feeling.

Finally, Nicky asked if I was okay, did I need anything? I shook my head and began crying again.

"I hate God."

"Shh, Gen, you don't mean that."

"I do. I hate Him." I was weak. It was a strain to speak.

"Gen, this is a tragedy. But this is—"

I interrupted. "If you say this is God's plan, I will hate you forever." Even though I was feeling weak, I could feel a fiery anger rising within me.

"Honey, I understand your suffering. I honestly do. This baby meant so much to so many." He squeezed my hand, tears welling up in his eyes. "This is a terrible loss. I'm learning how to accept things we cannot change. But before you interrupt again, hear me out. We are humans. Without complete faith in God, some things that happen to us seem insurmountable. That's what being a human is."

"I loved this baby as if he were already here," I said. "In my heart, in my mind, Nicholas Austin was my little person. Now he is gone. I will not accept this thing that I cannot change."

A nurse came in and said, "Excuse me, Father, but I need to examine Mrs. Austin. She needs her rest, but you are welcome to come back and sit with her."

It was only then that I realized Nicky was wearing black pants with a black belt and a white collar, partially hidden by the black shirt. Was he here as a friend? Was he here as the father who had just lost his son? Was he here as a priest?

I was in the hospital for five days. Mr. and Mrs. Austin came to visit. I remember how hard that was. With my family, I could be whoever I wanted to be. Genevieve who does not want to talk. Genevieve who is angry. Genevieve who is verbally attacking anyone who tried to be kind. Genevieve who is mourning. But with them, it was different. I remember when

Mr. Austin said it was a blessing that I was not farther along. "We have God to thank for that."

I thought I would reach over and grab him by his cheap, synthetic tie and choke him in front of his wife. Fortunately for all, Mrs. Austin said to her husband, in her calm manner, "Dear, you know nothing about being a mother."

I was back home in Newport, recuperating, when Emma told me I had a long-distance call and asked if we should accept the charges. I wanted to scream, "Of course, you idiot." In hindsight, I may have.

I knew it was Michael as I hobbled to the phone in the hallway. His mother had gotten in touch with him, gave him the news. She let Michael know the baby was gone. The connection was terrible. Michael couldn't tell me where he was, but he said that he hoped I was feeling well and that we might look at this as a blessing. He said maybe it was God's will that I lost the baby. I am not sure, but I think I hung up on him.

The holidays with my family in Newport were a struggle, and I felt drained. I felt so lonely, so sad, so unfulfilled. I spent days wandering aimlessly on the beach, bundled up against the New England weather. This was a bleak time for me, and again, I was alone with my pain. Yet at the same time, I was sick of being treated with kid gloves. Emma tiptoed around me. My father seemed terribly uncomfortable with me. Trey was oblivious. It was only my mother who helped, yet I still sensed she knew more than she was letting on.

At the first of the year, I knew I needed to get back to myself. I could not go on like this forever. I had reconnected with Sally from school and told her an edited version of my life since we had last seen each other. She was working in Boston and invited me to come visit for a weekend. She was single, loved her job, and loved her apartment. It sounded like this was just what the doctor ordered.

I waited until the spring to visit her. By then, I had recovered my strength, both physically and emotionally, and I was learning how to keep my anger in check. As a matter of fact, even as I lie here, ninety-four years old, I still struggle to keep my anger in check. The death of Nicholas shook every fiber of my being. I do not understand the intense connection I had with that child. I guess I was never meant to understand.

What is it that Nicky liked to say? It is God's will? I suppose I should make up with God if I plan to meet Him soon. I will be sure to ask Him what that pain, sadness, and despair was all about. Why did He let that tragedy shape my life? I hope God has a good answer for me.

BOSTON

"IF 'PLAN A' DIDN'T WORK, THE ALPHABET
HAS TWENTY-FIVE MORE LETTERS!"
— UNKNOWN

Genevieve took the bus from Newport to South Station, Boston. Sally was there to meet her. Despite her conservative reputation in school, Sally's appearance was now that of a sophisticated, young, career woman. She had on a wide-brimmed, red hat, stylish, red, floral dress, and navy pumps. Genevieve noticed immediately that Sally had cut her mousy-brown hair into a fashionable bob.

At first, Sally didn't recognize Genevieve. She had changed so much in the last year. She was shocked at how thin Genevieve was, how pale and tired she looked. Genevieve had her hair in a ponytail, wisps of washed-out, blonde strands hanging by her ears. She was wearing a gray, A-line skirt, with a soft-pink, cardigan sweater and black flats. *What happened to Genevieve Lemaire,* she thought as she waved and ran over to hug Genevieve. Sally was a no-nonsense Midwesterner who spoke her mind.

"Genevieve, look at you. It's so wonderful to see you. But darling, we need to get you back in the game."

"What game? What are you talking about?" Genevieve

asked as she struggled with her suitcase through the crowds at the bus terminal.

"The game of life, honey. No offense, but you don't look like yourself. Really, I understand you have been through so much, but honestly, Genevieve, you don't need to look it."

"Do I look that bad?" Genevieve asked, tucking a loose hair behind her ear.

"I'm taking you shopping. The first order of business is to burn that skirt. You can keep the sweater to wear around the house."

"Sally, money is tight. I am not working, and Michael … well, anyway, I can't go shopping. How bad do I look?"

"Don't worry about anything. We will go to Filenes Basement. They have designer clothes at bargain prices. But first, we are going to stop in at my hair salon on Newbury Street to do something with your hair. My treat. No objections. I am a working girl with a good paycheck."

And that's what they did. They went to Newbury Street Hair where Genevieve got a shampoo, a toner treatment to bring back her vibrant, blonde hair, a trim, a few rollers in strategic places, and twenty minutes under the dryer.

"Ta-da," her stylist said as she turned her chair around to face the mirror. Genevieve was surprised at her reflection. It was a complete transformation from the woman who had walked into the beauty salon just an hour before. Genevieve didn't realize how she had stopped paying attention to her looks since she had come home from the hospital. Now, peering at the woman in the mirror, she smiled. It felt good to look nice again. Right then and there, Genevieve made a promise to herself. She must always come first. She is the only one who is going to care about her, so she might as well add beauty to the long list of things that she needed and deserved.

Sally and Genevieve had a quick lunch and walked into Filenes Basement, arm in arm, like two women on a mission.

"Look, Genevieve, free mini facials at the Estee Lauder counter. Let's start there. Just be careful because they will try to sell you more products than you could use in a lifetime."

After the facials, they walked around the mayhem that the Basement was known for. Genevieve was like a deer in the headlights, but Sally knew her way around the place.

"Stick with me. The designer labels are mixed in with everything else. Follow me, keep your eyes open and you just might find a smashing Claire McCardell taffeta skirt!"

At the end of the day, Genevieve collapsed on Sally's couch, surrounded by her shopping bags, feeling better than she had in a long time. Sally went out to get them dinner and returned with two brown, paper bags. "Roast Beef sandwiches, with a side of fries and a coke. I figured you have had it up to here with clam chowder and lobster."

They stayed up late, talking. Genevieve let Sally do most of the talking. She had so much going on in her life. A job she loved, an adorable apartment in the city. She was making friends, although the dating scene was lacking. For Genevieve, the best part of being with Sally, other than the generosity she showed her today, was that Sally didn't pry. She didn't avoid eye contact. She didn't tiptoe around her. Genevieve knew Sally was a straight shooter, and if she wanted to know something, she would ask. She never mentioned the baby and only briefly asked how Michael was.

"Goddamn war," Sally said, taking a sip of coke. Genevieve laughed and agreed. When was the last time she had laughed?

That's when Genevieve jumped off the couch and said excitedly, "Sally, I have a plan. I know what I am going to do next."

Genevieve wasted no time putting her plan into action. After she left Sally and returned to Newport, she started looking for an apartment in Boston. This was part of the original plan between Genevieve and Michael. They would have an apartment in Boston ready for him when he started at Harvard. Unfortunately, the plan had changed. Genevieve was also looking for a job now that there was no baby. She did the best she could, pushing her hurt, which was slowly festering like an angry wound, aside and focusing on what was ahead for her—a new life in Boston to share with her handsome, soon-to-be-captain-in-the-air force husband. He would go to Harvard, and she would have a wonderful job as an interior designer.

With financial help from both her father and father-in-law, Genevieve found the perfect apartment on Commonwealth Avenue in Boston. It was on the second floor of a stately brownstone within walking distance to the Boston Public Garden.

Genevieve moved in during the heat of the summer and started working in a doctor's office as the receptionist. If she wasn't back in Newport on the weekend, she could be found in the best parts of Boston, poking around antique stores and thrift shops, looking for used furniture. Genevieve had an eye for quality pieces, thanks to her summers roaming the homes of Newport.

Her first purchase was an antique, mahogany dining table with six matching chairs from a thrift shop in Beacon Hill. She knew it was made by a prestigious, high-end furniture maker by the intricate, carved legs on the table and the backs of the chairs. Between the purchase and delivery, Genevieve had spent a week's paycheck.

This is how she filled her time, working and hunting for treasures to make the apartment her own. Genevieve still had a large hole, an ache in her heart, but she got up every day, went to work, and tried to cover the pain that was always with her.

The Christmas season came to Boston with a light dusting of snow. Boston put on its finest outfit to celebrate the season. The Common was lit with twinkling, white lights. They held a Christmas parade on Washington Street. The downtown stores' windows were decorated to delight both children and adults. The brownstones adorned their doors and window boxes with ribbons and greens. Despite the war, the city took on a festive holiday spirit.

Genevieve got caught up in the spirit, putting up a small tree decorated with antique decorations she had found in a thrift store earlier in the year. She loved shopping in Filenes Basement for gifts for her family. Money was still tight, but she found a scarf for Trey and a leather tobacco pouch for her father, both on sale. Emma would get a used book in excellent condition. Genevieve splurged a bit for her mother with a bottle of Jean Nate.

She took a bus from South Station to Providence on Christmas Eve to spend the holiday with her family. The Lemaire traditions remained as they always were, with a couple of exceptions. The gifts were less extravagant, more on the practical side, and the meal was scaled back. Their typical Christmas meal consisted of elaborate appetizers, usually including foie gras, as a course. This year, there was no foie gras, and the appetizer selections were less than usual. Dinner was a roast turkey with a variety of winter vegetables. The cheese course, which is an essential part of any French, multi-course meal, was also scaled back. But the dessert stayed the same.

The table had been cleared of the remains of dinner. Edward poured five glasses of champagne, and they toasted to Margaux as she placed her beautiful la Bûche de Noël in the center of the table.

After dessert, when the dishes were washed, dried, and put away, the family sat together by the roaring fire in the living room. Genevieve was curled up on the couch next to Emma, both sipping their champagne. Each sister silently wondered what the next year would hold for them. Emma wondered about college. Would it be possible for her? Genevieve wondered what Nicky was doing, and would she be able to purchase that dressing table with a stool and mirror she had spotted last week. It was from the 1920s and well over her budget. Genevieve hated that she had to watch how she spent her money. *I just need Michael to get home, get through school, and then we will be on easy street*, she thought as she sipped her champagne.

"Merry Christmas, everyone," she said, gazing out the window toward the Reynolds' house.

WELCOME HOME

"THERE IS NOTHING LIKE RETURNING TO A
PLACE THAT REMAINS UNCHANGED TO
FIND THE WAYS IN WHICH YOU YOURSELF
HAVE ALTERED." — NELSON MANDELA

"Hi, Genevieve."

"Who is that? Who is here?" I can hear someone, I think. Why won't my eyes open?

"It's Liza, Genevieve. Are you that far gone that you don't know who I am? Your favorite granddaughter," she said as she bent down to kiss me.

One thing that I know for sure is that none of my grandchildren are my favorites, but I have done something right because each one thinks they are.

"Liza, dear, sit down for a minute. I am sure I look a mess. See if you can find a brush and do something with my hair."

I fade from Liza. Maybe it is the gentle way she is brushing my hair, or maybe it is the morphine that Sara and Jessica keep squirting in my mouth.

I can feel a warm breeze and familiar sounds and smells, but I'm not sure where I am. Oh, now I know. I am on the Boston waterfront. It's summer. I live in Boston, and despite everything—the baby, the war, Michael, Nicky—I am happy at this very moment. My life is good. I have a job, a fabulous apartment, and lots of new friends ... some single, some married to men overseas.

We are all so different and yet alike in so many ways. Our independence is one thing that we have in common. Single or married, we are making our own way in this world, paying the bills, going to work every day, and keeping the home fires burning, as the saying goes. I remember how much I loved my freedom. My time in Boston shaped me, gave me a sense of purpose, a sense of who I wanted to be. And that was, and still is, to be Genevieve—the girl who could take on the world, and win.

THE WAR ENDED, and so did my complete independence. Michael came home. Oh sure, I was ecstatic, just like everyone else. The war was over. We had won, and now life would get back to normal. But back to normal for me was not having a husband. Back to normal for me was doing whatever I wanted, whenever I wanted, and not answering to anyone.

I met Michael at South Station. I waved to him as he stepped off the train. His uniform was baggy and wrinkly on his very thin, six-foot-four frame, but he was still so very handsome. He was wearing what was probably a three-day beard growth on his now gaunt face, and what appeared to be a nose that had been broken more than once. His brown hair was longer than I remembered, and shaggy. Yes, Michael needed a shower, a shave, and a haircut. Oh, but his blue eyes still sparkled, and his captivating smile made my heart beat a little faster.

He dropped his bags and picked me up off the railway platform. He spun me around, laughing, and put me down to grab my waist, pull me close to him, and kiss me. Michael kissed me hard. People were jostling by us, but we stayed like that just being in each other's arms until we knew we needed to move. We splurged and took a cab to the apartment. I was so proud of how much I had done with it and could not wait to show him.

"Welcome home, Michael!" I said as I spun around the foyer, which now had a small writing desk to leave your keys on. Next to it was a coat rack and a Chinese-style umbrella stand.

Michael dropped his bags on the floor, along with his coat, and asked, "Do you have any booze in this place?" I chalked it up to his exhaustion, his reentry into the real world.

I went into the living room where I had set up a small bar and mixed his drink. A feeling of unease got ahold of me as I handed him the gin and tonic, hung his coat up, and said, "Let me show you around." I walked through the apartment, pointing out the unique pieces, where they were from, what period, how I found each one, but Michael didn't seem interested.

He rattled the ice cubes in his glass, asked where the bathroom was and then asked for another drink. I made the drink and showed him to the bathroom. The shower was running as I made myself a gin and tonic. I stood in my—our—kitchen, looking out the window toward Boston Common. My husband is home, he is safe, I should be grateful. I wasn't.

Michael came out of the shower, empty drink in hand. "How about you make us a couple more, and then you can show me the bedroom?" He smiled and squeezed my hand. We, or I, tried so hard to make our reunion romantic, a night to remember. Instead, what stood out was that he had a condom? *Where did he get that, and why does he have one?* I thought.

Let me tell you, reunion sex is nothing to write home about. Actually, at that point in my life, sex in general was nothing to write home about. Let me see … there was the sex with Nicky. I will call that innocent sex. Or maybe it should be called how-to-ruin-your-life sex.

Next was Michael. That would be how-to-save-your-life sex. Or better yet, how-to-hook-a-guy-for-life sex. Then there was the honeymoon sex. It was okay, but no mountains moved for me, by any means. I remember thinking practice makes perfect, but we didn't have time for practice. So should I call that boring, married sex? And that is what our reunion sex was—boring, and over much too fast for my liking. One minute, Michael is ripping open a condom wrapper, and the next thing I know, he is snoring on the bed next to me.

I got up, put on a white, silk robe, and slipped my size-nine feet into my white, fluffy, peep-toed mules. I have always believed, at least as long as I can remember, that there is absolutely no reason for anyone to dress like a slob, even if the occasion is right after boring sex. I can remember shutting the bedroom door—my door, but now our door—and walking across the living room to sit on my, our couch. *What the hell have you done, Genevieve* is what I thought.

I had been offered a few days off from my job to spend quality time with my husband returning home from war. After one day of being with Michael, I went back to work. The routine of getting up in the morning, doing my makeup, and deciding what to wear was my anchor. Michael and I were like strangers. He didn't know what to do with himself during the day, and I didn't want to have much to do with him after a long day at work.

Michael went to New York to spend a few days with his parents and seemed to be in a better frame of mind when he returned. He signed up for the GI Bill and started classes at Harvard. I felt a weight lift off my shoulders, but there was a black cloud sitting just above where the weight had been. The baby. I tried to talk to Michael about Nicholas, about the unbelievable anguish I felt when he died. Our conversation went from bad to worse.

Michael had finished up his first full week at school. It was Friday, and he wanted to have some fun. I had put on a Frank Sinatra album, looking forward to the weekend.

"Let's go out, do something. What do you say, baby?" Michael asked after mixing us a couple of drinks.

"How about going to Newport for the weekend? We can pack up now, stop for a bite to eat on the way? The weather looks perfect for some golf, maybe tennis?"

"Why don't we do anything but that?" he replied just as the phone rang.

"I'll get it. We can figure this out afterward." I left my drink and went to answer the phone.

"Hello."

When I came back to the living room after my call, the first thing I noticed was that my drink was empty. I had only had a sip before I answered the phone. I knew he drank it but said nothing. Instead, I walked to the bar and made myself another.

"Hey, what about me?" Michael was on the couch. His eyes were a bit glossy, and there was just a hint of a slur to his speech. "Who called?"

I ignored his request for another drink. "That was Sally with some very sad news."

"Oh yeah, what?" he asked, getting off the couch. I watched him. It was just a short distance to the bar, a matter of feet, but I could see the subtle shift in how he walked.

"She miscarried last week. I wasn't even aware she was pregnant. She and Ralph had kept quiet about it for a while."

"If they wanted to keep it quiet, then why is she telling you? I don't get what the big deal is," he said, mixing himself another drink.

Michael sat down in the blue-and-white chintz armchair directly across from me. I had deliberately placed the chair there to encourage conversations. I watched him take another sip. There was a coaster on the end table beside the chair, but Michael never put his drink down.

"The big deal is that she miscarried, Michael. That is a big deal. Listening to Sally and her pain has brought up all the memories of when Nicholas was born. That hurt does not go away automatically just because you are no longer pregnant."

"Oh, for God's sake, Genevieve, that's ancient history. You had a miscarriage, it happens. But what doesn't happen is that someone in their right mind would name that thing, whatever you want to call it. You didn't have a baby; you lost it. And speaking of how crazy the naming thing is, why the hell would you call it Nicholas?"

I could not believe what I was hearing. How could my husband, or, for that matter, anyone, be so callous? "Michael, you weren't here. You didn't see how my pregnancy progressed. How my belly grew. You never felt the baby kick. I went into labor. He was born just like any other baby, but he was just too little. He had no chance of survival. That pain was real, he was real, and my life has changed forever. You were not there for any of it. I know that isn't your fault. But at the very least, I would think that you would have just a thread of sympathy for what happened. Your son died."

I was simmering with anger as I got up, walked to the bedroom, turned, and said, "I don't feel like having fun tonight. Good night." I sat on the edge of my bed and let the tears fall. My heart got a little colder as I swallowed my anger. I knew I needed to guard myself more than ever. I will not let Michael, or anyone, gaslight me by dismissing my feelings.

The morning sun pouring into the bedroom window brought me out of a troubled sleep. At some point during the night, I must have gotten up and undressed, then crawled back into bed. Michael's side of the bed was empty. My mind was groggy. Too many gin and tonics. Maybe add our terrible conversation to the mix, and you wind up feeling like crap.

Then there was a knock on the door, and a very sheepish-looking Michael peeked his head in. He pushed the door open with one foot, stepped in with a tray of juice, black coffee, and an antique grapefruit spoon and a half of grapefruit sliced just the way I like it—in segments.

"I'm sorry," he said, gently placing the tray at the end of the bed. "I am so sorry. I'm an ass."

He handed me my coffee. I remained silent, wondering how my hair looked. Was my face puffy from crying?

"I was wrong, and you were right. I don't understand what you went through. Since I've been home, I don't understand a lot of things. I don't know where I fit in, or how to get back to who I was before the war. I feel lost, numb. I think I just need time to readjust. I've talked to some guys, and they are feeling the same way. But that's my problem, not yours. I'll do better, Genevieve, I promise. I love you so much. I couldn't stand to see how upset you were last night, and again, I'm sorry I wasn't home to support you through that terrible time.

"Last night, while trying to sleep on that uncomfortable couch, I thought about everything you'd said. You didn't tell me why you named the baby Nicholas, but I think I understand. Nicky is your best friend. He was here, not me. Doesn't seem fair to me, but that's life. A guy dodges fighting for his country to say he wants to be a priest. That guy gets to comfort my wife while I'm dropping bombs on some poor people I can't even see." Michael's hand shook as he took a sip of juice. He saw I was watching and put the glass back on the tray.

"I was thinking that if you want to do something today with me, we could go to those antique stores or thrift shops, whatever they're called, and look for a more comfortable couch. Although, I don't plan to sleep on it again."

He flashed me that dazzling smile of his, and I thought, *We can do this.*

My mind drifts to that conversation as the morphine takes hold. It was a pivotal one in our relationship. We began to find our way back to each other. Between my job and Michael's schedule with school, we were like ships passing in the night. This worked in our favor because we appreciated our time together. I remembered why I was attracted to him when we first met, and I think the same was true for Michael. Not a great foundation for a marriage, but I had made this bed, so I might as well enjoy it.

Should I have walked away at that point? Listening to my children laughing in the kitchen makes me believe I did the right thing.

WELCOME TO THE FAMILY

"Genevieve, hurry. I don't want to be late." Michael was banging on the bathroom door.

As Genevieve opened the door, her husband's eyes widened at the sight of her stunning appearance. She was wearing a cream-colored suit and black pumps. The form-fitting jacket had a Peter Pan collar with nine black buttons from the collar to her hips, emphasizing her narrow waist. The skirt hugged Genevieve's hips before flaring out, accentuating her curves and highlighting her shapely calves. As she walked to the foyer to get her purse and wide-brimmed, black hat, she let Michael soak it all in. Genevieve knew she looked good. Actually, Genevieve knew she looked better than good.

"I hope, from your expression, I am worth the wait. Okay, Michael, time to get your diploma."

The Lemaires and the Austins were seated together in the Harvard stadium to witness Michael receiving his diploma. His grades were poor, at times, and they were worried he wouldn't graduate. But there he was in cap and gown, accepting the diploma from Harvard.

After a celebratory lunch, both sets of families went on

their way, leaving Genevieve and Michael to bask in his achievement.

"Look at you, my Harvard husband. I am so proud of you, Michael." Genevieve handed him a tall gin and tonic and sat next to him on the couch. "So what is next for you, for us?"

"What do you mean?"

"What are you going to do with your education now that you are finished with school? I know jobs are still hard to come by, but I would think that companies would be thrilled to hire a Harvard graduate."

Michael took a big sip, then set the drink down on the coffee table. Genevieve immediately placed a coaster under it. He stood up and began to pace around the room. He stopped and looked out the window, watching cars pass by and people walking down Commonwealth Avenue.

With his back to Genevieve, Michael said, "Most of the guys I graduated with had jobs lined up, probably before they even started school. They came out of the war as captains, or at least as majors. They were on the fast track to get ahead. Genevieve, I'm just a shitty private, a nobody." He walked to the coffee table, reached for his glass, and finished it in one swallow.

"You are not shitty, Michael. I know it's disappointing that you couldn't move up the ranks like so many others, but you are still a Harvard graduate, and that has got to count for something."

"You want another?" he asked, rattling the cubes in his empty glass, walking to the bar cart without waiting for her to answer.

Genevieve bit her tongue. She harbored a lot of resentment toward Michael for not doing what so many of her friends' husbands had done. They might not have a degree from Harvard, but most returned home from the war as captains, which gave them an advantage over those who didn't advance in rank. *People like Michael*, she thought, taking a sip of her drink.

The summer after graduation was one of disappointment for both Michael and Genevieve. He couldn't find a job, and she found out that she was pregnant. Instead of celebrating this news, Michael buckled under the pressure and began staying away from the apartment. He would come back late at night, drunk and belligerent.

By the middle of July, Genevieve was at the end of her rope. She had miserable morning sickness, which she tried to hide from her coworkers and a husband who was, in her mind, a waste of her time. She took a week off from work and went home to Newport.

Genevieve told her parents she was pregnant with as much enthusiasm as she could muster. Margaux and Edward digested the news and then put on their best faces. Lots of hugs and congratulations, all the right questions. How do you feel? When are you due? When can we shop for baby clothes? But behind closed doors, in their bedroom, they whispered their fears. Michael didn't have a job. How much longer could Genevieve work? How on earth could they afford a baby?

"Don't worry, *mon chéri*, I will see what I can find for work for Michael. You just focus on our daughter. I don't want Genevieve to go through what she did with her other pregnancy. She needs to be well cared for this time."

Margaux snapped at Edward. "What are you saying, Edward? That I didn't care for Genevieve during her last pregnancy? She is a grown woman. Nobody took care of me when I was carrying your children."

"Shush, she will hear you. I am simply pointing out that things did not go well before, and I would like to avoid another unpleasant event. Good night, dear."

THE PHONE RANG JUST as Margaux Lemaire bent down to take the hot corn muffins out of the oven. *Who can that be*, she thought, annoyed. The warmth from the oven warmed the kitchen on the chilly January morning.

"Edward, can you please get that?" She can picture him grumbling down the hall. Edward doesn't like to be disturbed when reading the morning paper.

She can hear him, "Hello. Oh yes, Michael, everything okay? Well, I'll be damned. A girl, you say? Had hoped for a boy, but we will take what we can get. How's mother and baby doing? Yes, of course, I'll tell her. Oh, and Michael, congratulations. This news comes with additional responsibilities—ones I hope you will take seriously. Yes, that's right, goodbye."

Margaux stood just outside the kitchen, waiting for her husband to hang up the phone. She was untying her apron when Edward turned around and said to his wife, "Well, *mon chéri*, it's a girl. You are officially a grandmother."

She went over to him, gently touched his arm, and said, "And you, old man, are officially a grandfather. Imagine that. I'm going to change so we can get to the hospital. Should we celebrate with warm, buttered muffins for breakfast?"

Michael hung up the hospital pay phone. "God, sometimes I hate that man," he said aloud. He put more dimes into the phone to call his parents, hoping for a more enthusiastic response.

As the phone was ringing, Michael began to feel sick to his stomach. He knew it wasn't anything that could be cured with a doctor's prescription. This was bigger than that. Edward Lemaire's words were on replay in his brain ... *more responsibilities, take things seriously.*

His thoughts were interrupted when his mother answered the phone. After sharing the news of a new granddaughter, Michael hung up, took a deep breath, turned, and walked out of the hospital doors, looking for the nearest bar. *I just need something to calm me down*, was his excuse to himself.

"Mrs. Austin, are you up for a visitor?" Genevieve looked up at the nurse and then saw her mother standing in the doorway. For a brief second, she had hoped it was Michael, but it wasn't.

Margaux Lemaire, holding a bouquet of calla lilies, hesitated before approaching her daughter's hospital bed.

"Mom, the flowers are beautiful. Nurse, could you please put these in a vase for me? Did you see the baby? Should I ask that she be brought down from the nursery?" Genevieve watched her mother hand the bouquet to the nurse and sensed an air of something coming from her mother. It wasn't warmth or joy. Her mother seemed ill at ease standing in the hospital room.

"That's unnecessary. I stopped by the nursery on my way here. Does she have a name?"

"No, not yet. I haven't had a chance to talk to Michael about a name yet. I'm not sure where Michael is."

Margaux chose to ignore that her daughter and son-in-law hadn't talked about a name and that Genevieve didn't know where Michael was. *I would think that as the time got closer, Genevieve and Michael would think of names and be ready once the baby was delivered*, she thought, walking to look out the window toward the harbor.

She knew Genevieve was stuck between a rock and a hard place in her marriage. When they had announced their engagement—their very brief engagement—she was suspicious. She never imagined Genevieve being married by a Justice of the Peace, but she washed over her concerns with the fact that it was wartime, and people did strange things. And then there was the unpleasant business of the stillbirth and how poorly Genevieve dealt with it. "Who in their right mind would name a stillborn child?" she had said to Edward. But time has a way of blurring the past, and now there was a new baby in their family. But Margaux felt no joy, just a foreboding of the future.

"Jessica."

Genevieve looked at her mother. "What?"

Margaux turned to say, "Jessica, name her Jessica. She looks like a Jessica."

"You could tell that she looks like Jessica from the nursery?" Genevieve doubted this.

"Yes, Jessica. Now make it official. Tell Michael that's her name and fill out her birth certificate." With that, she gave her daughter a quick kiss on the top of her head and turned to leave.

"Middle name?"

"You know the Lemaires don't do middle names," she said, walking out the door.

Genevieve lay back in her bed thinking, *Well, we might not do middle names, but what about the Austins? They have middle names.* She dosed off without asking to see her newborn.

Genevieve and Jessica spent five days in the hospital. Her mother came every day to visit, sometimes bringing Edward or Emma along. Edward was terribly uncomfortable, and Emma couldn't contain her excitement, especially when Genevieve asked if she would be Jessica's godmother. Michael stayed away.

"Oh, my goodness, of course I will. I would be honored, and trust me when I say I will accept this role with great responsibility. So let's start with the christening. When should we have it? Wouldn't it be wonderful if Nicky could officiate?"

At the sound of Nicky's name, Genevieve's head turned so quickly toward her sister that she felt her neck crack. Before she could respond, Margaux said, "Oh, that reminds me. Some mail came for you at the house." She pulled a few envelopes out of her alligator purse and handed them to Genevieve, who only smiled, said thank you, and put them on her hospital bedside table.

At that moment, a nurse came in to let them know visiting hours were over. After her family left, Genevieve got out of bed, put on her silk, floral robe, and walked over to the chair by the window. She curled her bare feet up under her and went through the envelopes, looking, hoping to recognize the writing on one. And there it was, addressed to Mr. and Mrs. Austin. She knew who it was from. For an instant, she was annoyed that Michael was included, but curiosity overtook the annoyance as she ripped open the envelope.

On the front of the card was a picture of what looked like an Angel Wing shell with the words written across it: *Congratulations on your new angel. May the Lord give you strength, patience, and understanding as you walk the path of parenthood with her.* Inside was Nicky's handwriting.

Dear Genevieve and Michael,

I heard the wonderful news and can only imagine the joy you are experiencing. A little girl, who I am sure is a beautiful baby. How could she not be considering who her mother is? I wish much love to the three of you.

Sincerely,

Nick

Genevieve didn't realize she was crying until she saw a tear drop onto the card. She looked out to the harbor, to the gray water, the gray sky, and felt an ache in her heart. She thought about Nicholas, the baby. How old would he be now? Who would he have looked like? She imagined him as a combination of the best of his parents—the best of her and the best of Nicky.

"WHY WON'T SHE STOP CRYING?" Michael was at the end of his rope with his three-month-old daughter. She was colicky, crying most of the the time, making a tense marital situation worse.

"You know why. She has colic," said an exhausted Genevieve, pacing the floor of their apartment, trying to console Jessica.

"The doctor said a few drops of brandy in her formula should help."

"Okay, Michael. Pour some brandy into her bottle and warm it up. Hopefully, she will drink some."

He did as instructed. Michael put a couple of drops of brandy mixed with formula, gave it a shake, and put it in a pan of water to heat the bottle. He put the brandy back in the cabinet and hesitated for just a minute, staring at the variety of liquors Genevieve had collected. Michael shut the cabinet door and went back to check on the bottle, all the while listening to Jessica crying in the background.

Michael was sober and had been since bolstering his courage in a bar the day Jessica was born. He had told the bartender, and anyone who would listen, that he was celebrating the birth of his daughter, which was only partly true. Michael got a few congratulations, pats on the back, "Give that guy a drink on me." He also heard a lot of, "Your life will never be the same. Maybe you should get out while you can. That's what I did." These comments came from men, drinking and smoking in a dark bar in the middle of a weekday.

Aside from the colicky baby, things were on the right track for Michael and Genevieve. Thanks to Edward Lemaire, he was working as an insurance salesman, a job he hated. He and Genevieve gave up the brownstone in Boston and moved into a spacious, two-bedroom apartment in downtown Providence. His father-in-law put down the first and last month's security deposit. Michael grew to hate Edward Lemaire more and more.

While Michael had hoped to stay in Boston or move to New York to put a bit of space between himself and his in-laws, Genevieve was dead set on being as close to Newport as possible. Michael didn't push that hard because he enjoyed the perks of being married to Edward Lemaire's oldest daughter, meaning, for one thing, he had full access to their country club for golf and tennis.

Before Genevieve got pregnant, before Jessica was born, they'd spent most summer weekends at the beach where Genevieve grew up. Afternoons might be doubles with another couple, or an early morning golf game with her parents. One thing that Michael loved about Genevieve was her athleticism and her competitive drive. He felt it pushed him to fit into her world … so far away from where he grew up in Brooklyn, NY. Michael wanted this lifestyle so much that he put up with Edward and his condescending attitude.

PASTA AND POLICE

"WE ARE WHAT WE PRETEND TO BE, SO WE
MUST BE CAREFUL ABOUT WHAT WE
PRETEND TO BE." — KURT VONNEGUT

"Jesus Christ, Genevieve," huffed Michael, out of breath as he burst through the front door. It was a workout, carrying seven-month-old Jessica up two flights of stairs.

Genevieve was on their couch, just finishing her nails.

"What's wrong, Michael? A couple of flights of stairs too much for you?" She meant it as a joke, but it came out like a dig, and they were both aware of her tone.

"No, dammit, it's not the stairs. It's her," he said, putting Jessica on the floor before getting a glass of water. Genevieve just looked at him, and then at Jessica, with a blank expression.

"We were walking down Main Street, and some old lady walks up to the stroller and asks if she can see the baby. I said of course and moved the cover back a bit. She bent over for just a second, then looked at me and said, 'Oh dear, I'm so sorry,' and just walked away."

"Oh, that is strange. Why did she say that?" Genevieve asked, waving her hands in the air to dry her new nail polish, Red, Hot, and Blue, advertised as the new, beautiful, American look.

"I don't know. Why don't you tell me, since she doesn't

look at all like me. She's a bit ugly." He knew these words would sting, but he hurled them at her anyway.

Genevieve didn't miss a beat now that her nails were dry. She glanced down at her daughter, sitting on the oriental rug, reaching for a toy, and said, "Well, you are right. She is a bit ugly, which is why she looks exactly like you. I have seen your baby pictures, Michael." With that parting shot, she scooped the baby up and walked out of the room.

Genevieve heard the front door slam. After giving Jessica a kiss on the cheek, she put her in her crib with her favorite stuffed animal and walked out into the empty living room. Genevieve just stood there, void of any feelings other than good riddance, and went into the kitchen to make pasta sauce. She wasn't sure why she was doing this. The apartment was warm enough from the summer humidity. Who makes pasta sauce on a hot, summer day? Why did she agree to not go to the beach this weekend? Why did she make the choices she made?

"What are you cooking?" It was Michael, reappearing in the kitchen hours later.

"I am making sauce. Where have you been?" Genevieve walked over to the stove to stir the sauce, which was simmering to a nice thickness.

"I needed some air." He was slurring. "What did you say you're cooking?"

"I told you, sauce, pasta sauce. Have you been drinking?"

Michael came up behind Genevieve and put his arms around her waist. "Oh, come on, baby. Don't act like you've never had a drink." He squeezed her tighter, and she could smell the alcohol on his breath. "Baby, what are you cooking?"

Genevieve exploded, pulled herself away from his embrace, and picked up the pot of sauce. Michael had just enough time to take a step back before she flung the pot at him. Hot pasta sauce went everywhere, but not on its intended target … only Michael's shoes, not his face.

It didn't take long for Genevieve to realize that she needed to get away from him. She was furious that he had been drinking. While he stood there, stupefied, Genevieve removed her apron and calmly walked out the front door, leaving her seven-month-old baby with her inebriated father.

Genevieve walked with purpose down Bellevue Avenue dressed in a red, polka dot halter top, white shorts, and open-toed wedge sandals, which made her long, tan legs look even longer, if that was possible. She had grabbed a silk scarf on her way out and knotted it around her hair, which resulted in a messy ponytail. This was not considered appropriate attire for a young woman to be wearing out in public.

She was furious with the world, but especially with Michael. *How could he be such an ass? What is wrong with him?* she fumed, walking past the best shops in Newport. *I need to get out of this marriage. I need him to go. But then what? I am stuck with a baby. How can I become who I want to be as a single mother? I cannot go back to my parents; that would admit defeat. My mother's attitude, when I told her Michael and I were getting married, was anything but congratulatory. I cannot give the baby to Michael's parents. He should not be anywhere near her. Maybe foster care. That could be a temporary solution until I can figure things out. I need time for myself. I need to take care of myself. Nobody else will.*

"Excuse me, miss. Oh miss, excuse me." Genevieve turned to the voice behind her. It was a police officer approaching her on the sidewalk. She just kept walking. The officer caught up with her and grabbed her arm. "Miss, please slow down. I want to talk to you."

Genevieve stopped and shook off the hold of her arm. "What is it, Officer?" The harshness in her voice was a clear sign that she was not in the mood for anyone to bother her.

"Genevieve? Genevieve Lemaire?" he asked.

"It is Genevieve Austin … and you are?" She spoke with a curt tone, suggesting a sense of superiority.

"Officer O'Malley, but you would remember me as Billy O'Malley."

"I would not remember you as anything because I do not know you."

Officer O'Malley smiled, thinking, *You haven't changed a bit, Genevieve Lemaire or Austin, whatever name you are going by these days.* They had gone to school together from first grade right through high school graduation. *You always acted like you were better than everyone, even your own sister and brother. But kiddo, you are a townie, just like the rest of us. Sure, you grew up in a nice house on the beach and pretended you were on the same playing field as the rich summer kids, no matter how hard you tried to drop your Rhode Island accent,* he thought.

"Exactly what is it you want, Officer?" Genevieve's voice brought him back to the present situation. "I am in a hurry, and if you do not mind, I will be going."

"You sure seem to be in a hurry. I stopped you, Miss Lemaire."

"Mrs. Austin," she interrupted.

"Right. I stopped you, Mrs. Austin, out of concern for your safety."

"My safety? What in God's name are you talking about?" Genevieve was dumbfounded. This was Bellevue Avenue, known for its high-end shops. Only people of a certain means frequented this street. She glanced around. Everything was closed, and it was getting dark.

"Well, I know you aren't here to shop, since it's Sunday and all the stores are closed. And you aren't exactly dressed for a Sunday stroll. I felt it was best to see if you needed some assistance."

Jesus Christ, thought Genevieve, *can this day get any worse?*

"Officer O'Malley, Billy. I just needed some fresh air. The apartment was quite stuffy, so I decided to just step out a bit. I must have been daydreaming, not realizing how far I had walked."

It didn't get past Officer O'Malley that her tone had changed. He saw right through her sweet, innocent act. "Let me give you a ride home." Before she could object, which she was about to, he said, "I insist, ma'am. It's in your best interest." So off Genevieve went, in the back of a squad car, ready to assess the damage waiting for her. When she got home, the sauce was cleaned up and both husband and baby were sleeping.

They never discussed the pasta sauce incident. Genevieve chose to put that at the back of her mind, along with the police car ride home. Michael didn't remember a thing. Not his first blackout and far from his last.

Between July and the end of 1950, Michael Austin's drinking was spiraling out of control. He would disappear for days at a time. Genevieve had stopped calling the police to find him and bring him home. She had come to a point where she didn't care if he was found, and she didn't want him home. She stopped calling his parents, since they were unaware of the extent of their son's drinking problem, or they chose not to acknowledge it. Michael was an expert at hiding his drinking. He rarely missed a day at work. For her part, Genevieve did her best to hide his descent into alcohol until she got a call from the Providence Police Department.

Genevieve was wrapping Christmas presents when the phone rang. She ran to answer it, hoping it didn't wake Jessica from her nap.

"Hello."

"Is this Mrs. Austin?"

"Yes."

"This is Officer Black, from the Providence Police Department. Your husband has been arrested."

"Arrested? For what?"

"Drunk and disorderly conduct."

"Jesus Christ, what do you expect me to do?" Genevieve studied her apartment as if searching for help. She looked at the pile of partially wrapped gifts on the floor, the beautiful tree she had decorated alone, and glanced toward the bedroom where Jessica was napping.

"Jesus," she said again to no one because no one was there to help her.

"We are going to hold Mr. Austin for twenty-four hours, pending an investigation."

Genevieve lit a cigarette. "What investigation? Do you need to investigate why he drinks? I have been trying to figure that out for a while now. Let me know when you come up with something."

She slammed down the phone, took a drag of her cigarette, and went to check on Jessica, who had started fussing. She extinguished her cigarette, picked up her baby, and put together a plan in her mind. Once again, Genevieve was calculating what she needed to do to make a difficult situation bearable.

"Hello."

"Nicky?"

"Gen, is that you?"

"Yes. I need help."

Within twenty-four hours, a plan was in place. Nicky, who had been transferred to a seminary in Rhode Island to complete his theology degree and be closer to his mother, made some calls. Over the last year, he had been working closely with a group of veterans struggling with the transition of returning home from the war. He made some powerful connections and knew he could help Genevieve by helping Michael.

Michael was released from jail on the charge of being drunk and disorderly. He walked down the front steps, expecting to see his wife waiting for him. Instead, he saw Nicky with his collar on and standard, black shirt and black trousers with two men dressed in air force dress uniforms approach him.

"Nicky, surprised to see you here." Michael stood tall, as if trying to mask why he was walking out of the Providence Police Station. They shook hands.

"Michael, this is Sergeant Steward and Sergeant O'Neil." The three men saluted each other. Michael smirked at Nicky, knowing he isn't allowed to salute.

"Private Austin, let's take a walk." Sergeant Steward's tone made it clear that this was not a request. Michael walked with the two sergeants, Nicky following close behind. Nicky couldn't hear what they were saying, but he knew what they were talking about. The three men stopped walking, and Nicky saw Michael's posture change—his shoulders slumped, he hung his head, and he shoved his hands in his wrinkled, trench coat pockets. After a few minutes, they turned to walk back toward the police station. Nicky stepped aside as they passed. Michael didn't look at him.

Meanwhile, Genevieve knew she had a part to play in this plan.

"Hello."

"Hi, Mom."

"Genevieve, dear, so nice to hear from you."

"Mom, please listen, and do not ask any questions. Not yet anyway. Jessica and I are coming home for Christmas this afternoon. No, Mom, do not interrupt. It will just be the two of us, and I will explain everything to you and Pops then. I will see you soon."

Genevieve hung up before her mother could say anything.

She lit a cigarette and looked at the luggage and Christmas presents, wrapped, bagged, and sitting by the front door. She took a drag and slowly exhaled the smoke out of her lungs and through her shiny, red lips. For just a moment, Genevieve wanted to leave everything behind—baby, alcoholic husband, the luggage, the presents—and just go somewhere to start all over. The knock on the door brought her back to reality. She put out the cigarette and opened the door.

The two friends hadn't seen each other since Nicky's visit to the hospital when Nicholas had died. But there he was, standing at the door … and there she was, looking strong and vulnerable at the same time.

There was just a moment of awkwardness between them. *She is still so beautiful*, Nicky thought.

God, he is so damn handsome, Genevieve thought.

"Nicky." His name came out of her mouth with a breathless sigh. "Come in. How did it go?"

Nicky took off his hat as he stepped into the hallway of her apartment.

"It's done. Michael agreed to commit himself for an initial two weeks at the VA Hospital. That should give him time to dry out, and hopefully, through counseling, help him get a handle on his drinking."

"Nicky, I cannot thank you enough." Genevieve took a step closer to him. Nicky put his hat on the hall table and opened his arms. Genevieve practically fell into his embrace. They stood like this, arms around each other. The only sound was their breathing. This hug, from both of them, healed years of hurt, angry words, and disappointment. Neither knew how long they had stood like that, hanging on to each other, but cries from Jessica pulled them apart.

"Go get the baby. I'll bring your luggage down to the car." As Nicky picked up the suitcases, he laughed. "How long are you planning on being in Newport, Gen? Until Jessica graduates from college?"

"Oh, be quiet. That is not all of it. Jessica's luggage is in her room." It was as if a switch had been flipped, bringing Genevieve and Nicky back together.

Nicky and Genevieve, with Jessica settled between them in the front seat of the car, made the drive to Newport. There was little conversation. Nicky seemed focused on the road. Jessica was happy with her stuffed animal. Genevieve watched the city fade away as they crossed the Newport Bridge. She took a deep breath, turned, and smiled at her daughter and her friend.

"Mom, Genevieve is here," Trey yelled from upstairs. The sound of tires on their seashell driveway pulled him away from his comic book.

Genevieve stepped out of the car to welcome hugs from her parents as she handed Jessica to Emma. Trey helped Nicky bring the luggage into the house. Genevieve lingered for a moment, observing her loved ones walking up the porch steps, past the potted holly tree adorned with seashells, and entering the home where she had spent her childhood. She couldn't help but feel that this was exactly how things were meant to be … *Christmas in Newport with my family, with the people I love.*

CHRISTMAS IN NEWPORT

"IT'S THE MOST WONDERFUL TIME OF THE
YEAR ... EXCEPT FOR THE PART WHERE WE
HAVE TO GO HOME." — JINGLE ALL THE WAY

There is a lot of laughter in my home, while I am lying here in my bedroom, waiting to die. I hear my children laughing, and I cannot decide if this is a good sign or a bad sign. I suppose it is a bit of both. I am going to die; that is a fact. But my children getting along is not typical, so I will take their laughter as a good thing. I am sure this is difficult for them, but life is difficult. I did the best I could.

Oh, how I remember the days leading up to Jessica's first Christmas. That was a challenging time. I left Michael to stew in the VA Hospital. That was not the hard part. The hard part was telling my parents that the man I married was in the hospital because he had been arrested for being drunk and disorderly.

My father was furious. His accusatory tone made it clear that he was angry with me for the mess. I remember him saying something to the effect of why I could not keep Michael happy. That was my job. "You have two jobs in life—one to be a good mother and the other to be a good wife!" he ranted, pacing back and forth in front of the seven-foot, blue spruce tree, decorated with our family Christmas ornaments.

I adored my father, but I wanted to punch him in the mouth that day. My mother tried to shush him, but she was not taking sides. My mother's facial expression gave me the impression she might have also thought all of this was my fault. I had come home for support, not this unexpected, hostile reaction.

"What about his job?" my father fumed. "How will you and the baby live?" I had not thought about that. I had always been resourceful, but that was before I had a baby to care for. I remember saying that I would figure it out. He was only away for two weeks. He would be better. We would all be better.

My mother finally got Pops to calm down, as she would say, "Simmer down, Edward, it's Christmas." This was a painful time for all of us. Pops struggled to come to terms with his son-in-law being committed to avoid jail time for a drunk and disorderly arrest. My mother played peacekeeper, Emma turned to Jessica for an escape, and Trey ... well, Trey was Trey. The bright spot was having Nicky join us for Christmas Eve dinner. Having him at our table, telling his stories about missteps to priesthood, lightened up everyone's mood.

The light snow on Christmas morning seemed to cleanse the world—at least my world—for the moment. My family showered Jessica with toys and oohed and aahed over her. Jessica was too young to know who Santa was, or what was going on that day, but she helped bring our family back together. I think Jessica was the catalyst that kept the Lemaires a tight family unit. My mother offered to watch her more often while we were there. Pops softened up with me. The tension eased itself out through the eaves of our home.

Nicky is the one who had called Michael's parents before Christmas to explain why they had not heard from Michael, or me. I could not muster up the strength to talk to either of them.

Nicky is the one who drove Jessica and me home after the first of the year.

Nicky is the one who picked Michael up from the VA and dropped him off at the front of our apartment.

Nicky. It was always Nicky.

THREE'S A CROWD
"IF AT FIRST YOU DON'T SUCCEED, TRY, TRY AGAIN." — WC FIELDS

The doorbell buzzed. Genevieve knew who it was. Nicky had told her when to expect him to bring Michael home. She put out her cigarette, shut Jessica's door, and stood in the hall, exhaling before turning the handle.

"Did you lose your key?" She instantly regretted the words and her tone.

Michael, hat in hand, rumpled trench coat, looked at her sheepishly. His eyes said it all. *This is hard enough*, he thought. He didn't need this side of Genevieve as soon as he walked through their front door.

"I am sorry, that came out wrong. But Michael, there is no need to ring the bell. This is your home too. I have been expecting you."

"Nicky told you." It was more of a statement than a question.

"Yes, come in, for God's sake. Give me your hat and hang up your coat." Genevieve didn't know what to do or say. Their go-to had been, "Do you want a drink?" She was at a loss.

"Jessica is napping. She has missed her daddy. Can I get

you anything?" she asked, putting his hat down on the hall table, walking into the living room.

Michael followed her. The first thing he saw was the bar cart. There it was, up against the window overlooking Main Street in downtown Providence, just where it had always been. Genevieve had found it in an antique shop while they were still in Boston. It was a beautiful, black-lacquer piece with two shelves. She had accessorized the top shelf with cut-glass martini glasses next to a black, leather ice bucket. The second shelf held a variety of alcohol, all top-quality vodka, tequila, gin, and whiskey. Michael sucked in his breath. All he wanted was to go over there and pour himself a drink—anything. He didn't care as long as it was alcohol. As long as it would get him through this painful situation.

"Oh, and there she is," said Genevieve, glancing toward Jessica's door. "Why not go in and surprise her? I'll get lunch started." Michael went one way, Genevieve went the other way, each wondering how they were going to do this.

Michael fed Jessica in the kitchen, glad to be away from the tempting bottles in the living room. Genevieve sat, watching them, smoking a cigarette. "I need to make this work," she said to herself, getting up to clear the plates. As she walked past Michael, she put her hand on his shoulder and smiled at him as he looked up at her.

After lunch, they bundled up against the cold, damp, Newport day, put Jessica in her carriage, and went for a walk. They didn't say much at first. Genevieve would stop to admire something in a store window, and Michael would agree with whatever she said. The weather was against them.

"I am miserable, Michael, and Jessica must be freezing. I want to go home."

"Genevieve, wait." He grabbed her arm. "This isn't easy for me. I've been away from both of you for only two weeks. It feels like coming home from war all over again."

Genevieve stopped walking, her back to Michael. She wanted to say so much. She wanted to scream so much. *Not easy for you? What about me? You left me with a baby so you could go take care of yourself. Who was here to take care of me? Nobody, except for Nicky. You are so selfish.*

But she heard her father's voice in her head. *Be a better wife.* She turned to look at Michael and said, "No, Michael, this is not easy. This is not easy for any of us. We, you and I, need to get back to the team we were. We need to support each other. There are two of us in this marriage, and if we are going to survive, we better come up with a plan."

Michael smiled. Genevieve always had a plan. Some were definitely better than others. "Okay, what's the plan?" he asked as they began walking home. Michael was gripping the handle of the carriage, his gloved fingers beginning to numb from the cold.

Genevieve slid her arm into his, hoping to steal some of his warmth. Why the hell did they decide to take a walk?

"To begin with, do you still have a job?"

"Yes, I go back tomorrow."

"What do they know? Why do they think you've been gone for two weeks?"

"I was allowed to call them when I was …" He hesitated. "I called them and told them I was taking family time over the holidays. Business is typically slow this time of year, and they agreed."

"That was quite generous of them. I guess you could look at it as your Christmas bonus." Again, she regretted her words and tone. *But too bad. I am not the one who screwed up here,* she thought.

Michael didn't tell her about the other call he made, the one to his parents, asking for money to cover the loss of pay. He had learned, one step at a time. Or in his case, one confession at a time.

Michael returned to work, just as he said. Every day, he went to a job that he hated. And every day, he came home and stared at the bar cart.

Life resumed for them as if they had never missed a beat. The only difference now was that Genevieve had decided to take Jessica, who was a two-and-a-half-year-old toddler, to her parents for the summer. Her reasoning was she wanted her daughter to have the same wonderful memories of the beach as she did. Michael didn't think anyone could remember what happened to them when they were two, but he wasn't going to argue.

Once they were gone, Michael called his sponsor for help. The two of them packed up all the alcohol, mixers, and anything that could trigger Michael to slip back to his old ways. He enjoyed this time by himself. He drove to Newport every Friday night, then drove back to Providence on Sunday afternoons with all the other weekenders.

Michael found a local AA meeting that he frequented when he was alone in Providence. The brotherhood of the group helped him keep his desire for alcohol in check. There was no judgment, no criticism. They were all equals. When he was in Newport, all he wanted to do was escape. How many times could he avoid the questions: Michael, want a beer? Michael, wine with dinner? Michael, how about an after-dinner drink? It was exhausting keeping up the facade of who Genevieve and her parents thought he was. Michael was an expert at adapting to his circumstances, but doing so weekend after weekend was taking its toll.

Genevieve was also enjoying her time without Michael. She thought it was a perfect way to live. When Michael came on the weekends, they did the usual routine—played tennis or golf, swam in the ocean, and read books on the beach. Emma and Trey were home for the summer, so she had a built-in babysitter with her sister and an occasional fill-in with her brother. Margaux had come full circle when it came to spending time with Jessica. She wasn't going to win any grandmother-of-the-year awards, but she loved to be the one to get up with Jessica in the morning while everyone else slept. She would get her out of her pajamas, put on a pretty dress, and bring her down to the kitchen for breakfast.

The one fly in the ointment for Genevieve was that Michael's brother was getting married over the Fourth of July weekend, and Michael was the best man. Try as she might, Genevieve could not figure out a way to get out of going to this wedding in New York City.

"Who in their right mind gets married over the Fourth, especially doing it in the city?" Genevieve would say to anyone who would listen. The only upside to this summer interruption was that she would buy something "smashing" to wear.

"Genevieve, you don't want to be overshadowing the bride," Margaux said as they browsed the fashionable shops on High Street.

"Seriously, Mother? He is marrying a mousy girl from Kansas. Michael will probably overshadow her."

Michael's jaw dropped when he saw Genevieve come out of their New York Hotel bathroom dressed for the wedding. She was a combination of elegance and sex in a soft-green, linen, Dior, sleeveless pencil dress that was cut just below her knees. He gazed down at her entire body from the neckline that gave a hint of cleavage and stopped at the nude kitten heels, making her legs look endless, and then back up at her smiling face.

"Well, what do you think?" Genevieve asked, giving a little twirl. She knew she didn't need to ask him what he thought.

"What do I think? Holy shit is what I think. I think I am one lucky guy," he said, grabbing her by the waist to kiss her. "But the wedding is in a church. Do you have a hat and maybe a sweater?"

"Prude." She smiled coyly, walked to the closet, and

produced a short, button-down jacket that matched the dress perfectly. Once that was on, Genevieve looked the picture of respectability. She put on a cream-colored, wide-brimmed hat that added an edge to that respectability, smiled at Michael, and said, "Mr. Austin, you look quite dashing in that tuxedo."

"And you, Mrs. Austin, are a knockout. I can't wait to get this wedding over with and get back to this room."

In August, Genevieve knew she was pregnant. She hadn't been feeling right for some time and opted to see her OB-GYN in Providence. Genevieve went alone and, once again, left the office with pamphlets in hand, wondering what she thought of this surprise. She and Michael hadn't discussed having more children, but regardless, they had been careful. *Ah, the wedding,* she thought as she pulled into her parents' driveway. *Michael didn't drink, but I had a couple of glasses of that cheap champagne. I guess we weren't so careful.* Genevieve stuck the pamphlets in her purse and walked up the stairs, across the back porch, and into the kitchen.

Margaux was taking a strawberry rhubarb pie out of the oven. "Oh, there you are, Genevieve. Jessica is napping." She gingerly placed the hot pie on the baking rack and looked at her daughter.

"Is everything okay, dear?"

"Yes, of course. Everything is fine. Thanks for watching Jessica. I'll peek in on her." *Jesus, does that woman have some kind of psychic power,* she thought, walking up the stairs. *I swear she can see inside my soul.*

After lunch, she took Jessica down to the beach. Genevieve put her on a blanket with a pail and shovel to keep her amused. She watched absently as her daughter put sand in the pail and then dumped it out onto the blanket. She sat on the beach that she loved and knew so well. Every day, the beach presented something new, something different. But the tides remained consistent, like an old friend you can depend on.

Someone who was sure to arrive and leave when they were supposed to.

Lost in her thoughts, Genevieve didn't realize that Jessica had left the blanket and was walking toward the water. She heard a voice, looked up, and saw Nicky scooping her daughter up in his arms. She got up, dusted the sand off her hands, and met them at the edge of the water.

Genevieve shaded the sun from her eyes as she smiled at Nicky. "This is a nice surprise. What are you doing here? Day off from God?"

"Apparently, I am saving your daughter from taking a dunk in the waves," he said, swinging Jessica in the air.

Jessica laughed and cried, "More, more."

Genevieve took in the scene-handsome Nicky, her best friend and undoubtedly her first love, playing at the water's edge with Jessica. *This is how it is supposed to be*, she thought. *Nicky, Nicholas, me, and our second child. Maybe it would have been Jessica. We are supposed to be a family. How the hell did this all go so wrong?*

"Actually, I was coming up to your house to see you," he said, breaking the spell. Nicky put Jessica down, and the two of them watched her pick up shells. "I wanted to talk to you."

"This sounds ominous." Genevieve bent down to take a shell out of Jessica's mouth.

"It's news. Not good, not bad, just news. I wanted you to know before the rumors started flying." Genevieve looked up and pushed her hair out of her face. "Oh my God, you are leaving the priesthood?" Was she asking him a question, or was she wishing for this to be the news? She stood up to face him.

"Gen." He sighed, but knew he would never stop loving her think first, then speak personality. "No, I am committed to my parish. The news is my mother is putting the house up for sale. It's too much for her now, and she can find a smaller place and relax, knowing that she will be financially set."

"Oh, well, that is news. I would have preferred you telling me you had come to your senses, but I don't seem to get any good news lately." Once again, Genevieve turned the conversation back to herself.

Nicky didn't take the bait … well, at least not immediately. "It's good news for my mother, and that's what matters."

"Yes, of course, your mother. Good news for your mother. Well, I am happy for her, Nicky." She could taste the bitterness in her words.

"Gen, what's wrong? You seem out of sorts. I'm sorry if this has upset you. I just thought it would be better if you heard this from me."

She looked down at Jessica, wet and sandy, knowing that she would need to carry a wet child, along with the pail and shovels, beach bag, and towels back to the house. Jessica would need a bath, meaning her own needs would have to wait. Genevieve would love to walk on the beach, dive into the ocean for a long swim in the waves, and then go home and take a hot shower.

"Sorry, Nicky. I didn't mean to sound so bratty, but I have some news of my own. And as you said, not good, not bad, just news."

"Okay, spill."

"I just found out I am pregnant."

"Do I say congratulations? You don't seem so happy about this." Nicky was grateful that he didn't say his first thought, which was, *Oh, not again.*

"Honestly, I am not sure what you should say. I suppose it's a good thing." Genevieve kicked at the sand. "I just don't know, Nicky. Please keep this to yourself. I haven't told anyone. Not even Michael. Do you want to come for dinner tonight? Might be the last time we will see you here on the beach." She picked up Jessica and started toward the blanket. "I need to get her home."

"Let me help you." He took Jessica from her while Genevieve packed up the sandy blanket, toys, and the beach bag. "I would love to come to dinner, and you aren't going to get rid of me that easily, Genevieve Lemaire … I mean Austin." They walked back to the house together, side by side, such a familiar feeling for both of them.

TRUE CONFESSIONS

My mind drifts in and out of what is real and what is not. I wonder why we didn't talk in my family. I mean, really talk. To say that we were reserved when it came to discussing feelings is an understatement.

I sensed a shift in my mother's behavior toward me after Nicholas was born, as if she was disappointed in my choices. She cared for me when I came home, but that was more out of duty than genuine concern. Stoic does not suit me, which is what was expected of me. I am strong, outspoken, opinionated, and impulsive. Stoic, I am not.

Sara was born in February 1953. My pregnancy with Sara was so different from my pregnancy with Jessica. I felt healthy, energetic, and the pain of Nicholas had slowly started to ease, just a little.

Sara was a dream child right from the beginning. She was healthy, happy, adorable, and loved to sleep. Mom was always asking if I could wake her up. "All that baby does is sleep," she said more than once. She helped more with Sara, which was so different when Jessica was born. I don't think I will ever understand her coldness with her in the beginning. That was when I really needed her but was afraid to ask for help.

After Sara's birth, Michael and I came together as the team I had imagined many years ago. He helped with bath time, read bedtime stories, and genuinely had fun being a father.

We were outgrowing the apartment and decided it was time to buy a house. Michael was doing well in his job, promoted to VP of Sales, and was making a name for himself. He was not drinking, and he had not been for quite some time. But I was always on edge, just waiting for the other whiskey bottle to drop.

Even though I considered us a team back then, in hindsight, I realize we were not. We never talked about his drinking or his sobriety. That was pushed under the rug, a very costly rug.

In a moment of what I considered weakness, Michael told me how much he hated his job. My response was to buck up … you have responsibilities, mouths to feed. Ha, I expected him to be stoic. It did not cross my mind to think about how I could help him.

Sara's christening was on a chilly March afternoon. I would have preferred to wait until the spring, but Michael, his parents, and our parish priest were beside themselves when I said that. I wanted Nicky to baptize Sara. She would be his first official act as a Catholic priest, having recently completed what seemed like a ridiculously long time with the seminary. So we all gathered at St. Mary's Church in Newport to witness my daughter being christened by the father of my first child. I wonder what God was thinking that day. I know what I was thinking as I watched Nicky lovingly sprinkle water on Sara's forehead. Priest or no priest, he was still my Nicky—my first love and I think my only love.

Despite my feelings for Nicky, I did my best to make my marriage with Michael work. In the summer of 1954, we purchased our first home, a wonderful, craftsman-style home, just about a forty-five-minute drive from where I grew up. I knew it was for me the minute I saw it. Michael wanted to be closer to Providence for work, but my priority was to be near my family, even if it meant a longer commute for him. I wanted my children to experience the freedom and magic of growing up along the Atlantic Ocean, just as I had. I honestly believe that if you can handle the power of a wave coming at you with confidence and skill, then you can handle anything this world is going to toss at you.

We moved out of the apartment in June and moved in with my parents until Labor Day while the house was being renovated. I spent hours sitting on the beach, poring over home interior magazines, which added to my grand ideas for that house. Emma was home after graduating from Smith College with a degree in early childhood education, and between her and my mother, I had plenty of time to focus on decorating.

I chose a timeless furniture style that will never go out of fashion. Every detail was crucial in my search for just the right piece, and I took my time examining each option. I scrutinized wallpaper books and fabric samples while sitting on the beach. I was so happy that summer, but I think Michael was wrestling with his demons. Oh, he kept himself in check, but I sensed a smoldering anger building inside him.

About a month before Sara's third birthday, Nicky called me out of the blue. We didn't see each other very often, and when we did, it was usually in Newport where he would come and stay with my parents. They loved him like a son, probably more so because he was not their son.

I remember the sound of Nicky's voice; it had a worry about it. Was it a quiver? I was unsure, but I knew that something was off. He asked if I was alone, could he come see me right away. Nicky was not much of a drinker, but when he got to the house, he asked if I could make him something ... something strong is how he put it. I checked to be sure that Sara was still napping, made him a Manhattan, and poured myself a small glass of sherry.

I listened to my dearest friend, my first love, pour out his heart and soul to me on that bitter January day. Was that the beginning of the end of my marriage? I am not sure there was ever a true beginning for us.

"YOU LOOK AMAZING, GENEVIEVE," he said, sinking himself into the custom-upholstered, down-cushioned couch. "But you always do." He smiled at her and she thought, *Oh, that smile.*

Genevieve sat across from him, trying to read his body language. "Well, of course I do, Nicky, but I am sure that you didn't come over here to remind me how I look."

He smiled, just for an instant. "No, of course not. I need to talk to you, and I won't be able to do that if you interrupt." He put up his hand as she started to protest. "Yes, you interrupt. I suppose that's just one of the little things that I love about you."

Genevieve settled back into the overstuffed chair that complemented the couch, took a sip of sherry, and said, "Go ahead, you have my full attention. You will not hear another word out of me."

Nicky sat up straight, took a large swallow of his drink, and said, "This isn't easy for me. You are probably the last person I should talk to about this, but you are the only person I can talk to about this. Before you ask if I have any friends, the answer is yes. But if they are from the seminary, they aren't going to be understanding, and if they are from my past, they just won't know what to say."

Nicky stood up. "Gen, I am very, very conflicted about choices I've made. No, remember you said you would hear me out? I'm torn between two worlds, and I don't see a way to either combine those worlds or to exit one of them. The worlds are …" Nicky stopped talking, sat back down, and looked Genevieve straight in the eye. "The two worlds are my calling. I love my parish and the parishioners. But"—here he took a deep breath and said—"you are my other world. I am in love with you."

Genevieve glanced down at her lap. Now it was her turn to take a deep breath. "Nicky, what are you saying? I don't understand. Yes, we love each other, as no two people have ever loved each other. But that love stems from our childhood together. It … it comes from how we grew up together, and how we made a baby together, and how we suffered separately from that loss." She moved to the couch and took his hands in hers. "Nicky, you are a priest, and I am married with two children. We are no longer kids who can just pack up, move away, and live on love alone. We both have obligations."

"And that is just a part of my torment, everything you just said. But answer me this, Gen. If things were different … if I hadn't chosen the path that was laid out for me … would we be together?" He let her hold his hands and waited for an answer.

Genevieve's reply was simple. "Yes."

"Well, looks like I interrupted something, huh?" Michael was standing in the foyer, glaring at his wife and the priest together on the couch. "Oh, a little afternoon delight? Some refreshments to boot?" he said as he walked into the living room, picked up the Manhattan sitting on the coffee table, and took a sniff. "Bringing out the good stuff for Father Reynolds? Is that right, Genevieve?" His voice had a nasty ring to it as he snarled out the words.

Genevieve let go of Nicky's hand but didn't make a move to stand up. "Of course you are right, Michael. Why would I serve a guest anything other than top shelf? Or, as you like to call it, the good stuff. Nicky is here to visit. Do not be so crass."

She had rolled sarcasm, anger, and self-righteousness into her response.

"Now, Nicky, where were we before we were interrupted?" She scowled at Michael but continued. "Oh yes, we were talking about Sara's birthday party. Nicky, I do hope that you can make it. It will not be the same without you."

Nicky almost felt bad for Michael. He was no match for Genevieve, but who was?

Just then, Jessica came in from school, thankfully breaking the tension in the room. Perfect timing for Nicky to say good-bye. He gave Jessica a kiss on her head, hugged Genevieve, and went to shake Michael's hand on the way out the door. Michael turned his back to Nicky and walked toward Genevieve, standing next to his daughter. He was ready for a fight, but Genevieve was having none of that.

How long had she waited to hear what Nicky had just said? She was not going to let her husband ruin that moment. Try as he might through dinner, and after the girls had baths and were tucked in bed, Michael could not get a rise out of Genevieve. At one point she simply said, "Grow up, Michael, and grow some balls while you are at it."

They never talked about what took place that afternoon, but Michael was on a slow burn, and Genevieve seemed to relish his frustration. Genevieve was in her own world of frustration, but nobody would ever suspect that anything was different about her. She couldn't stop thinking about what Nicky had said and how she'd reacted. But this was the fifties; divorce was frowned upon. And to add to her dilemma, Nicky was a Catholic priest.

HAPPY BIRTHDAY

"Genevieve, where are your napkins?" asked Rose. There was a lot of activity happening in Genevieve's kitchen as she finished up the last-minute details of Sara's third birthday party. Her parents had arrived an hour ago, right behind William and Rose Austin. Both sets of grandparents seemed to try to outdo each other with the amount of presents they came with.

"Jessica, help Meme and Pops, please. You can put the presents in the living room, under the picture window."

Nicky walked over to help Jessica and glanced at Genevieve. "What can I do to help?"

"You can find the birthday girl. She seems to have disappeared." Today was the first time that they had seen each other since Nicky confessed his love for her. But the two of them acted like their old selves with each other. No one would suspect a thing. No one would know of the love they had for each other.

The table was set, the cake was ready, and the family had settled in the living room. Edward was mixing drinks when

Nicky came in. "I found Sara. She's out in the driveway, no coat, and she refuses to come in."

"Oh, for God's sake. Why won't she come in?" Genevieve asked, somewhat exasperated.

"She wants her father." That was all Nicky said. The room went silent.

"By the way, I haven't seen Michael. Where is he?" Edward asked of no one in particular.

The Austins looked uncomfortable as they waited for Genevieve to respond.

"I don't know where he is, Pops. He has been out of touch for a few days." Genevieve spoke these words as if she was asking someone to pass the salt.

Margaux had put on her coat and was walking out the back door with Sara's snow jacket in hand.

"Do you mean to tell me he isn't here for his own daughter's birthday? What the hell is wrong with that man?" Edward intentionally directed those words at Genevieve, William, and Rose.

"Let it go for now," Genevieve said quietly to her father.

William cleared his throat and said, "This is not the time or the place to have this type of conversation. Jessica is right here, listening to every word. As the adults, we should set an example and discuss this at another time."

Edward grumbled something, Jessica sat next to Rose with her eyes down, and Nicky said, "Genevieve, can I help you in the kitchen?"

"Do you know where he is?" Nicky whispered as Genevieve put a wedge of Camembert cheese on a plate.

"No, I do not. Maybe a neighborhood bar? I don't care, either. He can rot in hell as far as I'm concerned."

"Gen, please, you don't mean that."

"Oh, I sure as hell do, Father Reynolds. I mean every damn word," she said, practically crushing the crackers she was attempting to put out on the cheese plate. "Will you go out back and see what is going on? I will try to play nice with my in-laws. Oh, poor Sara. This will be a birthday she will not forget anytime soon."

A short time later, Margaux came through the back door, holding Sara's ice-cold hand in hers. Nicky was right behind them. Sara's nose was running, and her eyes were red. Such a sad little girl on her birthday. *All because of her damn father*, Genevieve thought, as she stooped down to wipe her daughter's nose and give her a hug.

Michael came home three days later, looking like the bender he had been on. This time, Genevieve turned to William for help. Her father had done so much for Michael, she just could not bear to let him know what was going on in her home. And she was ashamed to tell Nicky. Genevieve had never felt shame before. She had felt paralyzing fear when she found out she was pregnant with Nicholas, but not shame. She was furious with Michael. This was his problem, not hers. He should feel shame, not her.

Once again, the VA came to Michael's rescue. The two-week dry out was under the disguise of an unexpected two-week vacation with his family. That is what his employer was told.

Genevieve kept a low profile for those two weeks, never letting on to anyone that her husband was a drunk. Jessica believed Daddy was working a lot. Genevieve tried to appease Sara with new toys. She spent her time thinking about how she got to this place in her life. A place that was not in her life plan. And as always, it went back to Nicky. Genevieve was well aware she played a role in what took place in that boathouse all those years ago. She still struggled with Nicky's decisions. His decisions had caused her so much grief, yet she couldn't hate him. Genevieve knew she could never hate Nicky. It was God she could hate.

Michael came home. Blue eyes clear and bright as she remembered. He looked well rested and healthy. They tiptoed around each other, letting their children be their marriage broker. They never discussed the drunk elephant in the room. Nothing changed in their relationship. They went on as though they were the stereotypical nuclear family. A handsome, successful husband with a beautiful, charming wife and two young daughters. No one would ever suspect the truth about Mr. and Mrs. Austin.

"Meme, we're home," yelled Sara, jumping out of the back seat of her parents' new Chrysler convertible.

"This is not our home, Sara. It belongs to Meme and Pops, not us."

"Of course it's your home. You are so lucky to have two homes," Margaux said, picking up Sara and smiling at Jessica.

"Genevieve, you look tired and pale. We need to get that hair of yours trimmed and get some color on you. A summer in Newport is just what the doctor ordered."

"I completely agree. I already made an appointment for my hair. And as for the color … well, that should take no time at all. You know how quickly I tan. Come on, Jessica, help me with the luggage."

Genevieve took in a deep breath of ocean air and immediately felt better. The ocean cures all.

IT'S A BOY

"HOW OFTEN I WISH TO FORGET THE DAY. TO
RUN AWAY. HOW OFTEN I WISH TO SAY
GOODBYE. TO STAY IS TO SLOWLY DIE." — J.L.

"It's a boy. A seven-pound boy. He was born just about an hour ago." Michael was so proud to be sharing this news on the payphone with his father-in-law.

"A boy. Well, I'll be damned. I was beginning to lose hope," Edward said, turning around to yell to Margaux, "A boy, Margaux, a boy!"

Margaux came out of the kitchen, drying her hands on her apron. "Edward, what are you yelling for?"

"It's Michael," he said, pointing at the phone, as if she didn't know he was talking on the phone. "Genevieve had a boy just about an hour ago."

Margaux took the phone from him. "Michael, a boy, you said? Well, that's just wonderful. How are they doing?" At that moment, Jessica and Sara came running into the kitchen from the back porch. Margaux motioned to Edward to go quiet them down. They had been with her for the last week, while Genevieve waited at home to prepare for her third child.

"I will be over for visiting hours. I have a name in mind now that we know it's a boy. Edward William. That covers both grandfathers. I'm not sure about the flow, and we don't typically do middle names in this family. What? You already have a name picked out? Did you say Parker? Parker Austin? Michael, I need to go. The girls are ready for lunch. Goodbye."

Margaux hung up the phone and sat down in the chair next to the phone table. She was utterly stunned—not at the news of another grandchild, but at his name. And what's worse, she wasn't consulted.

When Genevieve had told her she was expecting again, Margaux struggled to look happy with the news. Her thoughts went to Emma. Emma did everything by the book, just as it was supposed to be done. First, she got engaged. Her wedding was a year later—a large Newport wedding, as was the custom for young couples in their community. She and her husband had moved to Vermont for his job, and Emma began teaching first grade. Their first child, a boy, was born fifteen months after the wedding. The twin girls had arrived a year later. Margaux rarely saw them because of the distance, but she and Emma talked once a week. Emma had her mother-in-law nearby to help with the children in the beginning and now had a full-time, live-in au pair.

"*Mon chéri*, this is some news. We are going to need a bigger house," Edward had said, slipping his arm around his wife's waist as they waved goodbye to Genevieve and Michael, who were beaming with their announcement.

Margaux had smiled and waved, saying between her clenched jaw, "I'm not so sure about this news." The car disappeared around the bend, and she turned to her husband. "I'm worried. I'm worried about the pressure another child will put on their marriage. I know why Genevieve is doing this. It's to compete with her sister." With that, she left her speechless husband standing in the driveway as she went up the porch steps, through the kitchen, and to the liquor cabinet to pour herself a small brandy.

Parker was a handful from day one. He cried, screamed

most of the time, and barely slept. In the early days, Genevieve was giving him a bottle every two hours. She had moved the girls into a bedroom together and put Parker in his own room. Michael was beside himself with his son. Even though Genevieve was doing 90 percent of the feedings, he was exhausted. They began to argue.

"I do not understand what you have to be tired about, Michael. I'm the one doing all the work. Have you even changed a diaper for him?"

"Don't be like that. Of course I have. But I'm the one who needs to be on point every fucking day to support this family. If I don't get some decent sleep, we might all be out on the street."

"Be like what, Michael? Be like a mother of three children? At least Jessica can get herself up on time, have breakfast, and get to school. But there is still Sara. She can't be expected to wake herself up, get ready, and be on the bus in time. And this one never stops," Genevieve said in a very calm voice, swaying back and forth with Parker on her hip. Genevieve looked as exhausted as she sounded. She now had a hollow look in her green eyes, which were accentuated by her dark circles.

Genevieve's calm voice compared to Michael's yelling put him on alert. He knew better than to escalate this conversation.

"Okay, I'm sorry. I am so sorry that we are both so damn exhausted. I don't know how people do this and stay sane. But I have an idea."

That night, Parker slept fitfully in his bassinet in his parents' room. Genevieve was sound asleep in their queen-size bed. Michael tossed and turned on the twin bed that had been Sara's. Sara and Jessica shared a bed in Jessica's room. The only person who actually slept well that night was Genevieve, and that was all that mattered.

BEHIND CLOSED DOORS

"SUCCESS IS NOT FINAL; FAILURE IS NOT FATAL: IT IS THE COURAGE TO CONTINUE THAT COUNTS." — WINSTON CHURCHILL

"Genevieve, it's good to see you awake."

"I suppose it is good to be awake, considering the alternative. Parker, what took you so long to get here?"

"I've been here, but you've been pretty out of it. Can I get you anything?"

I struggle to sit up. What the hell do I look like? "Yes, your sisters are trying to starve me to death. It is as if they are in some kind of race with the cancer. But yes, I would love a bowl of warm, not hot, homemade chicken soup. Hand me my brush and that small mirror."

I am shocked by my reflection in the mirror. My olive skin is gray, my green eyes are watery, and my hair ... oh, forget my hair, it is a mess. But if I force a smile, I see myself, the Genevieve I used to be. By God, my smile could dazzle a room.

I can hear the girls fussing about something with Parker in the kitchen. My eyes are heavy, and I sink back into my pillows, freshly changed, smelling like lilac.

Parker, my first son, was a pain in the ass during my pregnancy and has been so since the day he hit this earth. He seemed to always be hungry, but the pediatrician chalked it up to Parker being a big, sturdy boy. Such bullshit those doctors used to feed us women. But once Parker was on solids, he seemed to simmer down. I was so afraid he would get fat, but he never did. The same was true for Jessica, but Sara was a different story. She was always chubby. As a toddler, she was adorable. We referred to it as baby fat. But as she got older, it was not so cute.

"Here you go, Genevieve, my famous homemade chicken soup."

"Parker, I changed my mind. Would you get me a bowl of hot Cream of Wheat with brown sugar, just a bit of butter, and heavy cream?"

I watch him leave the room with the tray of soup and crackers. He seems perturbed, but Parker always seems perturbed. Parker and Jessica are a lot alike. Both are head-strong, go-getters, out to prove to the world just who they are. I think they get that from me, certainly not from their father. They have another thing in common—neither of them was planned.

Before Parker, Michael and I were doing well, our marriage seemed solid. Jessica was older and rather independent. Sara was such an easy child. She seemed to be a gift to keep the light going in our family. We had settled into a routine. Michael left for work just before Jessica went to school, and I stayed home with Sara. I kept myself busy with rearranging different rooms in our home. I redid the girls' rooms. Honestly, it should have been featured in *House Beautiful*. Life was good … until it was not.

Michael started drinking again just before Sara's birthday. I cannot remember which one. His nose had been out of joint since he thought he had caught Nicky and me doing some-thing. We were not doing anything other than finally telling each other the truth. We loved each other—that was the truth —and we wasted so many years denying that truth.

As I lay here in this morphine haze, I look back at who I was then. Life had thrown me plenty of curveballs, but I was determined to hang on to the plan I had put together so many years ago. My original plan was not what was expected of young women then. Of course, I wanted it all. I wanted a good education, a job in design, and a wonderful marriage and children. But I did not want to have to put myself aside for the sake of marriage and children. I did not want to be the dutiful wife, dinner on the table, clean house, always smartly dressed, perfect makeup. The image of the little woman waiting for her man to come home was not in my orbit.

The ridiculous expectations put on women were endless. How did other women feel, or was I the only one pushing against these stupid, unrealistic demands? I was in a tough position, since there was no one I could talk to. My friends from school had turned in their diplomas for dirty diapers and catering to a husband whom they may or may not even like, never mind love.

Nobody would understand if I told them I was in love with a priest. I could not reveal that my supposed perfect husband was actually a drunk. But Nicky knew. Nicky knew, which made me uncomfortable. I hated looking needy in front of him. I hated that he saw firsthand how I had made such a mess of my life. All my mistakes started with Nicky, and I despised him for it. Yet I was still in love with him.

But I did as was expected, at least to a point. Michael and I were a team at putting on a show. Sometimes I think we actually believed what we pretended to be. Parker was born about three years after Sara. Secretly, I hoped a son would help to keep Michael on the sober track. He had been doing so well after the birthday incident, but I was always ready for the proverbial bottle to drop.

Life continued for us as a family. Summers were always at my parents' home for the children and me. Michael would come on the weekends, and we would be the beautiful couple on the tennis courts or the perfect little family on the beach. God, how I hated those weekends.

Nicky still came, usually in August, for a week or two. Sometimes he brought along another priest, but for the most part, he came alone. The kids loved their uncle Nicky. He would make a point of spending time with each one of them, making them feel special. He and I would spend days on the beach with the kids, swimming in the surf, reading, looking for sea glass.

When Nicky was with us, I could breathe. I was not waiting for an outburst, or perceived misunderstandings, or anything disagreeable. There was never anything disagreeable when Nicky was there. Between my parents and the kids, we were never alone. I suppose that was a good thing. It was the late fifties, things were changing. But for a Catholic priest and a mother of three, being a couple was not only unheard of, it was also unthought of.

Michael still came to Newport while Nicky was there. He put on a good front. Michael was very good at slipping into any situation gracefully. None of us changed our routines when he was there, but I sensed a change in the air. The big house, with the windows wide open, letting in the sea breeze, carrying the smell of salt air filtering throughout the house, felt suffocating to me when Michael was there. But the children loved having Daddy with them, and that was important to me. Unconventional as I was, I still wanted my children to have a loving father, even if their mother did not love their father.

SNAP OUT OF IT

"Genevieve, can we find a quiet place to talk?" Her father had a look that Genevieve could not read. But whatever it was that he wanted to say, she knew to listen.

Emma had arrived, pregnant again, with her husband and three kids in tow. The house was bursting at the seams. A quiet place to talk was a challenge.

"Why not sneak out the front door. Nobody will see us, and we can take a walk. Am I in trouble?" Genevieve asked, half joking.

Once they were out of the house, strolling toward the harbor, her father broke the silence.

"Genevieve, I've heard from Harry Simms." She stopped and turned to look at him. A sick feeling crept up from the bottom of her stomach.

"I'll be straightforward and get right to the point. Harry called to tell me Michael's attendance record at work this summer has been poor, to say the least. He doesn't give any warning or explanations to explain his behavior. Harry has let this go because of our friendship, but he said that it has affected Michael's sales quota. And the other salesmen are asking him what's going on. He doesn't know how to answer them. He is very concerned, and honestly, I didn't know what to say. Michael has put me in an extremely uncomfortable position."

Her father started slowly walking again. Genevieve held back for just a minute. Her mind was whirling, but she didn't know what to say. That original, sick feeling was being taken over by anger.

What the fuck, she thought, fists clenching.

"I do not know what to say. I am speechless and am so sorry that you've been put in this position."

"Is he drinking again?"

Those words were like a hot dagger to her heart, fueling her anger. *Of course he is drinking. What the fuck do you think he is doing*, she screamed silently at her father.

"Pops, I honestly don't know. I see Michael on the weekends, and he seems fine."

"So you don't talk to your husband during the week?" She wanted to shrink to nothing at the tone of his voice. Disappointment … Genevieve could handle anger from her father, but disappointment was a different story.

"No, not very much. The kids keep me busy most of the time." They both knew that was a poor excuse.

"You need to go home and deal with your husband. Leave the children here. I will tell your mother you need to go home to join Michael for a work event. You can leave this afternoon."

"Mom won't fall for that. She is going to ask questions. I swear, Pops, she can see right through me."

"I'll manage your mother. Let's go back to the house so you can pack."

Genevieve did as she was told, as if she was sixteen again and in trouble with her father.

She pulled into their driveway and parked behind Michael's

car. Genevieve had hoped that he wouldn't be home to give her more time to figure out what to say to him. The house was unlocked, not unusual, but there was loud music coming from the living room. Genevieve quietly put down her car keys and suitcase and walked toward the music.

Michael was mixing a drink, swaying to the music, and slurring a few lyrics. *Oh, great. Country music, of all things*, she thought.

"Michael, what are you doing home?" He turned so fast, the clear liquor spilled down his khakis.

"Jesus Christ, you just about scared me to death. What are you doing here?"

Genevieve calmly walked over to the bar cart, put the cover back on the gin bottle, turned the music off, and said, "I asked first."

"Hey, I was listening to that," he said, moving toward the record player. But the look on Genevieve's face made him stop in his tracks.

"I asked you, what are you doing home? It's the middle of the day." Her voice was calm, but there was a definite edge to it. A volcano ready to erupt.

"It's not a big deal. Things are quiet at work. I came home for lunch. So what? Are you spying on me?" Michael walked back to the bar cart, defiantly opening the gin and giving himself a healthy pour.

Oh, how Genevieve wanted to walk out that door, but not before tossing a match to the house, with Michael in it.

"Michael, I will ask you again. What are you doing?"

"What am I doing? You want to know what the fuck I'm doing? Well, I'll tell you what I'm doing." His voice was raised, and his words were slurred. "I am trying to fucking drink you away. I've tried vodka, tequila, rum. Now I'm on to gin, since the others didn't work. That's right, my darling wife, I am trying to drink you away.

"You know what's funny? This," he said, gesturing around the room. "This fakeness we have. You are a fake, Genevieve. Everything we have is a fake. I learned that from my sponsor. Ya know, I started drinking in high school, just like everyone else. I had it under control. And then you go and get pregnant, and then there's the fucking war. Let's not forget that. A damn good reason to drink, don't you think? And I come home to someone I don't even know, a world I don't know, so there is another fucking good reason to drink. You just go on like nothing is wrong, when every fucking thing in my life *is* wrong. There, now you know what I'm doing."

Michael slammed his drink on the coffee table and sunk into the down cushions on their rhubarb-colored, linen-upholstered couch. Genevieve winced at Michael's words, but her attention quickly shifted as he reached for the glass, hoping it wouldn't spill on the couch.

"Well, it doesn't look to me like your little drinking game is working because here I am, Michael. You have not succeeded at drinking me away."

She stood on the other side of the coffee table, glaring at him. Genevieve Austin rose to her full height, pulled her shoulders back, tucked her blonde hair behind both ears, and waited for Michael to say something. She was ready for battle. Instead, Michael began to cry. Tears don't work on Genevieve. They are a sign of weakness, especially in a man. But now she had a situation that was both annoying and uncomfortable.

She remembered her father's words from a long time ago, something about being a supportive wife. Genevieve sat in the chair across from the couch and softly said, "Michael, what is wrong? What has got you so upset?"

He looked up at her, those beautiful, blue eyes full of tears, full of pain, and said, "Jesus, Genevieve, I just told you. Did you hear anything I said? I am miserable, and I don't know what to do about it. What the hell do I need to do to make you love me? What does a man need to do to make you happy?"

She hadn't expected that. "How to make me happy? That's a good question." Genevieve was carefully choosing her words —not the ones she wanted to say, but the ones she needed to say. "Michael, your drinking does not make either of us happy. I understand it is a struggle for you, but if you want to make me happy, make the children happy, make yourself happy, you need to stop drinking. You need to find some self-control. Your boss is concerned, my father is concerned, I am concerned."

He looked up at her at the mention of her father. "What does your father know?"

"He doesn't know much. Harry Simms called him to find out why you're not coming to the office. Pops sent me to find you. I would also like to know why you aren't working."

Genevieve wanted to berate Michael. How dare he put her father in this situation? How dare he jeopardize her financial security? How dare he try to blame his drinking problem on her? She knew better. He was drunk and down enough as it was.

"I'm lonely without you and the kids here. It's hard to resist temptation. I'm sure I'd do better if you would just come home. Let the kids finish out the summer in Newport, but you should come home to be with me."

Over your dead body. The body that will burn up when I drop a match on it just before I walk out that door. "I am not leaving the children alone with my parents. That is too much to ask of them. And I am not cutting their summer short to come home."

Silence. Michael sunk deeper into the cushions. Genevieve sat up straighter, staring at him. "You won't come home because you might miss seeing your precious Nicky." Michael angrily wiped his runny nose with the back of his white, Van Heusen shirt, got up, and stood right in front of Genevieve.

This was an aggressive move, and Genevieve assessed the situation.

"I have a plan." Those four words took the wind out of Michael. Genevieve always had a plan. Sometimes they were good, and sometimes, not so much.

She stood up and started toward the door. "If you really want to know how to make me love you, call your sponsor, stop drinking. Call your boss, apologize, say this will never happen again. Do not tell him you have been on a bender. I don't care what excuse you give, but that one is non-negotiable. I suggest you avoid Newport for the rest of the summer. It is only a few more weeks. And for my part of this plan, I will call you twice a week to check in."

As she picked up her suitcase and keys, she turned to look at her husband. "One more thing. Nicky has nothing to do with anything. You are the one with the problem. Fix it."

CHAMPAGNE TASTE

"TELL ME, WHAT IS IT YOU PLAN TO DO
WITH YOUR ONE WILD AND PRECIOUS LIFE?"
— MARY OLIVER

Why am I so tired? I sleep all the time. I know people are coming in and out of the house. Some come and sit by my bed. I caught Emma praying over me the other day, or maybe it was just a few minutes ago. But there she was, sprinkling something on me and asking God to forgive me. But I can sense someone is in here, not talking.

"Who's here?" I think that my voice sounds strong. I do not want to sound the least bit weak or afraid.

"It's me, Ray."

My eyes open. Oh dear, my youngest is here. I must be declining quicker than I expected. I put out my hand toward him, surprised that I feel a tear falling down my cheek.

Raymond. Oh, dear Raymond. I wish I could speak to you. I wish I could speak to all of my children. I don't mean I wish I could talk. I mean speak, express myself. But I guess it is too late for long, drawn-out conversations. I do not have any regrets about my children. I did the best I could. Nicky is my biggest regret.

Raymond was the last of my plans with Michael. It was the

sixties, and our marriage had been on the right track. Michael was sober, or *on the wagon*, as they say. Jessica was in private school, and Sara and Parker were in our local elementary school.

Since my days were free, I dabbled in home decorating. It started with ladies from my parents' club. They had seen how I had redecorated the Newport house, and some of them asked for my help. I didn't get paid, but it made me feel worthwhile. I was doing something other than being a wife and mother. We were doing okay, or at least pretending that we were okay, but I think we both knew the road was coming to a dead end.

Little by little, Michael had started to disappear for a night here and there, which meant only one thing—he was drinking again. Instead of talking to him about it, I would have imaginary arguments in my head. I stewed. How dare he fuck things up for me, for us, for the kids? I was so sick of it all.

My last plan went into place after a visit with Sally. She and I met in Providence for lunch. No kids, just us. She looked terrible. I think her marriage and brood of kids had taken its toll. Her clothes were matronly. Her mousy-brown hair was cut short, what is referred to as a maintenance-free haircut. She had put on more weight, and wearing no makeup did not help with her look.

"Genevieve, you look amazing," she had said when we met at the restaurant. I think I said she did too. Yes, sometimes I can be known for my decorum.

She was happy, and I let her think the same about me. After all, I was the daughter of Margaux Lemaire. Outward appearance is most important. Allow no one to detect any flaws, weakness, or unpleasantness.

After two glasses of champagne, I hinted that things at home seemed different now that the kids were in school. I did not mean for her to think that was affecting my marriage. I was trying to say how wonderful it was to be doing something outside of the house. Somehow, Sally took it differently. I remember her taking a sip of her third glass of champagne, leaning closer to me across the table, and whispering, "Try for another baby, a boy." She sat up straight, took another sip, smiled, and said, "That worked for us."

Driving back to the house, I let Sally's words sit with me. Would another son pull Michael back into the family fold?

Damn Sally, damn the champagne, and damn some of my plans.

Raymond was born exactly nine months later.

UNCLAIMED MEMORIES
"THE COURSE OF TRUE LOVE NEVER DID RUN SMOOTH." — WILLIAM SHAKESPEARE

"Eileen, can you please help me prepare the children's rooms? Genevieve is coming on Friday, and I want to have everything ready," Margaux said to her cleaning woman. She was looking forward to her grandchildren coming.

Ray would soon turn one, which meant he would be crawling all over the place. She wasn't getting any younger, and as the other three got older, they brought their own set of challenges. Jessica was almost a teenager, but still too young to be expected to be in charge of her sisters and brothers. Parker was a handful … and Sara. Margaux smiled, thinking of Sara. Sara would be no trouble.

But Margaux wondered how many more years she could do this. It was Edward who came to the rescue. He loved having his grandchildren near him and secretly loved having Genevieve back home. He would put up with Michael on weekends, as long as it meant he had his family home.

"*Mon chéri*. I have an idea. We will hire an au pair for the summer. I will look into a college student who wants to spend the summer on the beach in Newport."

"We need someone who loves children, is responsible, and

can be depended on. I don't want just someone looking for an easy beach job."

That summer, twenty-year-old RISD college student Angela Brown arrived, fully prepared to care for the Austin children. She fit right in, and everyone was thrilled. Everyone except Sara. Sara still went to Margaux for anything and everything she needed or wanted. She had no use for Angela Brown. Margaux was secretly thrilled with Sara's rebellion.

Genevieve was just happy to have more free time to enjoy her summer. Since Ray was born, she had felt overwhelmed with four children. Ray was a quiet baby, meaning Ray was easily overlooked. More than once, Genevieve had driven out of the driveway with just three kids in the car, only to hear Jessica say, "Genevieve, you forgot the baby." A slam of the brakes, a few choice words, and Genevieve would turn the car around.

The arrival of Angela gave Genevieve some much-wanted one-on-one when Nicky came for his annual August visit. The last time they had been alone was two children ago.

"Genevieve, your father and I are going to meet the Chapmans for dinner tonight. Angela has a beach dinner picnic planned for the children. That leaves baby Ray with you," Margaux said as she applied large amounts of Nivea to her tanned legs. Just one of the many beauty routines that Margaux swore by.

"That's fine. I have no plans anyway. Pass me the Nivea."

The big house was surprisingly quiet. Ray was fed, bathed, and down for the night. The others were out, leaving Genevieve and Nicky alone.

"Nicky, do you want a drink? What should we do for dinner?"

"I'll mix up a pitcher of Tom Collins. Sound good?"

"Sure. I will see what we have in the fridge." *This is so normal,* thought Genevieve. *This is how it was supposed to be.*

"Here's your drink. Let's not think about dinner right now. Come and sit on the couch next to me."

Genevieve felt something. Was it nerves? Butterflies? Or was it anticipation of what she hoped would happen? She sat down, tucked her bare, tan legs under herself, and sipped the ice-cold drink, letting the gin sit at the back of her throat before swallowing.

"You make a damn fine drink, Nicholas Reynolds."

He smiled, saying nothing. *God help me*, he thought, *but when opportunity knocks on my door, I'm gonna answer it. Forgive me.*

"Gen," he said, reaching over and tucking her hair behind one ear. "I feel like it has been an eternity since we've been alone."

"Four kids can do that," she said sarcastically. She regretted those words even as they flew from her lips. "Sorry. Those kids are my fault, not yours."

"Your kids are nothing you need to apologize for. Can we please just be us for this moment? I miss you so much. I've loved you too long to waste this precious time." He put his drink down and looked deep into her eyes.

"I can remember a time, a very long time ago, when you'd asked me if I was sure. It was in the boathouse. I said I was sure. Do you remember?" she asked, placing her drink on the oak coffee table in front of the couch.

"I do." Nicky didn't take his eyes off Genevieve's face.

"So now it is my turn. Are you sure?"

"I have never been more sure of anything in my entire life."

Genevieve was about to say, *Really? More sure than when you chose God over me?* But Nicky's lips on hers chased those words away as she fell into his arms. They pulled apart and simultaneously asked, "Are you sure?" Laughing, Genevieve rose from the couch, held her hand out to Nicky. They walked up the stairs to his room, hand in hand.

"Genevieve, where are you?" It was Jessica back early from the picnic dinner on the beach.

Genevieve flew out from under the covers on Nicky's bed, grabbed her clothes, and snuck back to her room. *Jesus, I feel like a teenager*, she thought, hurrying to button her blouse just as Jessica came bursting through her door.

"Jessica, lower your voice. I do not need Ray to wake up."

"What are you doing? Why do you look the way you do?"

"What you are talking about? I do not look any different than I usually do. Now, what do you want?"

Nicky met Genevieve in the kitchen, after she had sent Jessica back to the beach. He came up behind her and wrapped his arms around her. "Everything okay?"

Genevieve turned to him and smiled. "Everything is wonderful. Jessica just needed a big spoon for the picnic. She is gone, and I have you all to myself again." They stood together in an intimate embrace, savoring what they had just shared. "How much more time do we have alone?" Nicky whispered in Genevieve's ear.

She pulled back, laughing. "Not enough time for that!"

"Let's go sit on the porch together, like we used to, and talk."

Nicky refreshed their drinks and met Genevieve on the porch. She was on the new swing, slowly pushing it back and forth with her bare feet, quietly singing in a low voice. Nicky strained to listen to the lyrics.

> *Oh, my darling, my love, my dear, I've longed for*
> *your touch, I've longed for your touch*
> *A long and lonely time, Are you still mine? Time*
> *goes by so slowly.*

Nicky took in the site. Genevieve was a natural beauty, especially in the summer, when her hair was bleached platinum and her body was a golden bronze. His mother had once described her as a classic beauty. *That girl should model. Not too many are blessed with such high cheekbones, alluring, green eyes with those thick, black eyelashes, not to mention those long legs of hers. Mother was right,* he thought as he smiled and handed Genevieve her drink.

"What are you singing?"

Genevieve looked surprised. "Was I singing?"

"Yes, and you know you were. It sounds familiar. Come on, what is it?"

"'Unclaimed Memories.' I know it's old, but I love it."

Nicky took her hand to his lips, kissed it, and said, "And I love you. Once, I told you we didn't have a song, we didn't have a first dance. Well, now we have a song. It's a good start."

"What are we going to do?"

"Shall we dance while you sing that haunting song?"

"Nicky, I am serious. I am a married mother of three, I mean four, and you are a priest. We just made love. I think in your case, that is a mortal sin."

"Gen, I love you. I don't believe that God is looking down at us, judging us. The Bible says that since true love is part of God's nature, God is the source of love. He is the initiator of a loving relationship with us."

Genevieve pulled her hand out of Nicky's and stood up. "Don't you dare talk to me about God. You know how I feel about Him." She knew her words were sharp, but she didn't care, at least at that moment.

"Okay, let's leave God out of this. I love you. Let's not waste time arguing. I don't know how to make us work, though. It would kill my mo—" He stopped midsentence when he saw Genevieve grit her teeth and clench her fists. "There are so many reasons I can't leave the church. I would be excommunicated. If you left Michael and we married … now that would be a mortal sin. At least for me."

"Then we are stuck between a rock and a hard place, are we not?" Genevieve walked to Nicky and took hold of both of his hands. "I have also loved you too long to fight. As Michael's AA sponsor says, one day at a time." Her eyes began to fill with tears, and then, "Damn, here come the kids, back from the beach." She pulled away from Nicky as she wiped her eyes with the back of her hand, feeling the coldness of her wedding ring against her face.

Genevieve helped Angela get the kids bathed and ready for bed. She put the leftover picnic food in the refrigerator while Nicky read a story to Sara and Parker. Jessica was already curled up in her bed, reading one of Emma's old Nancy Drew books. Genevieve found herself humming again, absentmindedly looking out the kitchen window, out to the ocean. *Why can't this be my life? Why aren't these Nicky's kids? Why in God's name is my life so off the rails?*

Nicky and Genevieve spent as much time as possible together before he had to end his vacation. But between the children, Genevieve's parents, and Trey, who was home for a few weeks, they had no time alone. They both ached to touch each other. The temptation to hold hands, to kiss, to walk back up those stairs to the bedroom was intense. But the chance of being discovered was greater than either of them dared to risk.

The entire Lemaire family stood in the driveway to say goodbye to Nicky. Promises to meet in the city, come for Christmas, and see each other more often were said, just as they were said every year. They weren't words just spoken for the sake of speaking. Everyone meant what they'd said, but life always seemed to step in and step on those words ... step on their good intentions.

LETTERS

"IT'S OFTEN JUST ENOUGH TO BE WITH
SOMEONE. I DON'T NEED TO TOUCH THEM,
NOT EVEN TALK. A FEELING PASSES BETWEEN
YOU BOTH. YOU'RE NOT ALONE."
— MARILYN MONROE

"Genevieve, before I give you your morphine dose, can I get you anything? Maybe some water? You should probably drink a little water."

I struggle to respond to Jessica. "Yes, perhaps some ice chips. Yes, ice chips would be nice." I want to stay awake and alert as much as possible, but I do enjoy the effects of the morphine. My memories of years past have never been clearer. I am not sure if it is the influence of the morphine or my march toward death.

Nicky is on my mind. I probably should have talked to him before things got this far out of hand. But he will understand. He always understands.

I feel like I am back at my parents' house, the old Newport house where I grew up, the summer after Raymond was born. The summer that Nicky and I gave in to our love for each other. I have not been sexually intimate with many men in my life, but that summer, that time. Oh my, it was wonderful. To make love and to be loved by a man who truly loves you is a once-in-a-lifetime experience.

That first time with Nicky, in the boathouse, was amateur

hour. Well, probably not even close to an hour. That time upstairs in Newport was real. We took our time. We realized the privilege of making love to each other was precious. It was not something to be rushed or to make light of. It was beautiful. I cried after. Not because I was ashamed of what we had done. Not because I was sad about our situation. I cried because my heart was full. My emotions were overwhelming. When we were together like that, I shed my hard shell, stripped bare, exposed and open to the love Nicky had for me.

Nicky and I had made a pact to try to see each other whenever possible. To the world, we were best friends. Only we knew how much more we were to each other. I knew we needed to be careful, and that is when I'd decided we should write to each other. He was worried about Michael reading the letters, so I decided to get a post office box and not tell Michael.

So there I was, thirty-seven years old, married, mother of four, with a priest for a lover. Oh, it was scandalous.

Dear Nicky,

Seems like old times writing to you again. We have lost so much time, but you know me, no regrets. I treasure the time we had last summer, and that will keep me going. The children are doing well, although it seems Jessica is the only one who is happy to be back in the classroom. Sara is dreaming of horses, not math, and Parker simply does not seem to grasp the concept of school. I am thinking of taking a job at a local wallpaper shop during school hours. I am just not sure of what to do about childcare for Ray. I think after last summer, Meme has had her fill of the grandchildren. I look forward to hearing from you now that you have my new mailing address.

Yours,

Gen

My Dear Gen,

Loved your "newsy" letter. I also think of all the time that has passed between us, and with all honesty, I can say that will not happen again. Forever, I will hold close to my heart the memories we made in Newport, and your love means the world to me. I wouldn't worry too much about the kids and their aversion to school. We weren't ones to embrace school, and I think we turned out okay.

"Your turn."

Nicky

Dear Nicky,

Big news. I took the job at the wallpaper store. The pay is pitiful, but I am not in it for the money. I am going to make a name for myself. Just you wait and see. I am going to start my own interior design studio. I am not sure of a name yet, but one step at a time. I can just hear you saying, "Gen, you take four steps at a time."

I hope you are well. We are going to Newport for the holidays. Any chance you can get away this year and join us? We would all love to see you. Emma and her children are coming. Trey is bringing a new girlfriend. Yes, I know, another one. We will make room for you, I promise.

Yours,

G

My Dearest Gen,

Well, look at you! A working girl. I have never once doubted your ability to make a plan, put it into place, and make it work. Some of your plans have been challenging, to say the least, but nobody and nothing will ever get in your way. So happy for you.

Thanks for the invitation for Christmas, but I will be in New Orleans this year. My mother isn't well, so I am leaving just before Thanksgiving and returning in early January. I have been given the opportunity to "help out" at her church, which should be interesting. The parish priest is ancient, but I promise they won't recruit me. I will call on Christmas Day. Let's try to get together after the holidays. My love to you and your family.

    Always yours,
    Nicky

Happy New Year, Nicky,

    Christmas was not the same without you. It was not just me who thought so. We all missed your big smile and wonderful laugh that fills the rooms in Newport. But your phone call was my favorite present this year. The children loved talking your ear off!

    Wishing you a wonderful new year and hope that we can toast to 1962 together, sooner rather than later.

    Yours,
    G

Happy New Year to you, Gen,

    The highlight of my holidays was talking to you. I have missed your voice, even when it's raised. Ha ha. The children were over the top with what sounded like a feast of presents from Santa. I made sure to respect that Jessica is now "too old" to believe. I think she will come around to believing in Santa again. Most adults do. I know I did. Priest or not, Santa is a beautiful spirit that I wish the entire world embraced. Maybe if they remembered he was watching, our world would be a more peaceful, loving place.

    I have found home care for Mama, so she isn't alone. She fought me on this, but finally agreed, and the woman she settled on is perfect for her. Lots of patience to listen to the stories that I have heard repeatedly throughout my entire life.

    I've enjoyed getting to know the members of this parish—much feistier than my Rhode Island members, if you get my drift. But as promised, I am coming home. It's just been extended to the end of January. I'm excited to see what 1962 (and God) have in store for us.

Always yours,
Nicky

THE BEGINNING OF THE END
"I'D RATHER REGRET THE THINGS I'VE DONE THAN REGRET THE THINGS I HAVEN'T DONE." — LUCILLE BALL

The shrill of the ringing phone made Genevieve's stomach twist with unease.

"Hello."

"Is this Mrs. Austin?"

"Who is calling?"

"This is Sgt. Cooper with the Providence Police Department. Is this Mrs. Austin?"

Genevieve sat down in the hall chair next to the telephone table, wrapping the curly, black phone cord around her fingers.

"Yes, this is Mrs. Austin. What is this about?" She kept her voice even and tried to slow down her racing heart.

"We have your husband, Michael Austin, here at the precinct. He and another fellow got into it at Linnwood Bar tonight, and we were called in to break it up. Your husband is fine, physically, other than a split lip and what looks like a hell of a shiner on its way. The other fellow didn't fare so well. He's been admitted to Providence Memorial Hospital, and he's pressing charges of assault and battery. He will also be charged with drunk and disorderly conduct. We'll hold Mr. Austin for the night, and he'll appear before the judge tomorrow morning at 9 a.m. Be prepared to bring bail money. Do you know where the courthouse is located?"

Genevieve lit a cigarette and listened as Sgt. Cooper walked her through what they should be prepared for at the hearing. She didn't need instructions. Genevieve and Michael had been down this road before.

"Thank you, Sergeant. I will be there tomorrow," she said, hanging up the phone and putting out the cigarette.

Genevieve sat in the chair next to the phone table in silence, except for the ticking of the mantel clock in the living room. She knew what she needed to do, but not yet, just not yet. Instead of facing the inevitable, she went up the stairs to check on the children. Raymond was asleep in his twin bed. She didn't go in, didn't fix his blanket to make him cozy, didn't give him a kiss. She just quietly shut the door. She peeked in on Parker, who was reading a comic book. He never looked up. The girls were next. Jessica was sitting at her desk in her room, doing homework, oblivious that her door had opened. Sara was in her room, lying on the pink, oriental carpet, reading *Black Beauty*. She looked curiously at her mother but went right back to her book.

At least the kids are okay, for the time being, she thought, slipping back down the stairs and into the den. It was a dark room, which is how Genevieve decorated it. A brown, leather sofa with matching club chairs sat opposite a large, round, mahogany coffee table, perfect for card games and puzzles, although she never encouraged the children to be in this room. Genevieve preferred they spend time in their rooms, rather than in what she called the grown-up spaces.

She went over to the bar cart and poured herself a glass of Scotch, no ice, lit another cigarette, and sunk into the couch, sipping, smoking, and thinking. She finished the Scotch and cigarette simultaneously, stood up, and walked out of the den and into the hall to make a phone call.

"Hello."

"Mom, it is me, Genevieve," she said, twisting the black phone cord around her fingers, this time tighter and noticing a chip in her hot-pink nail polish.

"Genevieve, do you know what time it is? Nearly nine thirty. Why are you calling this late? Are the children all right?"

"Yes, Mom, they are fine. I need to talk to Pops. Is he still awake?"

"Oh dear, let me get him for you." Genevieve could hear her mother, "Edward, the phone is for you. It's Genevieve."

She could picture the scene. Her mother was in the hall by the phone, calling out to her father, trying to cover the mouthpiece, unsuccessfully. She could hear her father grumbling, picturing him trudging to the phone, her mother mouthing something, which Genevieve is sure her mother is saying is trouble. As Genevieve waited for her father to take the phone, she wished she had made herself a double Scotch.

"Genevieve, what's wrong? Are the kids, okay?"

"Hi, Pops. The kids are fine. It's Michael. He's been arrested for assault, and I am going to need bail money for tomorrow's hearing."

"Jesus, Genevieve, what's next with him?" Her father sounded gruff, almost angry, which wasn't his nature.

"I don't know what is next, but the police called, and they seem to expect me to be there with bail money in the morning. I would like to just ignore it … let him rot for a few days." *Imagine what I would say if I had that other drink*, Genevieve thought. She had continuously tried to play down the problems with Michael. Her parents were always there for her family, but seriously, what is next? Her father's voice on the other end of the line brought her back to the present.

"Tell me where and when, and I'll be there."

It took every ounce of self-control for Genevieve to not call Nicky. Here she was, alone, expected to handle a mess that she hadn't caused. Again. She wanted to give up, give in, let someone take care of her for once in her life. But the only person whom she wanted to do that couldn't. Not the way she wanted or needed it at that moment.

"Mrs. Austin, how do you do? I am Mr. Benton, Charles Benton. Please take a seat." Genevieve gave only a hint of a smile as she sat down in the uncomfortable, sturdy, wooden chair facing a large office desk. Mr. Charles Benton walked around the desk, sat down, and looked at some papers in front of him before speaking.

"Can I get you something? Perhaps coffee?"

"No, thank you." Genevieve glanced at her watch. She had hoped to get to work by noon, but things weren't looking like they were going to move as quickly as she wanted.

"Well then, let's get right to it." Mr. Charles Benton scanned the papers, looked up at Genevieve, and said, "If everything goes right, your husband will be released at the end of the week. There are stipulations attached to his release. Are you aware of them?"

Genevieve fixed her gaze on Mr. Charles Benton. He seemed to be the epitome of a disgruntled man who loathed his job. He tried to lord his so-called power over the people he was supposed to be helping so that he could feel better about himself. Her eyes quickly took in the details of his ill-fitting, brown suit and imitation Brooks Brothers shirt, its buttons straining against the large stomach beneath it. She let him squirm for a minute, knowing he was aware of her look of disdain.

"I am familiar with the so-called stipulations for my husband to be released from the VA Hospital. I have no intention of changing my life, or my children's lives, to make

Michael's life easier. If anything, he should be the one doing all the changing. I don't have a problem with alcohol—he does. I have a job. He is the one who cannot keep a job, which, by the way, was handed to him by my father."

"I seem to have hit a nerve. Let's take a step back, Mrs. Austin. Your husband needs a home to go to if he is to be released as planned. He can't stay in the hospital indefinitely. We're not asking you and your children to change your lives completely. We ask that you make a few simple adjustments."

"I read your simple adjustments, but please refresh my memory." Genevieve was fuming, her anger banging against her self-control, screaming *let me out*. She looked down at her lap, smoothed her black, linen, pencil skirt, and took a breath. Genevieve Austin raised her head, fixed her gaze back on Mr. Charles Benton, and forced a blank look on her face.

Feeling that he had the upper hand, Mr. Charles Benton shifted in his chair, adjusted his glasses, and picked up one of the papers in front of him. "Well, let's see. As you understand, Mr. Austin needs a suitable home to return to, and we believe that is his home, to be with his wife and children." He glanced up at Genevieve. There was no change to her face. He looked back at the paper.

"Number two—no alcohol in the home. Michael has mentioned several times that there is a stocked bar cart out in the open to tempt him. The bar cart and the alcohol will need to be removed from the home." Again, he looked up. And again, no reaction from Genevieve.

"Number three—eliminate all practices of drinking alcohol in front of your husband. The notes show you drink a cocktail every night before dinner. When he visits your parents at their home, he is subjected to watching people consume alcohol at any given time. We expect you and your parents to discontinue this practice. It's not healthy for Michael to be exposed to these practices. And I might add, it's not healthy for your children, either. Their father is an alcoholic, so the chances of them carrying that gene is quite strong."

Genevieve's lips, with a hint of peach lipstick, curled into a wicked smile as she forced the words out of her mouth. "Is there a number four, Mr. Benton?"

"Well, yes, there are a few more that I think—"

Genevieve reached her hand toward him, interrupting, "May I see?"

He handed the paper to Genevieve and sat back in his chair. *Just need to let the little lady read this over*, he thought.

She gave a quick glance over the notes, looked up at Mr. Benton, and smiled. "Mr. Benton, I appreciate your time and your thorough review of my husband's case." Her voice had a hint of golden sarcasm.

"You mentioned you believe that alcoholism is genetic. That is concerning. My recommendation, which is not up for discussion, is for Michael to return to his home—his parents' home. That way, they can all deal with the genetics of alcoholism."

She stood up, handed the paper back to Mr. Benton, and said, "Have a lovely day." She turned and walked away, knowing that he was watching her leave the room, assessing her figure, and probably wondering what the hell had just happened.

Whether or not she liked it, life had to change for Genevieve and her children. Michael was released a week after her visit with Mr. Benton. His brother met him at the front door of the hospital and drove him back to the family's apartment in New York. William Austin had passed away right before Ray was born, leaving Rose to clean up her son's mess.

Michael had lost his job, leaving Genevieve in a financial bind. Her job was now crucial to help with the bills. And then there were the children to deal with. She seriously wondered how in the world she was going to keep going. "Now is not the time for your stubborn pride," she said to herself as she made another dreaded phone call.

Edward paid for the childcare needed for Ray when Genevieve was working. Margaux came every afternoon to be there when Jessica, Sara, and Parker came home from school. They loved to have Meme waiting for them. She always had freshly baked treats ready, which were served on China plates and crystal-cut glasses full of milk. She washed and ironed their clothes and helped with homework. It was tiring for Margaux, but she couldn't let her grandchildren down. Genevieve was another story. She struggled to hold her tongue with her oldest daughter. She was disappointed at what a mess Genevieve had made of her life, and now the children's lives.

Even with the presence of their grandmother, the children were floundering. They were accustomed to their father being absent, but not Genevieve. Despite their mother's emotional distance, they knew she would always be at home, or at least close by. This was a brand-new world for them.

Meanwhile, Genevieve thrived, completely oblivious to the despair of her children. She made sure that they each had lunch money and looked presentable before sending them out to the world to walk to school. Jessica caught her bus much earlier in the morning, avoiding her mother whenever possible.

Genevieve rose to the challenges that she faced. In her mind, the challenge was to be an influential, sought-after interior designer, which, in turn, would be a solid role model for her children. They would see all the sacrifices she made as she moved from the wallpaper store to the high-end furniture store on Bellevue Avenue, the center of affluence and well-heeled Newport customers. This is where Genevieve Austin shined.

THE LAST STRAW

"Good morning, Mrs. Austin." That is a voice I don't recognize.

"Please, call her Genevieve. She doesn't like to be referred to as Mrs. Austin."

Ah, that voice. I recognize Sara. I struggle to fully wake up and focus my eyes. And there she is, Sara, who, by the way, is not looking her best.

I stretch out my hand to Sara. "And who is this?" I ask, looking at a woman dressed in some god-awful outfit. I cannot even call it an outfit. I don't know what the hell she is wearing, but someone should tell her to burn it.

"Genevieve, this is Alice Munro. She works with the VNA and is going to help you get cleaned up, change your sheets, and anything else you need."

"You work for the VA?" I say through clenched teeth. What the hell is someone from the VA doing in my bedroom? Just the sound of those two letters makes me want to punch somebody.

"No, Mrs., I mean, Genevieve. I work for the VNA, the

Visiting Nurses Association," Alice Munro said quietly with just a hint of a smile on her round, pale face.

"Well, then, that is much better. If you were with the VA … well, I would … well, never mind what I would do." I try to smile, but I know it is not my best effort.

As Sara plants a kiss on my cheek, I tell her to do something about the way she looks. What is she wearing? I thought I said it as a helpful suggestion, but I guess not by the look on her face.

"That's funny, Genevieve," she snaps, standing up from kissing my cheek. "Funny because I am wearing your clothes. And the reason that I am wearing your clothes is that I can't tell you the last time I was home to change. The clothes I do have here are dirty, and I haven't had time to wash them. I haven't time for much of anything other than to care for you."

Oh dear, I thought. *Sara is still so sensitive. She really should have outgrown that by now.*

Alice Munro turns out to be lovely. She talks about her family, never mentioning the unfortunate behavior of my daughter. Alice gives me a warm sponge bath, helps me to the bathroom, changes my sheets, and fluffs my pillows, all the while gently talking. I cannot understand most of what she is saying, but her voice is so soothing. I slip back to my memories while she is brushing my hair.

I can hear rain on my skylight, and it brings back to mind a day in 1963, or maybe it was 1964. It doesn't matter. It was one of the best and worst days of my life. It was raining on that day too—a chilly day in March. It started with a phone call. Well, it did not actually start because of the phone call, but that call sent me spiraling into a rage the likes of which I had never seen in someone, let alone witnessed in myself. I remember it so well, and I do not want to.

"Excuse me, Genevieve, you have a phone call."

I was at work on a Saturday, which was something I rarely

did. But Mrs. Elizabeth Thomas, wife of Arthur Thomas, heir to an oil fortune, had contacted me to help her with redesigning the library in her new Newport home. The Thomases had sold their Newport mansion, as many others had done in the sixties, because of ridiculously high real estate taxes. They had purchased a more modest home, a mini estate, on one of the last waterfront properties available in Newport. She told me I had been referred to her by one of the members of the Newport Polo Club.

"Arthur has several ponies stabled during the season in Newport," she had explained to me during the call. She told me about the sale of the mansion, which I already knew about. That was big news, and the fact that it was going to be turned into a museum for tourists was even bigger news. Oh, how the mighty had fallen. I didn't think that, but plenty of people in the area did.

Mrs. Thomas had planned to meet with her architect to discuss updating the pool area on the grounds of the new property and had a brief window to meet with me, which is how I found myself showing swatches to her on a Saturday morning when the call came in.

I can remember my annoyance. How dare I be interrupted when I was working with one of Newport's elites? I smiled my best smile, which I am sure did not come across that way. "Would you mind taking a message, please? Thank you."

"I'm sorry, Genevieve, but I think it's important."

"Excuse me, Mrs. Thomas, this will not take long. Here is another book of fabrics you might enjoy. My recommendation is to see which leathers you like. I think tobacco brown is a warm and inviting look, but see what you like."

I was furious. Nothing could be so important to interrupt me with what could be—would be—my biggest commission.

"Hello."

"Genevieve?"

"Parker? What's wrong?" It was Parker, and I could tell that he was trying to not cry. I had dropped him off earlier at the bus station to meet his father. Michael was going to spend the day with Parker. He was the only one of my kids I couldn't find a place for so I could work this Saturday. Michael wasn't there when I left Parker, but I was a few minutes early and Michael was typically late.

"Daddy isn't here. I waited where you told me to. I didn't leave for a second, even though I really have to pee." Now he was full-out crying.

I remember standing at the receptionist's desk, watching Mrs. Thomas sift through pages of swathes, glancing up, looking bored, and probably wondering where the hell I was. Well, I was wondering where the hell Michael was.

"Hang on, Parker, just let me think for a minute." I needed a plan, and quick.

"Mrs. Thomas, I apologize for the interruption. Have you found anything that you are interested in?" I could feel that old familiar bead of sweat forming on my spine. I could not mess this up. I would not let Michael fuck this up for me.

"Oh, Genevieve, there you are. I'm afraid I am overwhelmed by all of these choices. I didn't realize this would be quite so stressful."

I wanted to scream stressful. I will tell you what stressful is. Stressful is knowing that your seven-year-old son is standing alone at a bus station because his fucking father could not be bothered to show up. That is stressful, lady. But instead, I smiled that damn fake smile, sat down next to her, and said, "I have an idea. I can bring just a few samples to your house this afternoon, and we can get a better idea of how you envision the library."

"Oh my, you would come to the house? That sounds wonderful. I wish you had thought of that earlier before I wasted so much time here." She stood up, put on her gloves, and said, "Come over at three this afternoon. That will give me time for lunch, and I will change my flight to later this evening. You have the address, I assume?"

With great patience, I watched her walk out the door. Once she was out of sight, I raced out the back door to my car and drove the ten-minute drive to the bus station. I will never forget the sight of Parker standing alone in front of the station. His tears had dried up, but his face … oh, his face … told me everything—dejection, disillusion, confusion.

I got the big commission from Mrs. Thomas, the first of many.

Parker survived his morning at the bus station. He accepted what happened. Sadly, he would need to learn to accept a lot of disappointment from his father. Damn you to hell, Michael Austin.

NEW PLAN

"Hello."

"Rose, this is Genevieve."

"Genevieve, this is a pleasant surprise." Genevieve could barely control her voice. She wanted to scream at her mother-in-law about what a waste of a human being her son was. She wanted to describe in painstaking detail the hell Michael had put her grandson through yesterday.

But instead, she asked if Michael was there. She sensed a hesitation on the other end of the line.

"Yes, dear, his is, but he is resting. I will tell him you called when he gets up." *Does Rose know what happened*, Genevieve thought?

"Rose, this is important. Will you please tell Michael to come to the phone?"

"Is everything okay? There isn't anything wrong with the children, is there?"

"Rose, please tell Michael I need to talk to him now." Genevieve heard a sigh and the sound of the phone being put down. She pictured her mother-in-law, tall and sturdy, with her black dress, sensible shoes, and most likely wearing an apron, walking down the long hall to the last room on the right, Michael's childhood bedroom.

It seemed like an eternity until she heard his voice. "What's going on, Genevieve? I was resting. My mother said it sounded important."

Genevieve felt her fingernails digging into her palms; her knuckles were white. With all the control she could muster, Genevieve began. "Michael, where were you yesterday morning?"

"I don't know. Probably here or out somewhere. What difference does it make? Where were you yesterday?" he snarled.

"I was picking my son up from the bus station. That is where I was yesterday. Do you want to know why I was picking him up? Do you remember why it was not me who was supposed to pick up Parker?" Genevieve's voice was rising, heart racing, blood pounding in her ears.

"Michael, say something. Where were you yesterday?" She needed to hear his response, not ask him why he left Parker alone.

"I had car trouble. I ran out of gas and left my wallet at home, so I had to thumb back to my brother's house to get help. That was my day yesterday. Why is this any of your business? We don't live together, thanks to you. I barely see the kids." He stopped in midsentence. "Parker ... oh shit, Parker."

"Right—Parker. How could you leave that child alone at a bus station? As usual, I am left holding the bag, cleaning up after you." Genevieve was struggling not to scream. She knew that staying calm, in control, sent more of a message than a screaming, crying wife would.

"I told you, I had car trouble."

"You didn't think to call me?"

"I didn't have my wallet, and how would I know where to call you? I don't know where you are or what you do. For all I know, you leave all the kids alone. I've called, you know. Sara tells me you aren't there. So don't act all high and mighty on me. You are no better than me. Look, I made an effort. I stayed at my brother's house in Boston so I could be closer to the bus station. Look at the thanks I get."

Genevieve smiled to herself. Michael was acting out the classic "not my fault" drunk's excuse.

"You knew I was at work. That's why you were supposed to be with Parker. You did not have a dime in your pocket? That is a shame. You know what, Michael? You sound just like one of those bad county-western songs you like so much."

In her best imitation of a twang she sang, *"I lost my wallet and my car ran out of gas. I ain't got a dime to my name. Man, I am an ass."*

"Michael, you have pushed me too far. I will figure out how to keep the kids from being hurt by you. Goodbye."

GENEVIEVE AND NICKY met for lunch around the corner from Paine's Furniture on a sunny, spring day. Nicky was already seated. He had requested a table away from the windows and toward the back of the large dining room. He and Genevieve had spoken briefly about where and when to meet, but he had no idea what he was in for.

Genevieve was far from predictable. He sensed her before he saw her. Genevieve Austin was following the maître d' to their table. He couldn't take his eyes off her, and neither could most of the other lunch patrons as she slowly removed her oversize, black sunglasses and stared straight ahead. She carried her five-foot-ten-inch frame with confidence and poise, dressed to the nines in a chic, crème-colored, Chanel, A-line dress, a boxy, black jacket draped over her shoulders, and a single strand of black pearls that dangled just below her collarbone.

Nicky noticed Genevieve had cut her long, blonde hair to fall just above her shoulders, and now had bangs that were swept to the side, emphasizing her eyes, thick lashes, and dark brows, giving her a seductive look.

He stood, pulled her chair out, and as she sat, he leaned in and whispered, "I've missed you and your beautiful self." Nicky was dressed as Father Reynolds.

"So nice to see you, Father." She smiled and gave him a little wink. They each ordered a glass of wine. Genevieve settled back in her upholstered chair, took a sip of wine, and gave Nicky a look—a very discreet look, but it was still a look.

He smiled. "Is the collar too much?"

"Just the opposite. I think you look quite handsome. However, I appreciate your decorum."

After another sip of wine, Genevieve leaned forward and quietly said, "I am leaving Michael."

Nicky looked up from the menu, unsure of what she said. "What does that mean?"

"I am divorcing him. I have spoken with an attorney, and once I tell my parents, I will give the go-ahead for the papers to be filed," she said matter-of-factly.

"Are you ready to order?" the waiter interrupted.

Nicky started to shake his head no, but Genevieve smiled and said, "Yes, I think we are ready. I will have the Cobb salad. Father Reynolds, what do you think you would like this afternoon?"

Nicky was speechless. Did he hear her right … divorcing Michael? "I'll have the same, thank you." He stared at Genevieve as he handed the menus to the waiter. Now it was his turn to lean in. "Are you serious? Divorce is a major decision. Have you thought this over?"

Genevieve kept her voice low, a smile on her face. No one would know of the earth-shattering conversation she and the priest were having. "Of course I have thought this over. Have you ever known me to do something rash?" She saw the look on his face but continued.

While Nicky pushed the food around on his plate, Genevieve filled him in on her marriage … or lack of marriage. Between bites of Cobb salad, she told him about how her father got involved when Michael stopped showing up at work. She explained about the phone call from the Providence Police Department, his assault and battery charge, and the drunk and disorderly charge.

Genevieve stopped long enough to put her fork down, have a sip of wine, and then went on about another stint at the VA. She complained about what that idiot, what's his name, expected her to do so Michael could come home. And then Genevieve stopped talking and stopped eating. She smoothed the napkin on her lap and told Nicky about what Michael did to Parker.

Nicky had secretly felt bad for Michael all these years. He knew Michael was a pawn in one of Genevieve's schemes, albeit one of her larger, more elaborate schemes. He knew that Michael unwittingly stepped in where Nicky didn't. He knew Michael accepted the responsibility of an unborn child. Nicky didn't. He knew Michael was given the proverbial short end of the stick. But he also knew that it was Michael who blew his chances at Harvard.

Nicky wondered how different life would have been had Genevieve's plan gone off without a hitch. Would she and Michael still be together? Would they be happy? Would Michael ever discover that "baby Nicholas" wasn't his? Would that child stick out in the family, or would he look like Genevieve, and no one would ever know? Except, Nicky knew. He would always know, and Genevieve had made it clear that he would have no part in that child's life.

"Are you listening to me? Have you heard anything that I

said?" Genevieve's voice brought Nicky back from his world of guilt to the present.

"Yes, of course I am listening to every word you've said. I'm sorry, I was just struck by the selfishness of Michael in this situation. How a parent could leave his child alone is beyond my grasp. How anyone could abandon a child alone in the city at a bus stop is a crime." Genevieve ignored the last part of what he was saying since she had left Parker alone first.

"So, I take it you are moving forward, and nothing anyone says will stop you?" he asked quietly, prepared for her reaction.

But Genevieve remained calm, saying, "Yes, nothing, and no one is going to change my mind. I need to be true to myself, not try to be what someone else expects of me. I have been doing that version of me for too long. The children are older, and Jessica can help babysit after school to give my mother a break. The attorney will draw up a schedule of visitations for Michael. He is going to have to pay for alimony and childcare, which will be a tremendous financial help. Actually, things are working out. Finally, a plan that will work."

"Is Michael working?"

"Michael will have to take care of that part of the plan." Genevieve shifted in her chair and sat up straighter, as if her body language would convince everyone, including herself.

"I have a favor to ask," Genevieve said.

Nicky reached across the table and took her hand. It was warm and smooth; her nails were a perfect shade of pink. He didn't care if anyone was watching the priest and the mystery woman. He needed to let the love of his life know that he was there for her, but only to a point.

"Will you come with me when I tell my parents? They love you and respect you. Having you there will keep the yelling down to a minimum. Any chance you can free yourself up this weekend?"

TEAMWORK

"I HAVE NOT FAILED. I'VE JUST FOUND 10,000 WAYS THAT WON'T WORK." — THOMAS EDISON

"Okay, I am off. Children, be good for your father. I will be home Sunday after dinner."

"Where's Parker?" Michael asked, holding Ray in his arms.

Genevieve donned her oversize, tortoiseshell sunglasses as she said, "You are in charge now; you find him. Be good, everyone. Bye-bye."

She had called her parents earlier in the week, telling them—not asking them—that she would be coming on Friday for the weekend. Nicky would join them as well. Edward was thrilled to have Genevieve coming home, especially with Nicky. They could all golf on Saturday and have dinner at the club on Saturday night. Margaux's radar was up.

"Why aren't the children coming, do you suppose?" she asked, passing the plate of roast chicken to Edward.

"Genevieve told me Michael is spending the weekend with them. I find it amazing that he is still living in Rose's place. How many months has it been? Well, regardless, it will be good for everyone. Michael needs to step up as a father, and I'm sure that Genevieve would like a weekend to herself," her father said.

"Edward, you have your head in the sand about Genevieve. She does just fine finding time for herself. It's the children I worry about." Margaux pushed her dinner plate to the side, put her elbows on the table, and let her head rest in her hands. She was quiet for a moment. Then she sat up straight, looked at her husband blissfully gnawing away at his chicken leg, and said, "I think we may have made a mistake."

Edward glanced up with a bit of chicken stuck to his lip, swallowed, and said, "What kind of mistake? Having Genevieve as one of our children?" He chuckled and returned to the chicken.

"Wipe your face. I am back on the fence about selling this house. Something tells me we should stay for a while longer. It can't hurt with summer coming. We can see if Angela would like to come back again this summer. The children are older, less of a handful. Although, Ray will be three, and that might be a challenge."

Edward put down his fork, wiped his face with the linen napkin, and looked at his wife.

"Margaux, we have talked about this to death. This house is more than we need at this point in our lives. However, I will do whatever you want, but only to a point. Let's put the conversation of selling off until after the summer. Now, *mon chéri,* is there any more of this delicious roast chicken?"

Genevieve arrived at her childhood home before Nicky. She sat in her car in the circular, shell driveway, going over her spiel again, even though she had done this more times than she could remember. Divorce wasn't something that happened in her family. Her parents had been together for forty years. All the aunts and uncles had stayed together, unless one of them had died. None of her parents' friends were divorced. Genevieve didn't know anyone who was divorced, which is why she thought that the calming presence of Father Reynolds, the beloved Catholic priest, might provide her with some ammunition. She yanked her suitcase from the trunk, muttering, "This is the sixties, for Christ's sake, not the Middle Ages."

"So, what's this all about, Genevieve? Why the visit without the children, and why with Nicky?"

Margaux was finishing up washing the lunch dishes when Genevieve had arrived. She was studying her daughter with the scrutiny that only a mother can.

"Mom, you are just going to have to wait for the news until Nicky arrives. Where is Pops?"

"I'm right here, darling," her father said as he came in through the kitchen door. "Margaux, can't our daughter come home for a visit without the third degree?" Margaux glared at her husband as he gave Genevieve a big hug.

"Looks like Nicky just pulled in. You are both saved by the arrival of Father Reynolds," she said, swatting her blue-striped dish towel at Edward.

After Nicky had unpacked in his usual guest bedroom, he clapped his hands together and said, "Who wants a Friday afternoon Sazerac? It has become my specialty since my time in New Orleans over the holidays. Edward, do you have anise liqueur? I'm pretty sure that bar of yours is stocked with rye. Margaux, I'm going to need sugar cubes and a lemon." Nicky was busying himself at the bar, before anyone had a chance to say yes or no to a Sazerac.

Genevieve was sitting on the new couch that she had bullied her parents into buying, appreciating the expensive fabric with coordinating throw pillows. She was also the only one in the room who seemed to sense that Nicky appeared nervous. She smiled to herself, feeling a deep emotional connection to Nicky. Here he was, to support her, in front of her parents, and to protect and keep the secret of their love for each other safe. She realized then and there that what she was feeling, witnessing, sensing was genuine love and true intimacy. With her Sazerac in hand, Genevieve shared her thoughts about what was next for herself and the children.

"Divorce? Are you out of your goddamn mind?" Edward exploded, slamming his drink down and simultaneously standing up. He stared incredulously at Genevieve and then at her mother. Nicky moved toward Edward as if ready to intervene if necessary.

"Edward, please, the neighbors." Margaux's voice was calm, the voice of reason.

"You know that there aren't any goddamn neighbors within a mile this time of year. And who cares? Soon enough, the entire world is going to know about this. Genevieve, you will not get divorced." He then turned to Nicky. "What do you know about this?"

Nicky took the last sip of his drink, wishing there was just another sip left for fortification.

"I am aware of the situation." He put up his hand before Edward exploded again. "Genevieve and I have talked over the years. You could say that I have been a counsel to her."

Genevieve finally spoke. Like her mother, her voice was composed. She spoke calmly, ignoring that annoying bead of sweat once again forming on the back of her spine. She listed her reasons for deciding to divorce Michael. She left the incident with Parker to the end, thinking that would be the nail in Michael's coffin.

"Are you telling us you have left your children for the weekend with Michael, knowing how irresponsible he is? What in God's name is wrong with you, Genevieve?" This time, it was Margaux speaking, looking from her daughter to her husband. Her look said it all. But Genevieve knew that look and wasn't going to cave.

"Whether or not any of us like it, Michael is their father,

and he will have visitation rights. That is the law, and there is nothing I can do about it," Genevieve said.

"Edward, Margaux, I understand this is a shock. But if we all take a step back and look at the facts, the history, I think we can all see the bumps in the road that have brought Genevieve to her decision. I am a friend, but I am also a Catholic priest. Divorce goes against everything marriage stands for in the church. But in my heart and in my soul, I believe God has no boundaries. Things are neither black and white nor absolute for Him. He will judge each of us for the good we do, how we face our challenges in life. God looks for grace, love, and compassion.

"Genevieve has not come to this decision lightly. She has considered the fallout for all involved. Yet, to continue to show her children that Michael's lifestyle and his choices are acceptable is not acceptable to Genevieve. She is proving her love to those children by making the hard choices. She is teaching them to face life head-on, do what is right with grace and compassion." *Dammit, I wish I had a drink*, he thought as he waited for a reaction from anyone.

Genevieve stood up and walked over to Nicky. "Thank you, Nicky. That was very well said. Now I would like to explain to you how I plan to make this new way of life work for the children and me. Who would like another drink?"

MEMORIES

"Emma, is that you?"

"No, Genevieve, it's me, Annie, your favorite niece. How could you forget me? I'm Emma's oldest."

"Oh dear, of course. You look so much like your mother when she was younger. And you have her sense of humor."

"I will take that as a compliment, I think. Can I get you anything?"

"Yes, I would like a Sazerac."

Oh, my goodness, that was quite a night, telling my parents about my divorce plans. Nicky calmed everyone down. My parents adored him. Sometimes I felt jealous of their feelings toward him. They never acted like that with me, or Trey, or Emma, for that matter. I wonder if Trey was jealous. I guess that is something I will never know. Who knew someone could be struck down so early from a fatal heart attack?

We didn't go to the club for dinner after the divorce revelation, as originally planned. Mom scrambled up eggs, toast, hash browns, and fish cakes. It was a bit of a hodgepodge dinner, but it worked.

"The hell with those Sazeracs," Pops had said as he poured a large amount of gin and vermouth into a shaker. We seemed to come to a détente that evening. I was going to be divorced, and Michael would still play a role in our family.

After dinner, Mom insisted on cleaning up alone. Pops wanted to read the paper, so Nicky and I went for a walk on the beach. It was chilly and windy, as a spring evening can be in Newport, but we found sou'westers in the hall closet and hats that were unbecoming but did the trick.

That night ... oh, that night. The sky was clear, lit up by a bright moon. The Big Dipper seemed to pour out stars over our heads. We held hands and walked on the edge of the sand, just far enough away from the waves to not get our feet wet. And we talked and talked.

"I think that went well," I remember saying. Nicky laughed quietly and told me I did well, I held my own, although he never doubted my ability to handle my parents. I told him how wonderful he was, acting as the lightning rod for the fallout. I also told him I did not believe any of that bs he had said about God, forgiveness, compassion ... and what was that about boundaries?

Nicky stopped walking, did a quick survey of the beach, and pulled me close. When his lips came down to meet mine, I wanted to crawl inside his sou'wester. I wanted to be under his shirt, my head resting on his chest. His kiss released tension I didn't know I had. I kissed him back just as passionately. It was a miracle we weren't swept away by the incoming tide.

We spent that weekend doing what was expected of us—Saturday breakfast with my parents, a round of golf in the afternoon, and a lobster dinner at home Saturday evening. By then, my parents had reasoned out that once I had made up my mind, they had little choice but to accept my decision and make the best of it.

Sunday came too soon for Nicky and me. He and my mother went to mass, leaving me alone with my father. We took a walk, reminiscent of the walk years before when he'd sent me home to "fix" my marriage. He never said he loved me or told me he was proud of me, but I could sense it. When Pops says, "If you ever need anything," well, I knew that was his way of loving me.

Nicky left after our early Sunday supper, and I departed a few moments later. My parents walked me to my car, Pops carrying my suitcase. I looked out at the ocean and said, "The moon should be full tonight. Why don't you two bundle up on the porch and watch it rise over the ocean?"

Pops came around to stand next to my mother at the driver's side door. "They call the March full moon the Worm Moon."

"It's also known as the Chaste Moon," my mother said, shutting my door and giving me a look.

Driving back home, my mind was all over the place. What a weekend of lows and highs. I turned into my driveway with a smile on my face. The highs were much better than the lows.

I remember being relieved to see Michael's car in the driveway. At least he was where he was supposed to be. I pulled up next to it, just as Sara came running to the car, Parker right behind her. Jessica came after them, slower, carrying Raymond.

I had no sooner got out of the car when Sara threw herself at me in tears, crying, "Daddy said you're a whore. That's bad, isn't it? Why are you bad, Genevieve?"

Parker jumped on the bandwagon, crying, "Whore, whore."

I was dumbstruck. What had happened while I was away for a weekend? I looked at Jessica and she simply said, "Daddy took us for a drive, that's all."

"He drove to Memes and Pops, and we saw your car and Uncle Nicky's car. That's when Daddy told us you were a whore." Sara was sobbing.

"He got us ice cream." Parker had recovered and was over

the hysterics, but not Sara. I got a tissue from the car, told Sara to wipe her nose, and ordered the children to wait outside while I talked to Daddy. I remember Jessica looking worried.

Michael was inside, oblivious to what had happened in the driveway. He sat on the couch, watching golf on the television, and didn't even look up when I slammed the front door shut. I was a heat-seeking missile locked onto my target, ready to blow up his world. I remember losing all control. I was screaming at Michael. At one point, I thought about throwing the television at him. The best I did was hurl my designer throw pillows at him. In hindsight, it was a pitiful scene.

He cowered on the couch, telling me to stop. Was I crazy? Oh, I was crazy all right … crazy enough to kill him. I told him to go say goodbye to the kids. Nothing other than, "Goodbye, kids." Not "I'll see you soon, I'll call tomorrow," because he could not be trusted to do that. Not a word other than "Goodbye." Oh, tell them you love them, then get the hell out of my life.

Michael received the divorce papers later that week.

MANHATTAN RENDEZVOUS

"Okay, hurry up. Get in the car. We have a long drive ahead of us."

Genevieve got behind the steering wheel, waiting for her four kids to get settled in for the drive to Rose's apartment. Jessica was in the front, and the others were crammed in the back seat. Genevieve was eager to get this ride over with. Once the kids were deposited at their grandmother's, she was driving into Manhattan to meet Nicky. He had booked them a room at the Park Plaza Hotel as Mr. and Mrs. Alber and had left his black shirt and collar behind. Father Reynolds was out of reach for two glorious nights.

"Jessica, stop changing the station. I cannot stand that rock music."

"Genevieve, it's folk, not rock. Get with it, for Christ's sake." Genevieve took her eyes off the road for just enough time to glare at Jessica and change the music back to her choice. The other three were in the back seat, bickering. Genevieve's blood pressure was rising. It was bad enough that she had to drive the kids to Rose's. Michael was without a car and a driver's license, thanks to his most recent drunk and disorderly charge. She hadn't planned on the mayhem happening inside her car.

Jessica changed the music back, Ray started crying, saying he had to pee, and Sara was torturing Parker, telling him if he didn't move over, she was going to spit at him.

Genevieve blew up. "Stop it, all of you! If you do not stop, I am going to drop you off at a police station." The threat lasted about ten miles, then it started all over again.

"Genevieve, let's compromise. We can listen to your music for five miles and then mine for five miles. We can alternate till we get to Rose's."

"Genevieve, make Sara stop," Parker whined from the back seat.

"Genevieve, make Parker move over. His sweaty body is touching me."

"I still need to pee, really bad," Ray piped up.

Genevieve pulled over alongside the freeway. She turned off the ignition and moved to sit sideways on the front seat, able to look at all four of her kids at the same time.

Calmly, she said, "If I hear one more word out of any of you, I will leave you here on the side of the road. Do you understand me?"

"Don't be ridiculous. You can't just leave us," said Jessica. "You'll get arrested for child abandonment."

Genevieve was silent for a moment. *Well played, Jessica*, she thought. "You are right, Jessica. It would be wrong of me to just leave you all like that."

Jessica smirked, just a bit, and the others were in awe to hear their mother admit she was wrong. The mood in the car changed, as if someone had rolled down all the windows to let out the foul air and bring in the pleasant air. But that didn't last more than a minute or two.

"This is what I have decided to do. I am going to leave you all at Rose's for the rest of your lives. Rose is old, so she will need help." She put her eyes on Jessica. "That means you will have to quit school to help her, Jessica. Sara, you are going to have to get a job after school, and Parker … well, you will need to get a paper route. Since Rose doesn't have a bike for you, you are going to have to walk the long route before you go to school. You will need to get street smart. New York is a tough city."

Silence until a little voice said, "What about me?"

"Oh, dear, good question. What to do about Raymond? We will probably have to give you to another family. One that tolerates terrible children." Ray's thumb went straight to his mouth. He hugged his blankie tightly.

"That's crazy talk, Genevieve. And anyway, Meme will take care of us," Sara said defiantly.

"Meme might take Raymond since he is still little." Genevieve thought for a minute, and then said, "She won't take you, Sara, or you, Jessica. You are both older now, and Meme only likes children when they are sweet, little babies. I know this for a fact. Meme stopped liking me, Emma, and Trey once we hit a certain age."

"Will she take me? I'm still little … too little for a paper route."

"Ah yes, Parker, what about you? You might get a few more months out of Meme. She does like boys better than girls."

Genevieve let her words sink in until Jessica said, "You win. Your music, and we will be quiet for the rest of the ride." She turned to look at her sister and brothers. "Don't worry, we will go back to our house on Sunday. Isn't that right, Genevieve?"

The ride to Brooklyn resumed in silence, other than the music coming from the radio's classical station.

Genevieve followed her children up the three flights of stairs to their grandmother's apartment, where their father now lived. She left them lined up on the couch, looking like they were waiting for an interview or maybe a chance to try out for a play.

"Be good for Rose. I will pick you up on Sunday."

"Are you going to be a whore again?" Parker asked.

Genevieve whipped around and gave him *the look*. She then turned to Rose. "Do not pay any attention to him. It is a nasty word that he learned from your son."

As she shut the heavy door and walked down the stairs, she thought about Rose. "Good luck with those kids," she said to herself.

Genevieve liked Rose. At least she did when they'd first met. She didn't blame Rose for Michael's alcoholism, but she did blame her for coddling him. She knew that the death of her oldest son had sent her into a downward spiral. According to Michael, she never recovered from that tragedy.

Just as Genevieve's foot hit the last step, she shook off any feelings for Rose. Rose had twenty years to love and enjoy her son. She got birthdays and Christmases, little league games, and report cards to cherish. She had photos and a closet filled with his clothes. What did Genevieve get with her first son? Genevieve's grief for Nicholas was a sorrow so deep, so intense, that at times, it seemed to burn into her soul, leaving her with a deep hole of emptiness that she felt would never be filled.

She started her car, looked in the mirror for any imperfections she might find—none, which was good—put the car in drive, and headed to Nicky.

Genevieve walked up the stairs and through the impressive front doors of the Park Plaza Hotel. She wore a black, cashmere, turtleneck sweater, white, wool trousers, and black stilettos. Jackie Kennedy might be setting a trend for pumps and kitten heels, but Genevieve was never one to follow a trend. Her vintage, leopard, swing jacket and Chanel purse screamed *look at me*. But Genevieve, being Genevieve, had pulled her blonde hair into a very high ponytail. Her bangs fell over to the left, slightly covering her eye. This little touch gave the illusion of *I just threw on this outfit, with no concern about what I look like*. The result was a chic, sophisticated woman with an intoxicating, girl-next-door charm who checked in as Mrs. Alber.

Confident, well-heeled Mrs. Alber, wearing lingerie that would make a grown man blush, smiled as the bellhop took her bag and showed her to her room … to Nicky.

MOVING FORWARD

"IN THREE WORDS, I CAN SUM UP
EVERYTHING I'VE LEARNED ABOUT LIFE: IT
GOES ON." — ROBERT FROST

"Labor Day is both a blessing and a melancholy day," said Margaux, waving goodbye to the grandchildren as Genevieve drove them back to their home. Summer was over.

"This won't be our last Labor Day," Edward said, walking slowly up the porch steps, steadying himself on the newly installed handrail. "It's only the last one in this house. But we have some wonderful memories to take with us."

"Memories stored in boxes," Margaux huffed as she hurried past her husband on the steps. "Get a move on, old man. I need help with the packing."

The family gathered to say their goodbyes. Nicky's words at the funeral mass and luncheon brought solace to the mourners, who numbered over one hundred. But now it was just them—the Lemaire clan—daughters and son, grandchildren, Nicky, and Margaux.

The last wishes were specific, right down to who should be invited and where the luncheon would be held. The only thing missing was *when* these events would take place. That was in God's hands. Bright colors were required, no black allowed.

Crying was discouraged, tears of joy would be accepted. Laughter, loud voices, music, singing, and stories were mandatory. The last request was for Jessica, the oldest grandchild, to read a simple poem.

I ask for no tears, no sorrow,
For we shall see each other on some tomorrow.
I ask for you to stay true to you,
The person I loved and knew.
Carry on with courage and a kind heart,
And always remember to return the golf cart.

Jessica folded the paper in half, looked at her family, then at the headstone, and said, "We love you, Pops."

I can sense something or someone in my room, but I don't see anyone. I have been drifting in and out of a blissful euphoria, a feeling of movement between my external world and something. Not sure if I would call it another world, but something entirely foreign to me. There is an odd sensation in my room. Are my parents here? I know that is impossible, that is ridiculous. They have both been dead longer than I can remember.

Pop's death shook our world. We were not the least bit prepared to lose him. The thought crossed my mind that he might have been aware of the growth inside his head, but chose to turn a blind eye to it. If not, then why would he have been so organized? Pops was prepared to die, but not us.

The Newport house—my childhood home—sold quickly once it was officially on the market. Pops had made sure that Mom would want for nothing, other than him, after he was gone. She settled into the home that they had already purchased, which is where they planned to live out the rest of their lives … together.

Mom was close by, but it was all so different. I had tried to get either Trey or Emma to buy our Newport home, but neither of them was interested. It seemed I was the only one who was truly invested in that beautiful home, but I didn't have the money to buy it. I was furious that Mom would not give me a break on the price. She stuck to her guns. "I am following your father's instructions," was her mantra.

I would whine, complain, and lament to Nicky whenever we were on one of our getaways. Secretly, I had hoped that he would buy the house, but he didn't even try. Although, once he'd said that maybe the church would buy it and turn it into a priest's retreat. I think I said something to the effect of *over my dead body*. That was the end of the discussion.

Life went on without our rock. Some things stayed the same, yet so much had changed. The death of my father spurred something inside of me. I had always taken on the world headfirst—sometimes with a plan, but often without one. This time, however, I felt like I could not waste a single minute. I was struggling as a working single mother. My finances were slim, and my patience with three teens and an adolescent boy was wearing thin.

Michael was not paying child support, and on the rare occasions when he saw the kids, he would spoil them rotten. Jessica and Parker seemed to thrive on pushing my buttons. I think they secretly hoped to wear me down until I didn't care what they did. At times, I wanted to give in and let them just go off and do whatever vile things teenagers were doing in the sixties. I had heard horror stories of girls running away, never to be heard from again, and boys living in drugged stupors. Honestly, more times than not, I wanted to run away, and the drug stupor did not sound so bad. But of course, I did none of that.

I ruled those kids with an iron fist. I held them to their curfews, insisted on good grades, and weeded out unsavory friends. Jessica was caught shoplifting when she was about sixteen. She came home from an afternoon at the mall with friends and told me what had happened. She and another girl were grabbed by a so-called security guard and brought to his office, where he kept them for over an hour. Jessica said that he was demanding they sign a paper admitting to stealing. Thanks to me and the influence I had on her, Jessica refused to sign and told her friend to do the same.

He finally released them. I was furious. I knew she had done this, but I also knew that idiot had no right bringing two teenage girls into a room without someone else present. One phone call was all it took for that little, sniveling, poor excuse for a man to apologize to me and his supervisor. Jessica and I never spoke about this incident, but I can guarantee that she never shoplifted again.

Parker, on the other hand, went through a stage smoking pot. I could never prove it, but my instinct told me he was. He denied and denied, until he got caught—not by me, but by the school. It was a stupid move on his part, smoking pot out behind the high school during class. But I guess pot makes you do stupid things. He was expelled for a week and assigned detention for the rest of the semester.

This time, I was not the mother bear defending her cub. No, I was infuriated with him. Since I was working full-time during his expulsion, I was not going to let him enjoy staying home alone. Instead, I got his teachers to give me his assignments, and I would drop him off at the library every morning when it opened and pick him up right before closing. I am sure I was late a few times, but too bad. Anyway, Parker was used to waiting for a parent to get him, except usually, it was Michael.

Sara stayed in the shadows. She was quiet and low key. She stayed out of the house as much as possible, and out of my hair. As long as she maintained good grades and stayed out of trouble, she remained in my good graces.

I know I dropped the ball with Ray. By the time he was ready for middle school, I had already moved on from Paine's Furniture and had opened my design studio. Belle Maison was, and still is, my pride and joy. Mom would say I gushed over that place more than my kids.

Starting my business as a woman was not a common occurrence then. I was damn proud of what I had accomplished. I poured my heart, soul, and every bit of energy I had to make Belle Maison a success. And with that success came paid tuition for Jessica's school, horseback riding lessons for Sara, sports gear for Parker, and a damn decent allowance for Raymond. Those kids wanted for nothing.

It has always burned me how successful men are treated versus how successful women are treated. I fought for recognition, and by that I mean just being seen and acknowledged by my colleagues in meetings at work. Every commission presented its own challenges for me, just as it had for my male coworkers, but it was even more difficult as the only woman to stand out and gain the attention of the newly arrived client in a showroom full of men. And add the pressure of my family. My coworkers went home to a spouse, or a mother, or someone who would have a martini chilling and dinner in the oven. I came home to four surly kids, usually sitting on the couch, watching television, and asking what was for dinner as soon as I walked through the door.

SKELETONS IN THE CLOSET

"THREE CAN KEEP A SECRET IF TWO OF THEM ARE DEAD." — BENJAMIN FRANKLIN

"Okay, you are each assigned to clean out your rooms, including your closets. Pack up what you want to keep at your houses, not mine." They were home, each of her children, adults with their own homes and families. Genevieve had labeled each piece of furniture that was coming to her new home. She wasn't taking much. She was starting a new chapter in her life and needed no sentimental pieces of her history coming with her. New home, new start.

Jessica, Sara, Parker, and Raymond had come back to their childhood home to take what they wanted and discard the unwanted. Sara had protested, "We can't just throw things out people could use."

Genevieve was adamant that she wanted their bedrooms empty by the end of the weekend. She had begrudgingly left a bed in Ray's and Jessica's rooms since they had both come from the West Coast and needed a place to sleep. Sara's and Parker's rooms were empty, having already declined to take any of the furniture. It seemed nobody wanted to hang on to any memories of that house.

"Sara, when I say empty, I mean empty. I do not care where

anything goes, but it is going! I will be back on Sunday. Have fun." So there they were, the four Austin kids, alone in their house … Genevieve off somewhere. Some things never change.

"Sara, come help me for a minute," Jessica whispered.

"Jess, I have my own stuff to take care of, and why are you whispering?"

"Shh, just come with me and don't let the others hear you." Sara followed her sister across the hall and looked at the mess that Jessica had created.

"Are you throwing anything out? This is a disaster here. How the hell do you think you're gonna have it emptied by the time Genevieve gets home?"

Jessica shut her bedroom door and pulled a box out from under her bed. "I found this tucked away in the back of my closet. Genevieve had been using it for herself. That woman had more shoes than anyone I know. Here, look at this."

Sara took the sheet of yellow paper that was folded in quarters. She unfolded it gently. The paper appeared old and felt as if it might disintegrate in her hands. Sara silently read what she could of the document. The handwriting was mostly illegible, and the typeset was smeared.

"Certificate of Birth, the State of Rhode Island," she said, looking up at her sister quizzically. "It's hard to read. What's this all about?"

"Give it to me," Jessica snapped, putting out her hand for the document. "Yes, it's a birth certificate. I can't make out the full date of birth, but the year is 1941 and both parents' last names are Austin. Dad and Genevieve were married in 1941."

"So?"

"So why does Genevieve have this hidden in the box?"

"What are you not saying? Why do you think it's hidden? Just tell me what is going on in that mind of yours?"

"Is there another one of us out there somewhere?" Jessica got up and looked out her old bedroom window, across the yard to the two birch trees her father had planted when they'd first moved in. They were skinny, spindly twigs, no more than two feet tall, with just a couple of wilted leaves on each one.

Jessica remembered how Genevieve had made fun of the trees, saying something about them being as spineless as her father was. But now, those two trees were at least forty feet high, their trunks covered in a beautiful, silvery-yellow bark that could be peeled off in thin layers. These trees seemed to mirror her father. As a child, she would look out her window, see these trees, and think of her father. Yes, at times he was weak, but when he was strong, he was her hero. As she grew older, Jessica understood that her father's layers were as thin as the birch—too thin to form him into a person who could stand tall and weather the storms life threw at him. Too thin to withstand the force of Genevieve.

The sound of clinking glassware brought Jessica back to the present, packing away the past.

"Chardonnay, okay?" Sara asked, opening the bottle, not waiting for an answer. "Let's see what treasures this box holds. Maybe we'll discover that you're a twin! Crazier things have happened." The sisters clinked their wine glasses, sat down on the Persian carpet, and got to work.

Genevieve,

I want to say happy anniversary, but that would be foolish. I'm writing this to you on the anniversary of our divorce. Most couples celebrate their wedding, not divorce. But today, I am celebrating these last years that we have been apart. How many has it been? Five, six? I just know that it was November 16. I also know that is the same date you lost the baby. Yes, Genevieve, I do remember things that matter.

By God, I wish things had turned out differently for us, but it seems God had other plans for me. I've learned to accept the things I can't change. You knocked me off my feet that first time I saw you. We were both so young and naive, each of us with big plans for our future. And that was stripped away.

Between the war and the pregnancy, our lives were forever changed. I came home from Germany a different man. I was a shadow of the man you fell in love with. You changed too. You weren't the girl I fell in love with. I wonder if we ever loved each other. I tried so hard to please you, but Genevieve, I didn't know what I could do to turn things around for us. I felt powerless for so many years. I allowed alcohol to rule my brain, and I allowed you to rule my heart.

I'm working on The Twelve Steps through AA, but to be honest, I'm struggling with a few of them. I admit I'm powerless over alcohol. I have turned myself over to God for help. AA expects us to make amends with the people whom we have harmed, and mostly, I can do that.

I've tried to be a better father, but the kids are older now and don't seem interested in spending time with me. It's sad to say, but I don't feel much of a connection with Raymond. When he was born, things were spiraling for me. At least I had some good times with the others.

But it's you, Genevieve, whom I have the most overwhelming feelings about. I go back and forth, wondering if you tricked me into marrying you. Was that even my baby? I suspect not, but what's done is done. Sometimes I want to send you The Twelve Steps and say, "Take a good look at yourself, Genevieve, and tell me that these words don't hit home with you." But of course, you wouldn't think so because you don't think that you are ever wrong.

As I write this, I feel my blood starting to boil. Anger is rising in me, and yet I can't hate you. I just wish I had known what a man had to do to make you love him. Evidently, I am not that man, but I am pretty sure I know who is. He will never be entirely yours. You are no competition for God. Let that sink in.

The real purpose of this letter is to let you know I'm done, and I am going away for a while. I don't know for how long, but that is for me to figure out. I'll send money when I can. I will let the kids know that I'll be in touch from time to time.

Michael

PS. I used to think that love was constant, like the sea, which always returns when the tide is right. But our love was not like that. Our love was a series of waves washing over the jetty. Sometimes they were soft, rolling waves, gently caressing the rocks. But most of the time, those waves lashed out at the jetty, wearing down the rocks, pulverizing them to grains of sand.

Sara took a large swallow of wine, looked at her sister, and handed her the letter. "Read this. We are more fucked up than I ever suspected." Her brain felt like it had shut down, leaving her with a dull, numbing sensation. She felt an ache in her chest as she watched her sister silently read the letter. Other than the sound of Sara's pounding heart, an eerie silence filled the room.

Jessica read the letter, looked up at Sara, folded it, and placed it back in the box. "I'm getting us another bottle. There's more in there to look at."

"Wait! You can't just get up and leave. Say something."

"You already said it, Sara. We are more fucked up than I suspected. I'll be right back."

Sara's hands trembled as she emptied her glass and gingerly removed the papers from the box, her mind swimming with the impact of the letter's contents.

"Anything earth-shattering?" Jessica asked, standing in the doorway with another bottle in her hand.

"Why are you acting so calm? That letter was from Dad."

Jessica interrupted. "That letter from Dad is a letter written by an angry alcoholic. Don't you remember how he'd changed when he actually stopped drinking?" Before Sara could answer,

Jessica added, "He was an angry son of a bitch. I learned the term as a dry drunk when Genevieve forced me to go to stupid meetings for kids of alcoholic parents. He was nicer when he drank. So who knows what the fuck this letter means? Don't worry, I'll figure it out. Here, give me your glass. What else did you find?"

"The signed-off mortgage on the house. The paid-off loan for Belle Maison." Sara sipped her wine. "Oh, and their divorce agreement. Funny, I don't see a marriage certificate in there. Figures she wouldn't save that."

Jessica refilled their glasses and began rummaging through the small box. She removed a velvet bag. "This must be her wedding ring. I wondered why Genevieve had never had a big diamond ring. Now I guess I know why." Her sarcasm was so biting that it hung in the air.

"Why don't you ask her about it?" Sara said, as a challenge.

"I think I just might do that." *Challenge on*, Jessica thought. "What else is in here?"

Sara opened a manila envelope and shook the contents out on the floor. "Wow, old polaroids and postcards." They both went through the pile. "Oh, look at this one … Genevieve and Nicky in front of the Eiffel Tower. She really was beautiful," Jessica said, picking up more photos.

"In this one, Genevieve and Nicky are on some beach. Jesus, she had an amazing body. Maybe this is before kids." Turning the photo over, she said, "Nope, this is dated March 1964, St. Tropez. This is after Ray was born." The sisters sipped their wine and swapped photographs and postcards, remarking how stunning their mother was—something they had never noticed.

"Sara, do you remember her taking all these trips?"

"I remember most of them. She usually vacationed in February, missing my birthday."

Jessica laughed. "That's right. I remember we never really

knew when your birthday was. I think Genevieve would just pick a date when she knew she'd be home. Do you think it's strange that there aren't any pictures of Dad?"

"I don't know what to think," said Sara. "Was their entire marriage a sham? Why would they have four kids? I know Nicky is her best friend, but I don't know. It seems a little unsettling seeing them together in these pictures. Maybe when you ask her about her diamond engagement ring, you can ask her about these pictures. And then you can go into the Witness Protection Program." The sisters fell silent, looking at their mother's past, each with their own thoughts about who she was.

"I am back." Genevieve was about to drop her key on the hall table before realizing it was gone, as was most of the furniture.

"We're in the kitchen."

She found her adult daughters sitting on folding chairs in the kitchen, sipping tea.

"Where in God's name did you find those?" She laughed, opening the refrigerator door, and then shut it. She had thrown out all the food that was in there. "How did your purging go? Where are the boys?"

"Parker brought Ray to the airport earlier."

"Did you check their rooms, make sure everything is out of them?"

Jessica got up, went to the refrigerator, opened it, and then closed it, exactly as her mother had just done. Jessica wanted some wine, but she and Sara had finished off what was in the house. "I didn't check, but from the number of boxes Parker stuffed into his Range Rover, I am pretty sure the room is empty."

"That one could never part with anything. I cannot imagine what his basement must look like."

"And Ray?" Genevieve found a bottle of Scotch and was pouring herself a glass.

"Ray only had one box, and he's leaving it with Parker."

"It's sad, you know."

"What is sad, Sara?" Genevieve sipped her Scotch, looking at her daughter with suspicion.

"It's sad that Ray only had one box."

"Oh, Sara," Genevieve said, softening a bit. "Raymond has never put any stock in material things. Even when he was a child, he didn't have a favorite stuffed animal or toy. I believe he suffers from emotional detachment."

"Emotional detachment is when someone can't engage with people. It has nothing to do with their stuff. And speaking of stuff, whatever happened to your engagement and wedding rings? I don't think that I even remember you having a diamond. But ..." Jessica glanced at Sara and then pulled a pink, chiffon dress out of a bag that was next to her chair. "We found this."

Genevieve was speechless. Her face relaxed. She took the dress from Jessica and held it for a minute. "My goodness, where did you find this?"

"Parker found it in the back of his closet in a trunk. What was it doing there, and whose is it?"

"This is a dress I had worn to a school dance," she said, holding the dress up to her, twirling just once.

"A little risqué for a school dance, don't you think?"

"Oh, I was unaware that I had raised a prude. But if you must know, it was for a college dance. Now put it back where you found it. As far as my rings are concerned, I had to sell my diamond years ago because your father was such a deadbeat. I needed the money to put food on your table. I have no idea where my wedding ring is. Perhaps at the bottom of Narragansett Bay."

"We found your wedding ring," Sara said, immediately regretting her words.

Genevieve's green eyes darkened as she handed the dress back to Jessica, all the while keeping her gaze fixed on Sara. "Where did you find the ring?"

"It was in a box in the back of Jessica's closet."

"I must have forgotten I put things back there. What else did you two amateur sleuths find?" Her tone gave no hint of dissatisfaction, but her eyes said otherwise.

"Genevieve, you are the one who told us to clean things out. We were just doing what you wanted." Jessica wasn't one to let Genevieve typically intimidate her, but she felt she was on shaky ground.

"I asked you, what else did you find in the back of the closet? It is a simple question, girls." The tone had changed, and Sara and Jessica, adults and mothers in their own right, felt as if they were kids again. Genevieve had never raised a hand to her children, barely raised her voice, but her tone, her words, and her looks were sharper than a slap across the face.

Before Sara could respond, Jessica put her hand on her sister's arm to stop her. "We found some pictures." She handed over the envelope of old polaroids.

Genevieve began going through the pictures, her expression becoming gentle and her smile returning. "Oh, look at these. Such a long time ago. This one was when Nicky and I were skiing in Switzerland. And this is us in Paris. Meme came on that trip, but I don't think we got any pictures of her. She hated the camera. Just like you, Jessica."

"Meme went on a trip with you and Nicky?" Jessica was dumbfounded.

"She did for that one. There was a group of us. It was such a wonderful time."

"You and Nicky traveled together a lot when we were

younger. Was that normal back then?" Sara's eyes grew big. What was her sister hinting at?

"Normal? I don't know what you mean by normal. I was fortunate enough to benefit from having my best friend, who loved to travel, invite me along. Most of these trips involved some type of networking," she said with air quotes. "Nicky would go off and do what was required of him, but the rest of the time, we would sightsee and just have the best time. Oh, look at this one. Here we are at high tea at the Ritz in Boston. I remember meeting Nicky there for the afternoon in the spring." Her face clouded over as she stared at that photo.

Genevieve put the pictures back in the envelope and said, "Put this box back where you found it. The movers will take care of it. Now you two need to get out of here. I have to get ready for the move tomorrow, and I do not want any distractions. Remember to take your things with you."

Sara and Jessica stood for a moment, for the last time, in the front yard of their childhood home. There was no sentimentality or nostalgia. There were no feelings, good or bad. Neither felt much of anything, other than they were glad they had dodged a bullet from Genevieve concerning the box.

Jessica adjusted her purse, bulky from the letters she had taken from the box, got in the car with Sara, and simply said, "Done."

LET SLEEPING DOGS LIE

"THERE ARE SOME SLEEPING DOGS THAT
SHOULD BE LEFT TO LIE; THERE ARE SOME
QUESTIONS THAT SHOULD NOT BE ASKED."
—STANLEY ELLIN

The day started out with a warm breeze, bringing the smell of salt air across Genevieve's back garden patio. She had just sat down with her coffee, black with cinnamon, something that she had picked up in Mexico on a trip with Nicky many years ago.

Genevieve was hoping to take in the morning's peacefulness, occasionally interrupted by the cries of a seagull flying overhead. However, she felt an underlying sense of uneasiness, one that she couldn't shake off. She thought it might be the state of her flower beds around the patio. She had been in her townhouse for almost two years now, and Genevieve imagined the beds would be much lusher than what she was looking at. The roses were full of fat, pink buds. The lavender had survived the last winter snows, and the hydrangeas looked promising. But of course, Genevieve wanted more, and she wanted it right then.

"Genevieve, where are you?" She heard Parker yelling from the front foyer. She got up and opened the French doors that led from her patio into her living room to see Parker flushed and somewhat agitated.

"Parker, stop yelling. The neighbors will hear you. What has got you so riled up?"

"I found him."

"Found who?"

"Dad. I found Dad."

"I did not realize your father was missing," she said, looking around her living room for something—anything—to help ground her, to keep her from showing her hand to Parker. *This is why I am feeling so uneasy this morning*, she thought to herself. "I am having coffee on the deck. Come join me, and do keep your voice down, Parker."

"Did you hear what I said? I found Dad," Parker reiterated, waving his arms in the air.

"Yes, of course I heard you. I am sure the Bernsteins next door heard you too. Now pour yourself a cup and come sit outside."

Genevieve Austin listened to Parker go on and on as he told her how he had tracked down Michael, the long-lost daddy. Her words, not his. *No good can come of this*, Genevieve thought to herself.

"He lives north of Boston and has remarried. And the most amazing part is that he stopped drinking years ago. His wife, Lois, gave him an ultimatum—stop drinking, or they were through, and he wouldn't be a part of her life." Parker took a breath while nodding his head, as if in disablement. "How about that for some news, huh? He should have cared enough to do that for us, but he didn't. He must really love this woman."

Genevieve felt like the rug had been pulled out from beneath her. She wanted to hurl her coffee cup at Parker and get up and hug him at the same time. God, she hated Michael Austin. How dare he stop drinking for someone other than her? How dare he tell Parker any of this bullshit?

"Well, that is some news, dear. How did you find this out?"

Genevieve's voice remained steady, but her heart was pounding in her chest from the rage that was building.

Parker pulled a folded-up newspaper page from his back pocket and handed it to his mother. "I read this article a few months ago and knew I needed to find out the truth. Read it."

"What is it?"

"You need to read it, but in a nutshell, it's an article about Dad. Someone from *The Boston Globe* did a series of interviews with veterans from New England fifty years after World War II. This one is about Dad."

My goodness, thought Genevieve, *fifty years. Some days it seems like yesterday. How old does that make me?* With a heavy sigh, she shook her head, feeling the weight of her age and the years gone by.

"Genevieve, are you listening to me?" Parker asked, clearly agitated.

"I am listening, Parker. May I suggest you substitute your coffee for a glass of water? You are perspiring. This news appears to have put you in a state of agitation."

"Agitation? Yes, I am agitated. Jesus Christ, Genevieve, has this sunk in? Our father, YOUR ex-husband, the professional drunk, has given it all up for another family. I would think that would send you over the cliff."

"What other family?"

"Read the fucking article. I'm getting some water." Parker gave a hearty push to his wrought-iron chair, sending it skidding back from the table.

"Language, dear."

Parker walked into the house, shaking his head. He stood over the kitchen sink, running cold water on his wrists, wondering if his mother actually did have ice water running through her veins. He went back outside and sat down to face Genevieve.

"Where is the newspaper? Did you read it?"

"It is in the trash, where it belongs."

"Did you read the f—? Did you read it?"

"I did."

"Jesus, Genevieve, it's like pulling teeth to get you to open up. What do you think?"

Genevieve took a moment to respond, a moment to choose her words carefully. "The article talks about two Michael Austins. It is unfortunate that his family—you, your brother and sisters—are referred to as his former family. And this group of people he has taken up with are considered his current family. The article is in poor taste, but I am grateful that some of our skeletons stayed in the closet." She softened her tone and asked, "Why did you decide to look for him after all these years?"

"The newspaper article made me curious. How could he just leave like that, as if we don't exist? He doesn't even know his own grandchildren. But here's this other family, getting the best of him, when we got the worst. Just doesn't seem right."

"No, it doesn't seem right, but that changes nothing. Your father is, or was, a troubled soul. He was so young when he enlisted, and I think the war took a terrible toll on him. Today they call it PTSD, which I think came to the forefront after Vietnam. There was no help like that for the veterans of your father's war. At least nothing that I was aware of. But I find it curious how some men came home and went back to life as it was for them before the war, while others, like your father, could not seem to pick themselves up by their own bootstraps." Sensing she was headed down a bash-Michael Austin road, Genevieve decided to let Parker tell her more. "Did you talk to him?"

"I did. Turns out the person doing the interviews is the daughter of his new wife. I didn't know that when I called *The Globe*. She was nice, took my phone number, and said she would talk to him. That is so messed up. I am his son, and she's the one who is going to talk to him?" Parker gulped his water and said, "I'm getting a beer. What can I get you?"

Coffee and ice water turned into mimosas and beers. Genevieve and Parker spent a good part of that beautiful, summer Sunday talking about the past—the good, the bad, and the ugly. Genevieve treaded carefully to not let her guard down, but she talked about the difficulties she had faced being married to an alcoholic. She let Parker know how she'd struggled financially, trying to raise four kids with little to no financial support from Michael. She also let him know the sacrifices she made to provide for them. And if those necessary sacrifices diminished her influences as a warm and nurturing mother, well, so be it. In true Genevieve fashion, she said, "I did the best I could."

Parker, on the other hand, spilled his guts. He let loose years of pent-up anger, which he had channeled into being the best that he could be. Parker took Genevieve's 'I did the best I could' and turned it into 'I will be the best, possibly better than I imagine.' He told her that Michael eventually called. It was an awkward conversation. Michael had told him he was sorry for everything, but he was in a much better place. He had met a woman who put him first, gave him strength and confidence to help him fight his demons.

Genevieve felt that familiar trickle of sweat on her spine. It wasn't from the warm, midday sun, but rather, anger forming in her belly. Michael had the nerve to place responsibility for his miserable life on her? Parker's voice brought her back to the present.

"He asked how you were and said that despite it all, you had some wonderful times together."

Genevieve's voice was sharp and strong as she responded, "The hell we did," putting an end to the mother–son bonding conversation.

Parker knew his mother's cues all too well. He got up,

kissed her cheek, and said, "Bad timing, but I need to meet the guys for a tennis match."

Parker left. Genevieve made another mimosa without the orange juice and made a call.

DROWNING

"HAVE I WASTED MY LIFE, I DON'T KNOW. I
HAVE ALLOWED YOU IN AND WATCHED
YOU GO. THAT'S THE TROUBLE WITH YOUR
LOVE. IT HANGS AROUND, KNOCKING AT MY
BROKEN HEART, LEAVING ONCE I LET
YOU IN." — UNKNOWN

My mind is scrambled. I cannot make out if it is day or night. I get flashes of insight when someone is talking to me, but when I am alone, I am engulfed in deep isolation. It can be quite dark, and yet at times, there is a soft light in the distance. I hear muffled sounds, also in the distance. I am confused. Not scared, just confused. I have lost all control of my surroundings. I do not like to lose control, and I will fight like hell, for now, to keep going.

Parker has been sitting by my bedside. His voice brought me back to the day he came to tell me he had found his father. I was unaware that Michael was missing, or that anyone, let alone my son, was looking for him. Oh, how it burned me when he'd told me that Michael had stopped drinking for someone other than me. I don't think Parker was intentionally trying to hurt me, but his words were as if he had put a hot poker to my heart.

When I had filed for divorce, I was not heartbroken. I was never in love with Michael, but I think, at one point, I did love him. My marriage had failed. That is defeat, and I do not like to accept defeat. I made a mistake. I married the wrong man, but what choice did I have? Nothing can change that. I could not fathom sacrificing my own happiness to make the marriage last. I know I am not capable of that type of surrender, of losing myself to make someone else whole. Michael and I tried to give it a go, but he loved alcohol more than he loved me. And I did not love him enough to help him.

It takes a lot to bring me to my knees, but Parker's news about his father giving up drinking, getting married, and living the good life was about more than I could take. All of my hard work, my well-adjusted children—okay, somewhat well-adjusted children—were successful adults with their own families. Nobody had gone to jail, we had no drug addicts in the family, and I had established one of the finest design studios in the state of Rhode Island.

I, Genevieve Lemaire, had done all of this on my own. Yet this news about Michael was crushing, obliterating all that I had accomplished. So I did what I had always done. I called Nicky. Of course he would come riding in, my knight in white armor, or should I say, knight in white collar. He'd made reservations at the Ritz-Carlton in Boston under the name of Warren. We were Mr. and Mrs. Warren. When we first began our secret getaways, Nicky had started at the beginning of the alphabet. The first name he registered us under was Mr. and Mrs. Alber, and now here we were, all the way to the letter W.

Nicky and I had traveled the world together, staying in five-star hotels across more continents than I can remember. I had been seated next to former vice president Spiro Agnew at a White House dinner, flirted with Frank Sinatra at the Desert Palms in Las Vegas, met Princess Margaret at the Royal Lancaster in London, and skied the French Alps, literally running into Steve McQueen.

My time with Nicky was precious, and I am grateful for our wonderful adventures together, but it is the Ritz-Carlton that is etched in my mind, overshadowing all those amazing memories. My heart was broken at the Ritz.

It was a beautiful, fall day when I had driven into Boston and pulled up for valet parking in front of the elegant Ritz-Carlton. Nicky and I had not seen each other for quite some time, and I was surprised to feel a bit nervous as I'd handed over my keys. But nobody would have guessed it as I walked up the stairs and confidently strode to the reception desk.

"Good afternoon. Reservation for Warren, Mr. and Mrs. Warren. I am sure Mr. Warren has already checked in." I remember removing my sunglasses and giving a look of cool, yet elegant, poise.

"Welcome, Mrs. Warren. You are in Suite 111, one of our finest rooms." She handed me the key, nodded to the bell clerk, and said, "Mr. Warren hasn't checked in yet. Enjoy your stay."

By the time Nicky had knocked on our hotel room door, I was already in a mood. The news about Michael had me agitated, out of sorts, and Nicky's lateness was pushing me over the edge. The time alone had given me time to stew about all that I missed out on being the fake "wife" and, at times, simply the best friend. I expected and deserved so much more than that. When I was a kid, I had told my mother that I wanted to go to New York City for our school vacation. I remember my humiliation when she laughed and said in front of my family, "Get a load of you. Who do you think you are?" She and my father laughed and laughed until Emma and Trey joined in, chanting, "Get a load of you."

I hated that I didn't come first for either Nicky or Michael. For Nicky, it was, and still is, God, and for Michael, it was alcohol. And to add insult to injury, Parker telling me his father had married some person whom he completely gave up alcohol for. "He's like a new man," Parker had said. God, that burned me.

When I'd answered the door, I was struck by the change in

Nicky. He was graying around the temples and had put on a bit of weight—not much, but still, there it was, around his middle. We hugged each other, Nicky apologizing for being late while kissing my neck. I remember how much I wanted to just let go, fall into bed with him, like we had done for so many years, but I could not stop stewing.

I pulled away, saying, "Let's open the champagne." I watched as he struggled with the cork. Even that annoyed me. I remember grabbing the bottle out of his hand. "Here, let me do that."

We drank the champagne, making small talk. That annoyed me. I went in to use the bathroom and looked in the mirror, surprised at what looked back at me. For the very first time, I saw that I was looking older. That annoyed me. I colored my hair every six weeks, never missing an appointment. I had a facial once every two months, did yoga when I could get to a class, and never went a day without makeup—never. So there I was, working on keeping a youthful appearance, and there was Father Reynolds on the other side of the door with graying hair and a bit of a ponch. But what really irked me was that he was aging well, without doing a damn thing.

I came out of the bathroom and assessed the situation. The haunting melody of "Unclaimed Memories" filled the suite, churning up a memory of love and time gone by. Nicky had brought a portable CD player with him.

"May I have this dance?" he asked, extending his hand out to me.

How could I say no to him? I could not. I had never been able to say no to Nicky. Stepping into his arms, I was reminded of the safety and comfort I'd always found in his embrace. He smelled like Nicky. He breathed like Nicky. His heartbeat was Nicky's heartbeat.

By this time in our relationship, the passion between us had morphed into a loving, comfortable place. I was home when I was in his arms. But the feeling of home did not last long.

After the dance, Nicky had said he needed to tell me something. I felt my armor return, prepared for whatever he had to say. We sat on the love seat in the suite. I was doing my best to not let panic take over. But there it was, I was panicked. Was Nicky sick? Or worse, was he dying? But I was the one who had initiated this getaway. I was the one who needed him to console me. I was the one whose drunk ex-husband gave up drinking for another woman. I remained calm, realizing this could be very serious. For once in my life, I needed to listen first and then react.

Nicky leaned forward, looked straight into my eyes, and said, "Gen, I've decided to retire."

I let the words set in. With age comes patience. Nicky was going to retire. What could this mean for me? Would we … could we … finally come out of the confessional booth and let the world know how we feel about each other? Oh, this was wonderful news. In your face, Michael Austin. My priest, who has always loved me, trumps you giving up alcohol for some person you'd just met.

"Oh, Nicky," I said, smiling and taking his hands. "This is the best news I have heard in a long time. When do you officially become Mr. Reynolds and say goodbye to Father Reynolds? You can move in with me. I have plenty of room, so you can have your personal space and we can still be together. Oh my, there is so much to do and figure out. Never mind all that. "Let's call room service for another bottle of champagne. We need to celebrate properly!"

I practically jumped up to go to the phone to call for more champagne when Nicky said, "Gen, please, let me finish." Those words, *let me finish*, stopped me midstep.

I kept my back to Nicky, not sure what was next, and turned to look at him. "Okay, of course. You know me, always jumping the gun." I sounded like a fool and had a sick feeling I was about to look like one.

Nicky stood up and walked over to me, taking my hands in his. "Gen, I'm sorry if I misled you. I am retiring, but I'm not leaving the priesthood. They are sending me to a small retirement community in Naples, Florida, where I will live as an emeritus priest."

I pulled my hands from his, with no resistance from Nicky. That old familiar bead of sweat began to form on my spine. I was humiliated again. Here I was, thinking finally … finally, I would get what I wanted, what I deserved in life. How many fucking years had I waited for this man? How many fucking years had I been in competition with God?

My breath became shallow, and I couldn't tell if it was my heart or my head that was pounding with such intensity. It didn't matter; I was done. Nicky and I had gone around and around so many times about his choices, or should I say, his choice of becoming a priest.

Right then and there, I had decided I was sick of pretending that the handsome, charming, sexy man who was always my escort was simply my friend.

I poured myself a glass of water and calmly told Nicky that he should leave. I never wanted to see him again. If he tried to contact me, I would shout from the rooftops that he had been having sex with me for years, threatening to ruin his career. I told him that the world would hate him for using me with no intention of marrying me. I told him I felt like the mistress waiting for her lover to leave his wife. The lover who kept saying he would, but he never did.

Nicky tried to interrupt. "I never said I would leave the church."

"You are right, you never said that, but I had hoped that. I had hoped you loved me enough to do that. But you do not and you will not. What a fool I have been for all this time. I am sick of coming in second place. You need to leave now, before I show you just how much you have broken me. In the name of your fucking God, leave."

He left, he actually left. There was no begging, pleading, yelling, give me a chance. He just stared at me, tears streaming down his face, and left. Nicky walked out of the room, turning just once to look at me before leaving me shattered to pieces at the Ritz-Carlton Hotel.

WHILE I WAS STILL in Newport Hospital, soon after I was told I had stomach cancer, I asked how I could die quickly. When would they do a Dr. Kevorkian for me? Oh, I remember the looks of confusion on those doctors' faces. Sara had remained stone-faced. Once they understood what I was asking, they let me know that Rhode Island was not a Right to Die state. That's when I had decided I would go to the Ritz-Calton in Boston to die. I would spend my last days in luxury, drinking champagne and living large. I had my heart broken at the Ritz. Might as well have it stop beating there as well.

TIME CAN DO SO MUCH

"IN ORDER TO BE IRREPLACEABLE, ONE MUST ALWAYS BE DIFFERENT." — COCO CHANEL

"And that concludes the tour of the updates to my townhouse. What do you think?" Genevieve was in her element, showing off her exquisitely redecorated home to her old college friends. Sally, Betty, and Jane had arrived together with yearbooks and overnight bags, ready to reminisce and catch up on the years that had flown by for each of them.

"What do we think? How about green with envy. I mean, your house in Little Compton was wonderful, but this house is all you, Genevieve. Congratulations," said Sally, meaning every word she said.

"You have outdone yourself, but I would expect nothing less from you," Betty said.

"Oh, Genevieve, look at you, this home. You did it, girl! But I can't believe you've been here for four years, and we are finally seeing it." Jane was beaming.

"It is a shame so many years have passed since we have seen each other. Let's enjoy this weekend. I think it is warm enough for us to have lunch on the deck. The table is set. Sally, can you open up the wine? I will bring out our salads, for starters."

The four old friends took turns bringing everyone up to speed on their lives. It had been a decade since they had been together, and although they talked on the phone from time to time, they felt like their old selves, sitting at Genevieve's glass dining set, which was perfectly arranged, overlooking a peaceful garden, giving off a sense of serenity.

"Okay, Genevieve, your turn. You can skip the part about redecorating your beautiful townhouse, again, and get right down to the meat of your life."

Genevieve took a sip of her chardonnay and smiled. "The meat, you say. Well, I am not sure what you mean by that, but I can say Belle Maison has become the go-to for the Newport elite for their decorating needs. I just hired a new designer, and I love him."

"That's wonderful, but tell us about the kids. We were all so sorry to hear about your mother's passing. Betty is the only one of us whose mother is still alive."

"Trust me, there are days I wish otherwise. I know that's a terrible thing to say, but she has dementia. She's living at my house and driving me to drink. Speaking of that, is there more wine?"

As Genevieve poured more wine, she told her friends that she still missed her mother, even though she had been gone for nearly eight years. "I am not sure if it is her I still miss, or if it is those wonderful summer memories in Newport. Everything changed when the house was sold. But my kids are doing well. Jessica divides her time between Scottsdale and Laguna Beach. She and her husband love to travel, and her two children are quite successful. Sara is close by with her husband. She works for a marketing firm, surprise, surprise. Of all my kids, I thought Sara would live in a commune. Her daughter, Liza, has two children. Parker and his wife just sold another one of their start-ups. They are planning a long, well-deserved hiatus next year. Their son is in private school ... honor roll, I am told."

"The Newport home was a wonderful place. That beach was breathtaking. Speaking of breathtaking, whatever happened to Nicky Reynolds? I know he became a priest. Do you two still travel together?" Betty asked.

Genevieve set her fork down and put her hands on her lap, hoping not to give anything away. What did they know about her relationship with Nicky? They couldn't know anything. Betty is just fishing. Too much wine for her.

Genevieve flashed her radiant smile, her head cocked slightly to the side, and said, "You are right, Betty. Nicky Reynolds was breathtaking back in the day. We try to stay in touch, but he's retired to Florida, so our days of traveling together are over. I am so fortunate to have had such a wonderful relationship with my childhood friend."

"I didn't know priests retired," said Sally. "Can you retire from God?" she asked, laughing.

Jesus, these ladies cannot handle their wine, thought Genevieve, getting up to clear the table. "Well, he is living in a community of fellow priests. I guess you could call it an old home for priests. I am the last person you should ask about God. Who would like coffee?"

After the heart-wrenching scene at the Ritz-Carlton, Genevieve never saw Nicky again. He never called, never wrote. She couldn't believe that he wasn't crawling to her door, begging forgiveness. *I guess he took my words seriously*, she had thought. Genevieve was tempted many times to call him, or at least write to him, but her pride wouldn't let her. Her kids asked about him from time to time, and Genevieve would lie and say, "We stay in touch. He is doing well."

Genevieve had moved on with her life, focusing on Belle Maison. She met a few different men whom she'd spent time with. One in particular, Bob Mitchell, was someone she enjoyed traveling with. But after a while, she tired of him. He was in his late seventies, and Genevieve caught on that he was looking for someone to replace his wife, who had passed away a few years ago. According to Bob, his wife was a saint who ran their household, loved to make him gourmet meals, and catered to his every need. Genevieve finally broke it off, telling him that at this stage in her life, she was looking for someone to cater to her every need. Truth be told, Genevieve had been looking for that most of her life.

So there she was, Genevieve Austin, still a breathtaking, natural beauty in her mid-seventies, a successful designer, world traveler, mother of four, alone. Genevieve didn't enjoy being alone but had decided that if this was the hand she was dealt, she might as well play those cards to her best advantage. She joined the tennis club in her complex, started playing golf again, and made friends in her area.

Genevieve had found a new way to look at life, enjoying the company of women more than men. She and a couple of neighbors became the best of friends, embracing their independence without a care in the world. Genevieve looked forward, not backward, with the same gusto that she always had.

Genevieve Austin was a force to be reckoned with, right up to her last breath at the age of ninety-four.

ETERNITY

"Whose cell is ringing?" asked Sara as she threw out the last bit of food left in her mother's refrigerator.

"Not mine," was the response from her family. They were gathered at Genevieve's house to try to wrap their heads around the fact that their mother was actually gone. And this time, she was gone for good. Genevieve was not coming back.

The ringing of the cell phone stopped, just as Genevieve's landline rang. Sara stood up from peering inside the refrigerator. Everyone just looked at each other as though they had never heard a phone ring.

"Who would call this number?" asked Jessica.

"Just answer it, you're the oldest," Parker said with a smirk.

Jessica glared at her brother but did as he asked.

"Hello."

"Good morning. May I speak to Genevieve Austin?"

"Um … who's calling?" Jessica felt a chill run up her spine.

"This is Monsignor Williams. I'm calling on behalf of Father Nick Reynolds. Is Mrs. Austin available?"

"Father Reynolds? Is Nicky all right? Is there something

wrong?" Jessica was referred to as chicken little in her family. The sky is falling. Doom and gloom was all around her.

"I have been asked to speak with Mrs. Austin. Is she available?" he asked again.

Jessica hesitated and then said, "My mother passed away yesterday. I'm Genevieve's oldest daughter. If there is something I need to know about Nicky, please tell me. He is a part of our family, our uncle."

Silence on the other end, and then, "Oh, dear, I am so sorry for your loss. May God be with you and your family. We will say a novena for your mother at this evening's mass."

Jessica was rolling her eyes, making a gesture to indicate hurry up and get to the point.

"Father Reynolds had left instructions on who to contact, and your mother is the first name on the list." Jessica could hear a large sigh on the other end of the line. "I am sorry to tell you, but Father Reynolds passed yesterday afternoon."

Jessica was dumbfounded. She turned and looked at her family, staring back at her. She still held the phone to her ear. Her mouth was open, but she couldn't speak.

"Are you still there? I'm sorry, but I didn't catch your name."

Jessica snapped back to reality. "My name is Jessica Austin. Oh my, what happened?"

"After lunch yesterday, Father Reynolds said that he was going to lie down. When he didn't show up for evening mass, I went to check on him. That's when I found him, lying peacefully on his bed, as though he was sleeping. He had just a hint of a smile on his face. I know that he and your mother were the best of friends. My, my, my, God works in mysterious ways.

"Per his instructions, he will be buried in Newport, RI. He has a plot right next to your family's plot. Nick told me he felt like one of the family with Genevieve's parents and was committed to spending his eternal life with her. If you like, I can give you the details of his arrangements."

Jessica wrote down the information and said goodbye to Monsignor Williams.

"Fed Ex just delivered this package, a special delivery to Genevieve. The return address is Naples, Fl. It's got to be from Nicky," Sara said, closing the front door of Genevieve's townhouse. She walked through her mother's foyer, decorated with only Genevieve in mind. The dark, eggplant walls provided the perfect backdrop for the impressive art piece of a stylish woman walking two leopards.

"Open it up. What are you waiting for?" Impatiently, Jessica tapped her cell phone to turn on her playlist and turned up the volume. The house didn't feel as empty with music playing. But the house was empty. Everyone had left, leaving Sara and Jessica alone.

"Jesus, give me second. I just signed for it." Sara took the package over to her mother's kitchen table. Most of the furniture in her townhouse had been sold, taken by family, or donated. The kitchen set would be the last to go. Sara dumped the contents on the table.

"Want some wine?" asked Jessica.

"Yes, of course. Oh look, there's a ring in here." Sara turned the gold band around to inspect it and found the initials NCR. "This must be Nicky's ring. Wonder what his middle name was?"

"Charles." Jessica was reading a document. "This is his certification from seminary school. His middle name was Charles. It's eerie to be seeing this stuff, with both of them gone—and gone on the same day. You know that's crazy, right?"

"Uh-huh." Sara took a sip of wine and began to read a letter in Nicky's handwriting.

My Darling Gen,

Time has not healed all wounds. The word sorry does no justice to what has happened between us. I have led a life of torment. I love you, still love you. I am in love with you and will always be in love with you.

I have another love, a love that you don't understand, nor should you. My love for God is overwhelming, as is my love for you. I am incapable of choosing one over the other. When you told me to leave and to never see you again, I died that day. I drove away as a broken man, and truth be told, I am still a broken man, which is how I will die. Without you, I am broken.

I have confessed my sins but wonder if there will be absolution for me. I have broken my vows to God for you. But that is on me. I am the one responsible for my actions. I have done so many wrongs in my lifetime. But I still struggle. How can it be wrong to love you? How could we have been wrong about creating another life?

From the minute you told me you were pregnant, I fell in love with that baby. When our son was born, was it God who took him away from us because we had "sinned"? I wonder if I will ever have an answer to that question. The pain of his death was shocking to me. I could never dare imagine the pain you had felt, but I know that his death changed you for life. The events leading up to that day changed you for life. Every plan you tried to put in motion backfired on you, but you did one hell of a job, Genevieve Lemaire. Your secret—our secret—goes to the grave with us.

I sense that my time is coming to an end soon. What I would give to have one last chance to look deep into your eyes, hold you in my arms, and dance slowly by the ocean. Until we meet again, my darling Genevieve. I know that this is not the end for us.

I leave you with our song …
Oh, my darling, my love, my dear,
I've longed for your touch
A long and lonely time
Are you still mine?
Time goes by so slowly
Like my tears flow
To the sea, to the sea.
Wait for me, wait for me,
I'll be coming home, wait for me.

Eternally yours,
Nicky

Sara gently placed the letter back in its envelope as though the contents needed to be kept safe, no chance of anything spilling out. And then she glanced at her sister.

Jessica was going through the package and sensed Sara staring at her. She looked up and said, "What?"

"So now we know," she whispered, taking a sip of wine.

"Now we know what? What are you talking about?"

"Mom being pregnant before they got married."

"We already knew that. Remember, I had that tech guy remove any hint of that from the deep, dark world of the web. I destroyed those letters between her and Dad when he was in the air force. Our kids will never find out about this. This is old news, Sara. What else you got?"

"She had the baby. He was stillborn."

"Ancient history. What were you just reading? Anything interesting? Why are you acting so weird?"

"The baby was a boy."

"We know that already."

"His name was Nicholas."

"Yup, again old news."

"Nicky was the father, not Dad."

Jessica's head snapped up from the papers she was looking at, a look of shock on her face. "Nicky? You said Nicky, not Dad? What the fuck? Why would you say that? You've had too much wine, girl."

"It's in the letter I just read, a letter Nicky wrote to Genevieve a couple of months ago. He writes about his love for her and their son. Nicky and Mom have been lovers since the beginning."

The two sisters, now in their sixties, looked at each other, not saying a word. The look said so much, as if they both now understood their mother for the very first time.

Sara broke the spell. "What's that song? It sounds familiar."

"That's odd. I don't remember adding it to my playlist. It's an old song, 'Unclaimed Memories.'"

THE END